Inked Expressions

A Montgomery Ink Novel

By
Carrie Ann Ryan

Author Highlights

Praise for Carrie Ann Ryan....

"Carrie Ann Ryan knows how to pull your heartstrings and make your pulse pound! Her wonderful Redwood Pack series will draw you in and keep you reading long into the night. I can't wait to see what comes next with the new generation, the Talons. Keep them coming, Carrie Ann!" –Lara Adrian, New York Times bestselling author of CRAVE THE NIGHT

"Carrie Ann Ryan never fails to draw readers in with passion, raw sensuality, and characters that pop off the page. Any book by Carrie Ann is an absolute treat." – New York Times Bestselling Author J. Kenner

"With snarky humor, sizzling love scenes, and brilliant, imaginative worldbuilding, The Dante's Circle series reads as if Carrie Ann Ryan peeked at my personal wish list!" – NYT Bestselling Author, Larissa Ione

"Carrie Ann Ryan writes sexy shifters in a world full of passionate happily-ever-afters." – *New York Times* Bestselling Author Vivian Arend

"Carrie Ann's books are sexy with characters you can't help but love from page one. They are heat and heart blended to perfection." *New York Times* Bestselling Author Jayne Rylon

Carrie Ann Ryan's books are wickedly funny and deliciously hot, with plenty of twists to keep you guessing. They'll keep you up all night!" USA Today Bestselling Author Cari Quinn

"Once again, Carrie Ann Ryan knocks the Dante's Circle series out of the park. The queen of hot, sexy, enthralling paranormal romance, Carrie Ann is an author not to miss!" *New York Times* bestselling Author Marie Harte

Dedication

To Chelle, Dali, and Miley. It was a tough road and I wouldn't have been able to do this book without you.

Acknowledgements

I fall more and more in love with the Montgomerys with every book. And as I keep writing, my Team gets bigger and bigger. So without you guys I wouldn't have been able to do any of this!

So to Team Carrie Ann—Chelle, Charity, Tara, and Dr. Hubby—thank you! Also, thank you MJ and Liz for listening to me when I needed to talk about my plans and ideas. And thank you to my BFF for being there for me every morning. Without our coffee Skype sessions I wouldn't have been able to keep going!

And to the Skype Sprint Loop—thanks for the pushes!

Of course, I know I wouldn't have been able to do any of this without my readers, so thank you for reading my worlds and sticking with me! You guys are amazing!

Happy reading!

~Carrie Ann

Inked Expressions

The Montgomery Ink Series from NYT Bestselling Author Carrie Ann Ryan continues with the brother who keeps his secret and the one woman he shouldn't want.

Everly Law married the love of her life and on the eve of giving birth to their twins, lost him in a tragic accident. Now she's a single mother working overtime at her bookstore trying to make sure her boys have the life they deserve. Her life is busy enough without her adding dating a Montgomery. As past secrets come to light, she'll need Storm more than ever—even if she doesn't realize it.

Storm Montgomery has spent his life atoning for sins that only few know he's committed. When he lost his best friend, he promised his widow that he'd always be there for her—even when she wanted nothing to do with him. But when a single touch ignites passions they've both buried deep inside, he'll have to remember exactly who is in his arms and that taking chances might be far more dangerous than they bargained for.

CHAPTER ONE

Then

*T*he babies kicked, sending a shockwave through Everly Law's bladder. She winced, rubbed the large swell of her stomach, and tried to remember the last time she'd seen her feet.

"Storm?" she called out, now running a hand down her back since that ached, as well. Being eight months pregnant with twins wasn't an easy task.

"Yeah?" her husband's best friend called out from the back of the house. "You need me?"

That man, she thought with a smile. He always put everyone else first no matter what. Here he was on his evening off, hanging out at her house making sure things were ready for the new babies and finishing up the back deck that Jackson had never gotten around to. She honestly didn't know why the man was single. Some woman should have snatched him up years ago.

"I just need you to tell me if my shoes match," she yelled back.

He chuckled as he made his way into the living room where she stood, sorting through the mail.

"Your shoes match, Ev. I would have told you if they didn't."

She rolled her eyes. "You say that, but I still remember the time you let Jackson walk around campus with toilet paper tucked into the back of his pants."

While she was a few years younger than both Jackson and Storm, she'd been an undergraduate at the University of Denver while both men were in graduate school finishing up their degrees—Storm his Master's in Architecture, Jackson his Ph.D. in Anthropology. From the moment she'd begun dating Jackson over a decade ago, Storm had been a part of their lives. The men had been childhood friends, and as such, she'd formed a friendship with Storm also, though it was nothing like what the two men shared.

Storm ran a hand over her belly—the only person other than Jackson she'd *ever* allow to do that—and smiled. "Jackson deserved that. He pissed me off that morning." He shrugged, his dark hair falling over his forehead. The man needed a haircut, but he seemed to like it longer on the top than the sides anyway. "I don't even remember what he did, but I remember that not telling him about what he missed was decent revenge. I'd never do something like that to you." He winked, those blue eyes of his sparkling. "Not because I'm a nice guy, but because I'm pretty sure you could take me."

She waved her fist at him, her fingers so swollen she couldn't even wear her wedding ring. "And don't you forget it, Storm Montgomery."

He let out a breath and rubbed her belly again. The babies rolled, enjoying Uncle Storm's touch, apparently, since they weren't kicking her bladder again at the moment. "Your shoes match, and you even have pants on, but how about you relieve my stress and sit down on the couch while you look at the mail. You're like days from your due date and starting to freak me out."

She let him lead her to the couch since he'd just annoy her if she didn't—though her ankles had swollen up like her hands, so maybe he wasn't all that wrong about her needing to sit down.

"I'm a couple of weeks away, Storm, not days," she countered once he'd settled her on the couch with a couple of throw pillows at her sides.

"You're having twins, and they don't usually like to take their time. Believe me, I know. I am a twin." He winked again, and she snorted.

"Your poor mother," Everly teased. "Not only twins with you and Wes, but eight children altogether. I have no idea how she did it." She rubbed her belly, that familiar tension sliding through her. "I don't know how *I'm* going to do it."

Storm frowned and sat down on the table in front of her. "You're going to be a great mom, Ev. You already take care of Jackson and me. What's one more set of boys?"

She laughed, despite the worry in her veins. Something was off tonight, she could feel it, but she hoped it was just nerves from the upcoming labor and delivery—and then the whole raising twin boys thing.

"You handle yourself just fine, and Jackson's not that bad." She rolled her eyes as she said it, and Storm grinned. "I'm serious," she said with a laugh as Storm shook his head. "Jackson is always in his head, thinking and working, but he's not immature or anything. I just like to make sure he's taken care of because he sometimes forgets daily things."

Storm narrowed his eyes. "And who is taking care of you?"

You are.

She blinked at that thought and firmly put it away. "Jackson takes care of me, as well. And now we'll both take care of these babies."

Storm nodded. "And I take it he won't be going on as many trips as he has been lately? I mean, this is like the fifth or sixth conference he's flown to since you found out about the twins. I hope he's just getting it all out of his system before he comes home and stays here for a bit."

There was an edge to his tone that Everly couldn't place, but she was far too tired to deal with it. The babies had kept her up all night, and she frankly hated having half of the bed empty without Jackson there to warm it.

"He said it won't be as bad when the babies come." Though Jackson hadn't sounded all that happy at the time about not being able to do as many guest lectures and conferences, and that did tend to worry her a little. Everly loved the fact that he was so passionate about his work, but she was also happy that he was going to stay at home for longer periods of time to help with their babies. While she knew she was strong and capable, raising twins on her own was not something she desired to do.

"I hope so," Storm grumbled. "A man needs to take care of his family."

Everly sighed. "And a woman needs to do the same. We're fine, Storm, stop fretting. It's going to turn that beautiful mane gray one of these days."

His cheeks reddened, and he let out a curse. "You're just mean, Ev. Plain mean."

"I've had to be if I wanted to keep up with you and Jackson." She frowned and looked down at her watch. "Speaking of Jackson, he was supposed to have landed already and he hasn't texted. I hope his flight isn't delayed."

Storm stood up and rubbed his back. "He probably just forgot. You know Jackson."

She did, sadly, so him not texting or calling wasn't all that surprising. He just got so in his head with his work, he forgot those around him some days. Another thing she hoped would change with the arrival of the twins. He seemed so excited about them, so she figured they would at least keep him out of his head for longer periods of time than he was now.

"Thanks for taking care of me, Storm," Everly said after a moment. "And taking care of the back deck tonight, though I know you're not really in the mood."

He shrugged. "It needed to be fixed since that bottom step rotted out. Jackson's not exactly handy, and I *do* happen to own half a construction business. It's sort of my thing." He rubbed his back again, and Everly frowned.

"What's wrong? Did you hurt yourself?" She tried to lever herself up, but he held up a hand.

"I'm fine, Ev. Don't get up and jostle the babies. I'm just a little sore, is all. Nothing a few stretches won't fix."

"Are you sure you should be working on the deck tonight, then?" she asked, worried. "You're the architect of Montgomery Inc., not the contractor, so I don't know how much pressure you usually put on your back if you're this sore. I don't want you hurting yourself."

He fisted his hands for a moment before stuffing them into his pockets. "I'm fine, Ev. Stop fretting. Just sit there and relax and before you know it, Jackson will be home, and your deck will be ready for you to actually stand on."

She huffed a breath. "If that's some kind of fat joke, I'll hoist myself off this couch and kick your ass right now. Don't think I won't."

He pulled his hands out of his pockets and held them up in mock surrender. "Dear God, woman. I would *never* make a fat joke about a lady, let alone a pregnant one. I have three sisters and a mother who can kick my ass just like you can. I know better."

She smiled sweetly. "I'm glad they taught you a few things."

He muttered under his breath as he walked away, and Everly grinned, feeling a little better than she had before, though she wasn't about to tell him that her sitting down had helped. There was only so much ego stroking she could handle.

The doorbell rang a few minutes later, and she frowned. She wasn't sure who it could be, but Jackson's parents *did* live a few miles away and liked to show up unannounced. Just thinking about that set her teeth on edge, so she ignored it and somehow levered herself off the couch. She wasn't sure Storm could hear the doorbell from outside, and since it was her house, after all, she might as well answer it.

Everly waddled over and opened the door, blinking hard at the sight in front of her. The two officers gave her a sad smile, their chests broad as they took deep breaths. Her hands shook as she gripped the doorknob with one, the frame with the other.

"Can I help you?"

"Mrs. Law?" the older of the two officers said softly. "May we come in?"

Everly's throat went dry, and she tried to keep the sense of foreboding from rushing into her, but she couldn't quite manage it—or think.

"What's going on, officers?" Storm asked from behind her. He put his hand on her shoulder, steadying her. Everly's knees went weak, and she leaned into him, knowing she couldn't stand on her own.

Both men looked up at Storm, frowns on their faces. "We need to speak to Mrs. Law. May we come in?"

"That way, she's not on her feet," the younger one added softly, and Everly's heart raced.

She moved back, pushing Storm out of the way softly. "Come in," she whispered, her voice hollow.

The two officers could have been there for any number of reasons, and yet Everly knew. She knew that no matter what happened next, her life would forever be altered.

As soon as they sat down, the officers spoke, and Storm gripped Everly's hands, but she couldn't hear anyone clearly. It was as if she were in a vacuum and everything was taking longer to reach her ears than normal.

Her husband was dead.

Gone before she could take her next breath.

The commuter plane that Jackson had been on had crashed outside of Boston. There were no survivors. No hope of finding her husband alive and whole, or even his body to put to rest.

The babies kicked at her bladder again, and she pressed her hand against her stomach, numb yet knowing she had no right to be that way. She couldn't sit here and listen to them talk of grief councilors and who would be in touch with her shortly. Storm spoke for her, and she couldn't care. She'd deal with everything later.

Right now, she needed to protect her children.

Jackson's babies.

Babies he'd never see. Never hold. Never know.

She stood up then, only just aware that she'd interrupted whatever the men in the room had been saying. "I have to pee," she blurted. The officers gave her an odd look, but Storm kept his grip on her hand.

"Everly." His voice was deep, soothing, and a little bit worried. Yet she couldn't focus on that.

"I need to take care of the babies," she rasped. "I'll...I'll be right back. Can you..." She swallowed hard. "Can you take care of...just take care of it?"

He nodded before letting her hand go, and she waddled away from the living room, not looking at the officers who sat on her soft loveseat. Storm would take care of them and tell her what she needed to do. She couldn't focus on anything else just then, only her babies.

They were the most important things.

Tears slid down her cheeks as she locked herself in the hall powder room, her legs shaking. The numbness settled in once more, and she looked at herself in the mirror, wondering who stared back at her, because that wasn't the Everly she knew.

Jackson is gone, she reminded herself.

Gone.

And when the pinch inside her echoed throughout her body and liquid pooled around her feet, she once again knew nothing would ever be the same.

The babies were coming, but Jackson wasn't.

He never would be.

And Everly wept.

Now

"I need you to breathe in, baby," Everly said softly as she held Nathan to her chest. Her three-year-old wheezed into the nebulizer, and she tried not to let herself go numb again. She refused to allow that sensation to take hold as it had once before. She didn't have time to ignore the panic running through her veins, but she *could* take that panic and turn it into the focus she needed.

Nathan looked up at her, his big eyes full of fear, an emotion that made her want to cry right along with him. James, her other sweet baby boy, held onto her shirt from where he stood beside the bed, tears running down his face.

We've all been here before, she thought, though tonight seemed like a far worse asthma attack than usual. She held back a curse and bundled Nathan in a blanket in her arms.

"Okay, Nathan honey, we're going to go to the doctor just to make sure you're okay." She kissed his little face, a thousand things going through her mind as to what needed to be done.

"Uncle Storm," James said from her side. "I want Uncle Storm."

Everly looked down at James before looking at Nathan, who nodded beneath the mask. She honestly didn't want to call Storm because that's all she'd been doing for the past three years, at least until a month ago, but tonight wasn't about her. It was about her boys and the fact that, frankly, she needed help.

"I'll call from the car, now come on, babies. Let's go." She bundled them up quickly and got them into the car within five minutes. The fact that she'd gotten into such a routine because of her two boys' health issues made her heart hurt, but she ignored it. The twins came first.

Always.

And that meant if she had to call Storm for help once again, she would.

Even if it pained her to do so.

CHAPTER TWO

Storm Montgomery groaned as he reached around the other person in his bed to grab the phone off his nightstand. He only had an outlet on one side of the bed, and now he was seriously regretting the fact that he hadn't fixed that.

"Yeah?" he growled into the phone. It was after three in the morning, and he and Jillian hadn't gone to bed until a couple of hours ago. The fact that they'd been up all night talking and not having sex wasn't new in their relationship—if you could call it a *relationship* at all.

Jillian rolled over, rubbing a hand over her face as she gave him a worried look.

"Storm?" Everly's voice had a hint of panic, but also that matter-of-fact tone he'd associated with her since she'd had the boys.

He sat up quickly and rubbed at his eyes, trying to clear the sleep from his brain. "What's up, Ev?" He blinked, annoyed with himself for calling her Ev. He hadn't really done so since Jackson's funeral—it had been so awkward between them without Jackson as a buffer. He would blame it on his sleep deprivation, but hell, for the past month, everything had been weird between them.

"It's Nathan. I'm on my way to the ER." She sounded calm, and he could hear the sounds of driving in the background. He didn't bother asking why Nathan needed to go to the ER. The kid had severe asthma attacks often enough that he'd been through this before with the two of them. James might not have asthma, but he'd had two surgeries already on his ear and had another one coming up that was a damn serious one. He hated that his two godsons each had health issues and that ER visits weren't out of the norm.

He threw off the covers and tried to find his jeans in the dark. Jillian muttered something under her breath and turned on the lamp beside her so they could see. He nodded his thanks at her and tried to pull on his jeans without tripping.

"Am I on speakerphone?"

"Yep," Everly said, her voice tight. Hell, he hated that she was alone for this. She'd been alone for so much these days, and he couldn't help her.

"Which hospital?" he asked, pulling on his shirt. Jillian dressed beside him, and he didn't know if she planned to come with him or go home. Everly told him the hospital, and he had her hang up so she could focus on driving and the boys. He'd just put on his shoes when he looked back at Jillian. "Are you heading home?"

She gave him a weird look. "No, I'm going with you. I know Everly, too. And those boys. I couldn't hear what was going on, but I know it's not something you want to wait to hear about."

Storm frowned, not knowing if Everly would like that he was bringing Jillian with him. Hell, he hadn't had enough sleep to think anything through really, and if Jillian wanted to go, he wasn't about to stop her. It wasn't as if he could anyway.

"Nathan's having an asthma attack. Everly is on the way to the emergency room."

"She has James with her then?" Jillian asked by his side as they rushed out the door and to his truck.

"Where else would he be, Jillian? She doesn't have anyone else." His voice came out sharper than he'd intended, and Jillian glared at him.

"I didn't know if she had a neighbor or something. For fuck's sake, Storm. Are you going to be okay to drive, or do you want me to? I know those boys are like your own."

Storm shot her a look and started the engine before backing out. "They're Everly and Jackson's. I'm just their godfather."

Jillian held up her hands. "You know what, I'm a little too tired and worried to get into that whole mess with you right now, so just drive."

He got onto the highway in silence, his grip on the steering wheel hard enough that he knew his hands would hurt in the morning. Or, he guessed, later *that* morning. "You going to tell me what you meant by that?"

Jillian didn't look at him, her attention on the road and her jaw tight. "Nope. This isn't the time, and I need a hell of a lot more coffee before I get into anything."

He let out a curse but didn't say anything back. The two of them had been good friends for a few years, and whenever they were single—which was more often than not in his case these days—they ended up sleeping together every once in a while. They'd never really dated and were more friends who liked sex than anything, but he'd never once felt like he and Jillian had wanted anything more out of the relationship. His brothers and friends might not understand it, but they didn't need to. The only two people who truly needed to understand their relationship were him and Jillian. Though in the past month or so—ever since he'd introduced her to Everly thanks to a plumbing problem—they hadn't seen each other or talked on the phone all that much. Tonight had been the first night they'd hung out in a month, and they hadn't even had sex—both exhausted and not in the mood for anything more than sleep. She'd fallen asleep in his bed rather than the guest room more out of habit than anything, he supposed.

If he weren't so tired, he'd probably not let his mind wander to the fact that he was in a damn rut and Jillian was right there with him. He tried not to think about the fact that he and his twin, Wes, were the only two Montgomerys in his immediate family that hadn't settled down yet. Sure, the majority of the cousins hadn't married off yet either, but he didn't interact with them enough these days for it to count when it came to feeling as though he was a little behind.

Everyone else, though? That tended to grate. He was looking forty in the face soon, and he truly didn't want to go it alone. Of course, he probably had to start dating someone other than Jillian—who he wasn't actually dating—for that to work.

"Here it is," Jillian said from his side. "Don't miss the exit."

He turned off the highway and took the short road to the Emergency Room parking lot. Thankfully, the new hospital nearest to him and Everly was easy to get to. He hoped she was already there and figured she would be, considering it had taken him time to get on the road.

Storm pushed all thoughts of his own life out of his head as they made their way into the Emergency

Room waiting room. He wasn't firing on all cylinders tonight, and thinking too hard would probably piss him off.

"I need to see Everly and Nathan Law," Storm said as soon as he made his way to the admin desk.

"Are you family?" the on-call nurse asked, and Storm cursed. No, they weren't technically family, and now they were going to waste precious time making sure he could go back there and see the kids.

"He's with us," Everly said from the doorway, her eyes wide as she took in Jillian by his side. "They both are."

The nurse frowned. "That's too many people back in the room, miss."

"I'll stay in the waiting room," Jillian said quickly. "Storm should be back there to take care of James, right?"

"Right," Storm agreed.

The nurse let him go, and he nodded at Jillian, who waved at Everly, her face sad. "Give him my best," Jillian said. "Both of those little guys."

"Will do," Everly said tightly before looking at Storm. "Thank you for coming. The boys wanted you here."

The boys. Not her. Couldn't blame her since they hadn't been all that friendly lately.

"Of course, I'm here. How's he doing?"

Everly wrapped her arms around her waist and looked toward the room where Nathan lay sleeping in the large bed, his body looking far too small.

"Good. Sleeping. They got him stable right away, and James is sleeping on the couch right behind that curtain. You can see his little feet if you duck down."

Storm did, feeling like an idiot, but relaxing a bit as soon as he saw for himself that both boys were there.

"That was fast," he said softly.

Everly played with the bottom of her shirt. "They let us right in and, apparently, the nebulizer I was using at home was already doing the job. I just panicked."

Storm frowned and looked down at her, doing his best not to touch her. He used to be able to give her a hug or even hold her hand when she was stressed, but she'd pushed him away over time. It shouldn't have bothered him since they were only friends, but it did.

"You did good, Everly. Don't berate yourself for being cautious. You couldn't have known."

Everly didn't look at him, but her shoulders relaxed a bit. "I didn't know you'd be bringing Jillian." She let out a curse under her breath. "I'm sorry. That's none of my business. I'm just tired."

"We're friends, Ev." Damn it. He needed to stop calling her that. It made them both uncomfortable. "She wanted to come since she met the boys and liked them."

"She was great with them." Everly turned to him, her brow raised. "And, Storm, if a woman is sleeping over at your house at three a.m., she's not just your friend."

Storm stuffed his hands in his pockets. "We didn't sleep together. We *are* friends."

Everly closed her eyes, pinching the bridge of her nose. "None of my business."

"If you say so."

He was tired, confused, and still worried about the boys. He didn't want to go down this line of conversation, now or ever. "I'm going to head back out to the waiting room so the nurse quits glaring at me."

Everly laughed softly. "She's checking you out, not glaring. You have bed head." She reached up to fix his hair and froze, her face paling. She dropped her arm and cleared her throat. "I'll let you know when the boys wake up so you can talk to them."

"Okay," he bit out and turned on his heel, leaving Everly behind in the hallway. As soon as he made it into the waiting room, Jillian stood, her teeth biting her lip.

"Nathan's fine," he said quickly. "Everly will come out in a bit and tell us more."

Jillian searched his face before letting out a breath. "That's good to hear. Storm? We need to talk."

Hell, he hated that phrase. Why did women need to say that when something shitty was about to happen?

"What?" he asked. "Do you want some coffee? Might as well get some caffeine in my system if I'm going to be up for a bit."

"No, but Storm? I called a cab. I shouldn't have come tonight. It wasn't fair to you or Everly for me to show up like I did."

He frowned. "What are you talking about?"

Jillian shook her head, her eyes sad. "You don't understand yet, but you will. And I'm going to love that you will soon. But, Storm? I'm going to go, and I'm probably not going to call you for a bit. I want you to text me about the boys, of course, but I think it's time we stop this."

He froze. "What are you talking about?"

She reached up and patted his cheek. "I love you, Storm. But not the way I should. And I know you feel the same about me."

His mouth went dry. "Jilly..."

She shook her head. "You're one of my best friends, and I think that's all we need to be right now...or forever. We've been what we are because it was the easy way out, complicated explanations and all. And I think...I think I want to see if I can do better than this. And I think you should, too."

And with that, she turned and walked toward the sliding doors, leaving Storm at a loss for words and feeling as though he'd just been kicked in the gut. He loved Jillian, but not the way he should, she was right. He'd never been *in* love with her, and he knew it was the same for her.

She wasn't the one for him, and never had been. He let out a breath. And Jillian wasn't the only woman in his life he could say that about.

Not then, and sure as hell not now.

CHAPTER THREE

Everly needed a bucket of coffee, but that probably wouldn't help her unsettled stomach. She ran her hand over James's light hair, loving the way he smiled up at her with that adorable little boy smile of his.

"Can we have French fries after?" James asked, his smile turning even sweeter. Even at their young ages, her boys knew exactly what smiles to use to get what they wanted from her. Seriously, how was a mom supposed to say no to those smiles?

And though, normally, she might have just braved it and said no to fast food; today, greasy food might be just the thing to make it through the day.

"Maybe," she answered, smoothing out his hair. Both James and Nathan each had a little cowlick that was completely adorable but refused to bend to her ways.

"Yay! Maybe!" Nathan squealed from his seat next to the examination table. He had his superhero coloring books and his favorite crayons to keep him busy during James's doctor appointment. It had only been a couple of days since they'd been in the emergency room for Nathan, but he seemed no worse for wear.

"Maybe!" James squealed right back, clapping his hands. She couldn't help but smile, knowing they were taking her *maybe* as a *yes*. She didn't say maybe often, after all. But having to stand in a medical building with her boys for the second time in as many days made silly things like having fast food seem like a treat, rather than evil.

Today, on the other hand, was all about James. It was the last appointment before his surgery for his cochlear implant. He was almost one hundred percent deaf in his left ear, his right ear almost perfect according to the masses of tests they'd had run over the past two years. They'd tried hearing aids that had worked reasonably well, though James had constantly tried to scratch the thing off when he was younger. They were even learning sign language as a family and would continue to do so even after the surgery. It was an important skill even if her child ended up being able to hear with both ears after the surgery. She'd gone through the pros and cons of the invasive procedure over and over since the opportunity had come about and had finally relented when she'd talked to numerous other parents who had stood on both sides of the issue. There was *nothing* wrong with her baby, but if this would help him function better in the cruel world that was theirs on most days, then she would do it—she'd do anything for him.

And when her insurance company had agreed to pay for every cent of the operation, she'd almost fallen to the floor and wept. Between James's ear and Nathan's asthma, medical bills piled up, and it wasn't all that easy to keep up with it. She'd set aside Jackson's life insurance policy early on to pay for the boys' school since she knew that even if they had to live meagerly, she'd be able to raise her boys in relative comfort. She might be a small business owner, but she was doing pretty well for herself these days.

And at that thought, she quickly knocked on the wooden shelf beside her, hoping that the pressed wood panel would be enough to ward off any evil thoughts.

Dr. Edelman walked in and smiled softly at them as soon as she pulled her hand back. "Well, I'll be. I must be seeing double today." The boys laughed as they always did when Dr. Edelman made that joke. She couldn't help but smile even as her nerves grated.

"Well now, let's get started, shall we?" the doctor asked with a pleasant smile.

Everly swallowed hard and nodded. "Sure." She reached around for her binder with all of her notes and research and let out a deep breath. Books had saved her in the past, and she hoped that everything she'd read had led her to the right decision with regards to James and the surgery.

Being a single mother was an amalgamation of one leap of worrying and hard decision after another, and she just prayed that she wouldn't make another mistake. Others might be able to make as many missteps as needed, but she didn't have anyone else to rely on when it came to the outcome.

She only had herself.

As always.

"So, everything went okay today?" Tabby asked from across the booth. The other woman looked worried, but you couldn't tell from the tone of her voice, which Everly appreciated.

After the doctor's appointment, Everly had taken the boys over to their favorite burger place and then called Tabby and Alex to join them. She and Tabby had been friends for years, and Everly had watched her friend fall in love with not only a good man, but a beautiful family, as well. The fact that Alex was Storm's brother just made the world seem that much smaller.

Everly had known Storm because of Jackson and college and had only met one other Montgomery— Storm's twin, Wes, recently. She hadn't run in the same circles as Storm outside of her relationship with Jackson, so it had made sense that she hadn't met the rest of his immense family. Tabby, on the other hand, worked at Montgomery Inc., the family's construction company that Storm and Wes owned. She honestly had no idea why she'd never mentioned the fact that she knew Storm to Tabby before everything had come full circle a few months ago but, apparently, she'd been keeping secrets she hadn't meant to keep. No, that wasn't right. She'd known Tabby had a crush on Alex throughout the years but hadn't said anything to Storm since it wasn't her place. She'd done her best in the past three years to keep her relationship with Storm as minimal as possible because she hated having to rely on anyone, and because of that, she'd unintentionally kept him a secret from Tabby and the others.

In the end, she'd somehow been taken in by the Montgomerys in a sense, and she wasn't sure how that had happened. They were like the Borg—resistance was futile. The family now knew that she and Storm knew each other, and it hadn't been that big of a deal. After all, Denver was a huge city, and it wasn't like everyone talked about every single person they knew day in and day out.

It just made things a little weird for her some days, so she chose to ignore it. She had far more important things to do in her life than worry about who knew whom and how everybody was connected.

Tabby and Alex had gone through hell to find each other, and Everly was so grateful that, in the end, they'd fallen in love and gotten engaged. She didn't even have a thread of jealousy that the two across from her clearly had eyes for only each other. She'd been married. She'd loved. She'd lost.

She wasn't going to do it again.

And at that weird thought, she shook her head and finally answered Tabby. "The visit went well," she said slowly, her gaze going to the center of the U-shaped booth where her boys sat on booster seats, gobbling up fries while talking to Alex. They loved Alex and always wanted to spend time with him. Though they loved their Uncle Storm more than the others even if all of the Montgomery men looked so much alike.

And why did she keep thinking about Storm? It made no sense.

Tabby reached across the booth and gripped her hand. "I'm glad to hear it. Just remember, you aren't alone in this, Everly. I know you want to do everything on your own, but we're here for you. We love you, too, honey."

Everly blinked back tears, clearly too tired to be having this conversation. When Jackson had died, she felt as if she'd lost a part of herself but hadn't been able to focus on it. She'd literally gone into labor that terrible evening and had to learn how to be a single mother when she'd planned her life around Jackson. Any friends they'd shared had slowly backed away, unable to see her and not think of the man they'd been close to. They hadn't known how to act with her anymore, hadn't known how to help her when she wasn't even sure what she needed help with.

Tabby had always been there, though, and perhaps that was because Tabby had been Everly's friend, not Jackson's.

Storm was always there, too. Still is.

She could have kicked herself for once again thinking of him and vowed she'd drink more coffee once she got to the bookstore after lunch. She was just too tired to think normally these days.

"I love you, too," Everly said after a moment, her voice thick. "And thank you for meeting me here for lunch rather than Taboo." Taboo was one of the Montgomery hangouts that shared a wall with Montgomery Ink—the family's tattoo shop. They went there often since one of their mutual friends owned the cafe, but today was about the boys, not her. "I promised the twins French fries, and while Taboo *does* have them, they aren't the ones the boys were thinking about."

Tabby grinned. "No explanations needed. Some days, it's all about a greasy burger, and French fries." She eyed Alex's chicken sandwich and shook her head. "Well, at least for some of us."

Alex looked over at that instant before winking at his fiancée and stealing one of her fries. "There's nothing healthy about my sandwich, Tabitha. Don't worry. I went grease for you."

She blew him a kiss. "You're so romantic."

"You know it."

Everly just shook her head. She truly didn't need to know what they were talking about to know they absolutely adored each other. She tried to remember if she and Jackson had ever been like that, but her memories came back a little fuzzy as usual. As time sped by, her past with Jackson continued to slip through her fingers. She wasn't sure what to make of that, nor did she know what she would do about it.

She'd loved him so freaking much it hurt to remember him sometimes, but she did for the boys. James and Nathan knew about their daddy and would continue to know more as they grew older. She wouldn't let them think they didn't have a father even if one wasn't raising them.

Tragedy happened, and others had to live with it. Even if it felt as if she were walking through sand in order to find this healing so many people talked about.

Everly picked at her burger, not in the mood to eat anymore. Her stomach still hadn't settled since the doctor's office, and frankly hadn't really been back to normal since the late-night emergency room visit with Nathan. She let out a breath, trying to keep her mind calm. She couldn't freak out in front of her kids, even if that's all she wanted to do these days.

"Can we go play?" Nathan asked, pulling her out of her thoughts.

Everly turned, holding back her frown. Those places were germ magnets, and with Nathan's recent illness and James's surgery right around the corner, she wasn't sure she wanted them in the ball pit of doom.

Alex must have read her face and gave her a small smile. "I have a soccer ball in my truck from playing with my brother's kids. Why don't we go out to the field in the back and play?"

She gave him a dubious look. "Don't you think a soccer ball might be as big as they are?" Her boys might seem wise beyond their years, but they were still only three.

"We'll be good, Mommy," James said with a smile.

"Real good," Nathan added.

She snorted but smiled anyway. "Be safe. And since it's so warm outside, don't overdo it."

"We'll be good." Alex looked up at Everly. "I'll take them to wash their hands and use the bathroom first. Is that okay?"

She nodded, her throat closing up. "Perfect." Her boys were getting older and taking them into the women's restroom was getting more annoying day by day. She didn't actually care what others thought, but she could do without the pointed looks selfish women gave her kids. What else was she supposed to do in a public place, take them into the men's or let them go by themselves? They were three, for God's sake. Finally—thankfully—potty trained but years from being able to be on their own in a restroom.

Tabby and Everly slid out of the booth so the guys could get out, as well, the twins chattering a mile a minute as Alex nodded along, his attention on them even as he kissed Tabby's cheek and waved at Everly. She reached into her bag and handed over Nathan's inhaler just in case, and Alex pocketed it, making it look like it was the easiest thing in the world—as if there weren't a single thing wrong with needing a little help now and then.

She didn't trust many people with her children's safety, but she trusted Alex and the rest of the Montgomerys wholeheartedly.

"Alexander won't let them overdo it," Tabby said softly. "And this way, you don't have to worry about the germs in that playhouse behind us."

Everly gave a mock shudder. "So many germs and children with unwashed hands and God knows what else."

Tabby grimaced. "At that unappetizing thought, let's clean up the table. I don't think I'm going to finish these fries."

Everly laughed with her friend as they cleaned up, taking the booth over again since it wasn't that busy this late in the afternoon.

"So, Nathan is doing okay after his attack then?" Tabby asked, her voice soft. "I can't believe the week you're having."

Everly sighed, playing with the straw in her drink. "He's breathing easier, and I know Alex won't let him work himself up out there. I'm just exhausted, I think. Too many nights in a row of staying up and worrying about my boys. If Storm hadn't been there in the ER that night, I don't know what I would have done. They needed to take Nathan to the back for another test, and Storm was there to take care of James so I wouldn't have to wake him up."

Tabby's eyes widened. "Storm was at the ER with you?"

Everly winced. She hadn't meant to mention that as it had been habit to keep Storm to herself, but, apparently, she was a little too tired. And she'd have to think later on *why* she kept Storm to herself.

It really wasn't something she wanted to dwell on, though.

"The boys wanted him, so I called. At three in the morning."

Tabby let out a breath. "I'm so glad he showed up for you."

"He always does," Everly whispered, and Tabby gave her a sharp look. "He brought Jillian with him," she blurted.

Tabby's brows lifted. "Really? I didn't know they were still together."

Everly thought on the conversation she hadn't meant to overhear. "I don't think they are anymore. Not that it's any of my business."

Tabby gave her a look. "Not that it's any of your business?"

"Storm is just my friend. Or rather, he was Jackson's friend and likes to make sure the boys are okay. That's it, Tabby. Nothing more."

Tabby gave her a long look before nodding. "Okay." Though Everly knew the other woman wanted to say more, she didn't. Instead, they talked about the upcoming wedding and the other things going on in their lives for another twenty minutes before her phone beeped and she knew it was time to head into work.

"Are you sure you're okay taking the boys?" Everly asked as they walked out to their cars to switch out the car seats. "It's just as easy for me to take them to the babysitter."

Alex held both boys in his arms, his grin wide—dear God the Montgomery men were handsome. "We're having fun. Don't worry about us."

Tabby hugged Everly hard. "Really. We're practicing." She said the last part softly, and Everly blinked back tears. She loved that her friend was so stinking happy. If anyone deserved a happily ever after, it was Tabby.

"Okay, then. If you're sure." They got the car seats figured out, and she hugged and kissed her boys goodbye, promising to see them soon. They waved as if they didn't mind being away from her, and she ignored that kernel of self-doubt. Her boys were happy and relatively healthy, that was all that mattered.

By the time she drove downtown and parked in her tiny lot in the back of Beneath the Cover, her indie bookstore, her nerves were less frazzled than they had been but still not quite up to one hundred percent.

However, as soon as she stepped into her store, her spirits buoyed just a fraction. She loved her shop with all of her heart. She adored the way the scent of new books and old filled her senses as soon as she walked in. She loved the different areas of the space she'd decorated over time to signal the subject. She loved the fact that she and her assistants had made sure that each subgenre of the main genre was clearly labeled and had special decorations to match. She loved all the seating areas she'd added with comfy—sometimes antique—chairs and chaise lounges she'd placed so people could sit with a good book and bring in a cup of coffee if they so desired. There was a place up front near the window display that she'd made into a larger seating area when they had guest readings, author signings, and comedy nights. And she'd even added a used book section upstairs for people who wanted books that were either out of print or special to them for other reasons.

This place was a part of her soul, just like her boys were, and she was grateful beyond measure that she had it in her life. Jackson hadn't quite understood how she planned to make an indie bookstore work in downtown Denver where there was already a few chain and established indie bookstores, but she'd found a way. The early days had been hit or miss, but she'd eventually found her groove after she opened the place using her inheritance from her parents' wills and put her blood, sweat, and tears into the project.

Throughout the years, a few businesses had come and gone along their street off 16th Street Mall, but places like Taboo, Montgomery Ink, and the newer boutique, Eden—that happened to be owned by a woman who'd married into the Montgomerys—had endured. She freaking loved everything about the place. Even the bills.

"Hey, boss," Freddie said with a grin from behind the counter. She had a book open in front of her as she watched customers shop. Freddie was in her late forties, tall, curvy, and freaking amazing. She'd been an MBA and working on the top floor of one of the skyscrapers that dotted the Denver skyline, but after she found her husband cheating on her, she had decided to find her passion.

That her passion was medical school just made Everly smile. The woman had a full caseload, three grown children in college themselves, and worked at Beneath the Cover part-time to pay some of her bills since she had been forced to pay alimony to the dumb idiot she married.

Everly put her bag down under the counter and gave Freddie a hug. "Hey, hon. Everything going well?"

Freddie nodded, closing her Organic Chemistry book as she started to pack up. "Yep. We had a bit of a rush earlier, which rocked. There are a few phone messages for you that I left on the desk in the back office. Oh, and I tripped up the stairs again because I'm a dork, so I called someone in to fix it since it was on your to-do list. I knew you'd eventually get around to it, but I wanted to help."

Everly winced. "I'm sorry. Were you hurt?"

Freddie shook her head, zipping up her backpack at the same time. "Nope. But I know you don't want anyone else to be. I know you, and we probably could have found a way to fix part of it on our own, but we both know it's beyond our skill set."

Everly sighed and rubbed her shoulders, the tension there a permanent part of her life these days. "Who did you call?" she asked, already knowing the answer.

"Storm. He said he'd be here in a bit since he was already downtown at the shop." Freddie shrugged. "I assume he meant the tattoo shop, but I didn't ask. Anyway, I'm off to my lab." She scrunched her nose. "I hate late-night chem labs. They're the bane of my existence."

Everly ignored the worry in her gut that she'd once again be seeing Storm. She didn't understand why she kept having a reaction when she thought of him. He was just Storm. "You'll get through it with an *A* like you always do. Then you can be my doctor instead of the rude guy I have now, and everyone will be happier."

Freddie winked. "If you say so. Have a good night!" The other woman walked out of the shop at the same time a familiar face walked in, causing Everly's back to stiffen.

"Hey," Storm said once he faced her. He had a toolbox in his hand and a frown on his face. He always seemed to scowl at her lately, and she didn't know why.

"Thank you for coming, though I'm sure I could have done it on my own." And didn't she sound like an ungrateful bitch? She needed to get the stick out of her ass and deal with whatever was going on between her and Storm, but she kept putting her foot into her mouth.

Storm gave her a weird look. "I'm sure you could have, but I'm here now. Just because you can do something doesn't mean you have to do it on your own all the time."

Everly swallowed hard, not liking the way he seemed to see more than she wanted him to.

"I'll head upstairs," he said after a moment. Then a loud bang rang through the store, and Storm jumped, his eyes going wide and his skin paling.

Everly reached across the counter for him, wondering what on earth had just happened. No one else in the shop seemed to have noticed, but Storm clearly had. "It was just a car backfiring. Are you okay?" He looked as if he were ready to crawl right out of his skin, but when he looked at her again, he set his jaw and color infused his cheekbones.

"I'm fine." He stalked away, his shoulders stiff, and Everly's gaze traveled down his back and rested on his very firm butt.

She quickly turned around, hating herself more than she thought possible. Dear God. What the hell was wrong with her? Not only had she acted rude to him, but something had clearly made him freak out just then.

And what did she do? She checked out his ass.

She had never been so thankful for needing to ring up a sale for a customer as she was in that next moment. With clear determination, she pushed all thoughts of Storm and his fine butt out of her mind.

Firmly.

CHAPTER FOUR

The next day, Storm knew if he didn't get out of the office soon, he might wring his twin's neck. He loved his family and, hell, he *knew* he and Wes were closer than close, but some days, he was just tired of it all.

"Raymond fucked up again," Wes growled as he stomped his way through the office. They had an open floor plan in the main office where Storm, Wes, Decker, Meghan, Harper, and Tabby each had their own desks and could easily see and talk to each other if needed. Since most of the time many of them were out on jobsites, it usually wasn't a problem noisewise. They had offices in the back for meetings with clients and a place for Storm to work since he was the lead architect of the company, but most days, there was always a few people in and out of the main room.

Tabby raised her finger, her attention on her phone call and her computer all at once. Storm just shook his head, his attention on the plans in front of him and not his brother. Wes was in a mood, and Storm didn't want to deal with him. That was the problem with working with family, though—there was no hiding. Ever.

"Are you listening to me?" Wes asked, hovering over Storm's desk.

Storm let out a sigh and lifted his head, annoyed at the ache in his back. He'd been sitting too long working on this one design instead of going to the back where his standing desk was. He was getting too old for long days like this.

"I am," Storm said as he ran a hand over his face. "Not sure why you're freaking out right now. We knew Raymond was a fuck-up ten minutes after we hired him, but we needed a plumber for the Westcott job. Luc and the rest of the crew were keeping an eye on him because Raymond *can* do his job if he doesn't let his attention wander. Hell, the man was only hired on for a probationary period of two weeks because he said he'd gotten his life under control, but now we know that isn't the case." Storm let out a breath and pinched the bridge of his nose. "What did he do?"

Wes sat on the edge of Storm's desk, which annoyed him to no end. But Storm did the same to Wes, so he let it pass. His brother was getting on his nerves more and more these days, and Storm knew he needed to take a step back and breathe. Wes wasn't really doing anything wrong, he just kept prodding until Storm wanted to scream. It was a twin thing.

"He never showed up." Wes ran a hand over his face much like Storm had just done. The two of them were fraternal twins, but they had many of the same mannerisms and things that matched more than they did with others in their family. His family had called them "the twins" for so long that he answered to it just like he did "Storm." There was another set of twins in the Montgomerys, as well—cousins who were fraternal also. He couldn't help but think of yet another set of brothers he knew that were also called "twins." James and Nathan were identical, though and were stinking cute—spitting images of their mother.

Storm quickly pushed thoughts of Everly out of his mind. Things had been weird between them for the past few months—years if he were honest with himself—and they'd only gotten more awkward since he'd brought Jillian over that one time to fix Everly's sink.

Storm sat up straighter, knowing he was probably about to make a mistake but didn't have another choice. "I have a plumber we can use."

Wes's eyes narrowed. "You didn't bring it up when we hired Raymond."

"She had another contract at the time, but it ended last week." He pulled out his phone. "She'd be a good fit for Montgomery Inc."

"She?" Wes's voice held a hint of speculation.

"Don't tell me you think women can't be plumbers," Tabby said from her desk. "Because I'm just fine with using the fighting techniques Alexander taught me to kick your ass."

Wes held up his hands. "I wasn't thinking that. I'm thinking my brother is about to ask me if his ex-girlfriend can come and work with us." There was an edge to his tone that made Storm stand up.

"First, Jillian isn't my ex-girlfriend." He held up his hands. "I'm not going to get into that because, hell, we aren't in high school. Secondly, she'd a damned amazing licensed plumber."

Wes narrowed his eyes. "If she's so good, why is she available?"

"Now you're just trying to be an asshole," Storm bit out.

"I'm trying to get a full answer."

"Okay, boys. Step away from each other and take a breath." Tabby came up between them and gave them each a look.

Storm lowered his head, pissed off at himself for getting angry at all. Just because Wes kept needling him didn't mean he had to react. And knowing Wes, he probably didn't even realize he was doing it.

"She needed to finish out her contract for the other company, and they strung her along forever since they made it working hours and not days on hire. She's been working for a few other companies, as well, trying to get the right fit, but she doesn't want to start her own business."

"That's smart," Tabby added in. "And from what I know of Jillian, she's smart."

Wes pressed his lips into a thin line. "I know Meghan and the rest have a stake in the company, but you and I are the ones who decide on hiring for something like this. So if you trust her and think you can work through whatever the two of you are doing, then fine. I mean, with Luc and Meghan married and so many of the rest of our company married into our family, it shouldn't matter." He paused. "But it does."

"You just don't like her," Storm said after a moment. He didn't know why, but the two of them had never gotten along, even though they didn't spend that much time together.

"I wouldn't say that," Wes said slowly. "But I don't want us hiring her and have it end up hurting the company. Hurting our family."

Storm met his twin's eyes and hoped the other man saw what he needed to see. "She's good people, Wes. She's my friend." He hoped that was still the case since he hadn't seen her since the night in the ER, but he wasn't going to mention that. "And she's a fantastic plumber."

Wes blew out a breath. "We needed someone on the Westcott project like yesterday, so yeah, bring her in. I just hope we aren't making a huge fucking mistake."

Storm rolled his eyes. "Real confidence you have there."

"I worry. It's my thing."

"And *my* thing is to make sure you don't have a heart attack because of it," Tabby said with a smile, though she still looked worried as her gaze darted between the two of them. "Now get back to your desk and sign those forms I sent to you. Then don't forget that Decker needs a hand on the Bailey project later this afternoon. I told him I'd send one of you but didn't say which."

Wes gave Storm a look. "Looks like it'll be me, right? When's the last time you worked onsite?" His brother winked, telling Storm he was joking the way they always kidded around and no harm was meant, but Storm felt like he'd gotten kicked in the chest.

There were reasons he didn't go to sites as much as he used to, but he hadn't told Wes what they were. He wasn't sure he could.

"I'll help Decker," Storm said, his voice perfectly calm. Wes opened his mouth to say something, but Storm shrugged him off. "Go sign those papers since Tabby needs you. I'll give Jillian a call and see what she can do before I head to Decker."

He turned away and made his way to one of the back offices, his back aching and tension in his shoulders that he knew wouldn't be going anywhere anytime soon. But it was just another day at Montgomery Inc., and he'd have to get over it. Eventually.

Storm gave Jillian a cautious look as she walked into the office an hour after he'd called her. She'd agreed to come in immediately to see if she fit, but he was still afraid it might be a mistake. He hadn't seen her since she'd walked away from him after declaring that whatever they had was over. And the sad part about all of that was that he wasn't too upset about it. He was more worried that he'd hurt her in some way than bothered by the fact that they wouldn't be sleeping together anymore. He and Jillian were friends, and he would hate himself if he'd inadvertently hurt her.

She wore her normal working attire of jeans and a t-shirt. Usually, it would have had the company logo of her employer on the front, but since she no longer worked with them, she'd just put on a plain one. He knew she'd used to wear baggier clothes to hide her curves because men could be assholes and had stared at her body more than her work, but in the past couple of years, she'd worn what was comfortable to her rather than caring what others thought.

If she took the job with Montgomery Inc., he knew she'd be well taken care of. Any man or woman who leered or said crude things wouldn't be working for or with them anymore. The Montgomerys didn't stand for crap like that.

"Hey, glad you could make it on such short notice," he said as he walked around his desk. He picked up a notebook on his way so he wouldn't have the urge to hug her hello like he usually did. Things were already awkward with Wes, and Storm didn't want to add any more fuel to the fire.

She lifted her chin in greeting. "Thanks for calling." There was an awkward pause between them that Storm hated with every fiber of his being before she let out a breath and ran a hand through her hair.

She hadn't bothered to put it up in its usual ponytail that morning, apparently. "Okay, let's just get this out in the open, shall we?"

"Yes, let's," Wes said as he walked into the room, his eyes narrowed.

Storm prayed for patience.

Jillian studied Storm's twin as if he were a bug and snorted. "Storm and I are friends. Nothing more now, and not quite more before. Storm and I are adult enough to work together because we're professionals." She gave Storm a pointed look.

"No problem here," Storm said quickly, holding back a smile. There was a reason Jillian was one of his favorite people. She got to the point and hated dealing with subtext most days. Though as he thought that, he remembered how vague she'd been at the hospital, but he put that out of his mind because, based on the way Wes's eye twitched, he was pretty sure his brother was about to have a stroke.

"Are you saying I'm the problem?" Wes asked through gritted teeth.

Jillian folded her arms in front of her. "You've always had a problem with me, Wes. Don't try to deny it. I don't know why, and I'd say it wasn't my problem, but if I'm going to be working for you guys, I don't want to deal with any crap that has nothing to do with my work."

Storm looked at the ceiling, blowing out a breath before he lowered his head to glance from one of them to the other. They'd squared off, their shoulders tense as they glared at one another.

"We're not going to have a problem. Right, Wes?" Storm asked, annoyed. They weren't in high school anymore, but hell, sometimes two people just didn't hit it off, and things could escalate. "I'm not in the mood to be the ringleader here. I don't need the two of you fighting with each other all the time. We need a plumber, and Jillian is the best I know. She's finally free of her contract and came in today to get the paperwork done with Tabby who's in the back on a conference call." He gave Wes a look. "As you like to point out—often—you're the one on the jobsite more frequently, so you're going to have to work with Jillian daily. If you can't do that, then we're going to have to make some decisions, but I'd like to think that we're all old enough to get shit done without fighting. Am I wrong?"

Jillian let out a breath, her cheeks turning red even as she glared at Wes. "Sorry. I have a bad habit of getting my back up when I feel like people are going to judge me. You haven't seen me work, and we've never actually been on the jobsite together. So I'm going to take a leap and go with the idea that you don't like me for personal reasons. That's fine. We don't have to be friends, but I don't want it to affect the way you treat me on the job."

Wes's jaw tightened before he spoke, and Storm prayed he wouldn't have to stay between the two of them for long. They needed to hash this out so he could deal with his own busy schedule and problems.

"I've heard great things about you so let's see if you live up to your reputation."

Storm just barely held back the roll of his eyes.

"Generous of you," Jillian said sweetly.

"Just be on time, do good work, and don't get in my way and we'll be fine," Wes said before holding out his hand. "Welcome to Montgomery Inc."

Jillian took Wes's hand hesitantly, and Storm held his breath. "Thanks. I've heard good things about the company."

"Of course, you have," Storm said with a snort. "We're the best out there."

Wes grinned at Storm but stiffened as his phone rang. "I've got to take this, but Tabby will be out in a second to help you with your paperwork." He looked at Storm. "Still okay going to the jobsite to help Decker? I can do it."

Storm's shoulders tensed even as Jillian spoke. "You do construction work in dress pants and a tie?" she asked skeptically.

"I change into jeans when I go to a site. Today, I have meetings with suppliers so I wore this." He waved over at Storm. "Just because Storm tends to wear flannel doesn't mean I do. We're twins, not the same person."

Jillian held up her hands, her eyes wide. "Seems I stepped into something there. Sorry. Won't do it again."

Storm snorted. "You will, but then again, we all do here. And, Wes? It's fucking hot outside so I'm not wearing flannel, thank you very much."

"You're thinking about flannel, though. It's your favorite thing." Wes grinned, and Storm rolled his eyes. So what if he loved flannel? It was comfortable.

Tabby walked out of the back room right then and smiled widely. "Jillian! Yay, you're here. I have your paperwork all ready, so let's get started." She shooed both Wes and Storm. "You both have appointments, so get going. I can handle Jillian."

Storm shook his head, smiling as he picked up his things from his desk before heading out of the office, giving everyone a chin lift as he did. He wasn't really in the mood to deal with backbreaking work in this heat, but Montgomery Inc. was his company, and he'd get shit done if he had to.

By the time he made it to the jobsite, Decker had most of the crew on the roof, tearing off the old shingles so they could put on a new one. Wes and

Tabby hadn't mentioned that he'd be on the damn roof in this heat, and now he wanted nothing more than to crawl back to his desk. Hell, his back ached something fierce just thinking about all the weight he was about to put on it.

But this was his job, and he needed to get over it and get to work. He got out of his truck, pulling out this stuff as he did so. Thankfully, he'd grabbed his water bottle on the way out so he could refill it at the station Decker had set up.

"Hey, man," Decker called out. "Glad you could make it. Grab what you need and head on up." His brother-in-law wiped his face with the bottom of his shirt, sweat and dirt clinging to him. "Sooner we get through this, the sooner we can get out of this damn heat."

"On my way!" Storm yelled back, grateful he'd worn a thin shirt today instead of something like his normal flannel.

It was indeed backbreaking work to tear off an entire roof in the summer heat, but it needed to be done. Storm's body was drenched in sweat and dirt, and God knew what else had come off the shingles as he worked. By the time they were done, it had taken ten men and more swearing than Storm could measure.

And he knew he'd need an ice bath once he got home.

There was no missing that familiar twinge in his back that said he'd not only overdone it, but had hurt himself enough that if he weren't careful, he'd be headed right back into the doctor's office for treatment. And as that was *not* something on his list of things to do, he prayed that ice and a long soak would help him. His brothers had joked with him when he'd put in the large soaker tub in his master bath, but if they knew *why* he used it often, they might not have done so.

Not that he planned to tell them. Ever. Some things were just meant to be kept secret. Some truths were never meant to be told.

He said his goodbyes to the crew and made sure everything was set for the next day. Decker had it handled, but Storm liked to make sure the man didn't need anything just in case.

In need of a long soak and a cold beer, he drove home, the waning sunlight blinding him in rush-hour traffic. It just set him on edge that much more, and he gripped the steering wheel harder, his back having enough spasms that he needed to keep still or he'd end up crying like a fool.

By the time he pulled into his driveway, new sweat poured down his face, and he thought about leaving his shit in the truck but thought better of it just as fast. He didn't want to have to leave his tub or bed once he got in. He limped like an old man into his house, his hands shaking. He hadn't had an attack like this in over a year, and he wasn't necessarily in the mood for it now.

Then the whining started—thankfully, not by him.

"Fuck," he muttered under his breath. He'd forgotten about his damn puppy. He had a friend come over during the day to play with Randy and make sure he did his business and all that, but he was still young enough that he needed to be in a crate during the day. As the crate was about half the size of his mudroom in the back, the puppy had more room than even Storm did at his desk at work. But Storm still felt bad that he didn't get to run until Storm got home.

He set his things down on the dining room table and slowly made his way to the back of his house.

Randy barked and yipped, jumping around his large crate as he saw Storm.

Even in pain, Storm couldn't help but smile at the little guy. According to the vet, he was a shepherd mix of some sort and had those big ears that so many of them did as puppies. The program Randy was in, and the one Storm volunteered for, figured that Randy would grow into those ears and those big ass feet of his one day. When that day came, Storm was pretty sure Randy would end up being as big as he was when he stood on his hind legs.

Storm loved working for Pets for Progress, even though he couldn't always help out as much as he wanted to because of work and family stuff. He helped train puppies and older dogs to aid their humans with PTSD. Every person who suffered did so differently, and it was the program's job to ensure that they did everything they could to make sure the dogs could help. Having a warm body to comfort you while you were having a panic attack was like nothing else for some people. The Pets for Progress program was small, so they worked with only dogs, but there were others around the country that worked with cats, llamas, and other animals that provided comfort and warning if the effects of PTSD were just too much. Storm couldn't save the world, but he could at least help whom he could. He owed that much.

"Hey, little guy," Storm said with a smile as he opened the cage. "Sit, Randy."

Randy wiggled his little butt, so excited that his human was home, but he eventually sat down, his body shaking with happiness.

"Stay," Storm said in a low voice.

Randy stayed for about twenty seconds before hopping up on his two legs and batting his paws in the air for love.

Storm held back a smile. "Well, you lasted longer than yesterday, but we still have some work to do. Come on, then. Let's go outside, and I'll get you fed before I crash."

Randy trotted along at Storm's side, clearly in need of pets. And if Storm could bend, he'd have given them to him. The puppy did his business outside as Storm stood on the back deck, unable to go down the stairs just then. He knew he needed to put in a ramp eventually, but apparently, he was still in denial of some things.

"Come on, Randy. Let's get some chow."

The puppy scampered up the steps before jumping on the bench along the side of the deck, reaching up for Storm.

Storm smiled widely, finally able to reach Randy to rub his hands up and down the little puppy's body. "You're a good boy, Randy."

Randy let his tongue hang out in absolute joy as Storm petted the little guy. When Storm picked him up—grunting only a little at the slight weight—and carried him inside, Randy shifted so he was on his back and his belly was bare.

Storm got Randy his food and let the little guy scarf it down as he made something to eat for himself after finding leftover takeout in his fridge. He was still sweaty, dirty, and in pain, but he needed something in his gut. He popped an Aleve into his mouth and swallowed it down before stripping off his shirt and pants so he stood in his kitchen in just his boxer briefs, still sweaty, but a little less dusty.

He pulled out his trusty ice pack from the freezer and brought his dinner with him to the living room where he sank onto the couch in his underwear and ate his meal like the single man he was. At least he'd used a plate, instead of eating right out of the container.

Randy jumped onto the couch, and Storm was honestly too tired to teach him anything better right then. The puppy settled on his lap and snoozed as Storm adjusted the ice pack on his back.

His body ached.

His stomach rolled at the greasy, heated-up takeout.

He wore only his underwear on his couch.

And now, his puppy had just peed on his lap.

This was the old Montgomery he'd become. It was no wonder he was alone.

Again.

CHAPTER FIVE

Everly would have preferred a root canal sans lidocaine to what she was about to endure. And considering just the thought of teeth made her freak out, that was saying something.

Her in-laws were visiting today.

Oh, joy.

The boys were playing in the living room, and she prayed they weren't finding a way to stain their clothes. Her in-laws had specifically sent over these outfits since they'd told Everly that her clothing choices weren't always the best. And while Everly wanted to smack her mother-in-law, she'd put the twins in their suede jumpers and took away all liquids and food items just in case it dared to touch their clothing.

Why Jackson's parents had given the twins suede outfits, Everly didn't know, but if seeing the boys in the ugly things helped get the Laws out of the house quicker, she'd deal with it.

She ran a hand over the sundress that covered her shoulders and chest far more modestly than anything she would normally wear and tried to keep calm—and sane. While her in-laws hadn't sent over an outfit for Everly to wear, she wasn't in the mood to deal with the judging looks if she dared to show too much skin or wore something other than a dress that was ladylike. She made her way out to the living room, happy the boys were still playing with their soft book, mumbling to each other as they 'read' through the pages.

It wasn't as if Jackson's parents were bad people. They just tended to like things certain ways. *Their* way. All the time. No matter how ridiculous it was.

"Okay, boys," she said with false cheer. Thankfully, they were too young to notice. Hopefully. "Are you ready for Grandma and Grandpa to come visit?"

James rubbed his ear again as he nodded, and she felt that familiar pang in her chest at seeing her baby hurt. The surgery wasn't for three more days, but her mind kept alternately thinking that time either passed too slowly or far too fast depending on what she was feeling that day. Everything was on schedule, but she knew things could change in an instant.

"I wanna go to the book shop," Nathan pouted. "I want you."

She held back tears, her emotions all over the place lately. Since it was the middle of summer, her boys didn't have nursery school like they had in the spring. She had a babysitter throughout the week, and the boys also had little camps they attended but were only for a few hours at a time, and Everly usually went with them for social times. Sometimes, she took the boys into the shop since she had a children's area and reading hour, but today wasn't one of those days. Her in-laws took the children some days as well, but today, they'd wanted to stay with the children at her place rather than take them to theirs. They'd said it was because of Nathan's recent asthma attack and James's upcoming surgery and that being in a familiar setting would be comforting, but she didn't quite believe them. The Laws' home was familiar to the boys since they stayed there often enough, so she figured Nancy, her mother-in-law, just wanted to peep around her house—and not for the first time.

Everly's home was never clean enough. Never orderly enough. Apparently, she had horrid taste, but that was to be expected with Everly's upbringing. She held back a groan at that thought. If her mother were alive, she'd probably have beaten Nancy with the large bag she'd always carried with her.

It was days like this that Everly missed her parents more than ever. But she didn't have time to dwell on what she'd lost and had to focus on making sure her house was in some sort of order before she left her babies with her in-laws and headed to work.

That root canal was sounding better and better.

The doorbell rang at that instant, and she bent to kiss the tops of her boys' heads before going to let Nancy and Peter in. As always, as soon as she opened the door, Nancy pushed her way inside without bothering to say hello or wait for an invitation. While Nancy might have called that rude if anyone else did it, the other woman often lamented that if she'd been given a key to her son's home, it wouldn't be a problem.

One of the many reasons the elder Laws did not have a key—nor would they have one anytime soon.

"Peter," Everly said after a moment and moved to the side fully so her father-in-law could enter her home.

"Everly." He didn't speak as much as Nancy did, but Everly knew that wasn't because he didn't judge her. He judged just as much as his wife was prone to.

He just showed his thoughts on his face, rather than voicing them.

"I see you've put them in their jumpers," Nancy said as she studied her grandchildren. "Probably just put them on right before we came over, hmm? That's why they're so clean. Not a spot on them."

And if they'd had a stain, because God forbid her kids act like children and get messy, Nancy would have had something to say then, too. But these were Jackson's parents, the boys' only living grandparents, so Everly held her tongue. Again.

"They look adorable in your choices as always, Nancy," Everly said with a smile. She looked down at her watch and held back a frown. "I'm going to be late if I don't head out now to the shop. Thank you so much for agreeing to watch the boys today. I'm sure you'll have a wonderful time." Nancy had actually *insisted* on being with the children today rather than it being Everly's idea, but Everly didn't mention that. Nathan and James needed family, so Everly would do what she could to make sure that happened.

Even if it hurt.

"Hmm." Nancy pursed her lips. "Late? If you'd told us the correct time to come over, maybe you wouldn't always be running late. Jackson was never late, you know. He prided himself on always being on time." She looked down at her grandsons but didn't smile like a doting grandmother should. They also hadn't told Everly what time they would be coming over and hadn't given her an option, but that was neither here nor there. "My son was always on time, early if he could make it work. That's why he achieved so much in his short life." She took out a handkerchief and dabbed her eyes.

As much as Jackson's parents grated on her nerves, they clearly loved their son and made sure her boys knew as much about their father as possible. Sometimes too much, in her opinion. Jackson didn't have a single flaw according to her in-laws, and they said as much often to Nathan and James. While Everly would never disparage Jackson to their children, she also didn't put him on the golden pedestal his mother clearly did. He had been human, after all.

"Thank you again for coming over. I shouldn't be out too late." She hoped. Quarterly taxes were looming, and that always gave her a headache. Her accountant did the brunt of the work, but she still had to prep everything.

"Working in a bookstore," Nancy tsked as she sat down on the ottoman nearest the boys. "I'm still surprised Jackson allowed that." She looked down at her grandsons and spoke to them. "Your father was a well-respected professor and the best in his field. He did wonders for his department and won every grant he tried out for."

The boys blinked up at her, clearly confused. They were only three, after all.

Everly didn't point this out. Nor did she mention the fact that Jackson had *not* won every grant, nor was he the best in his field. He was at the top for sure, but he'd had a rivalry with someone in his department, which he'd said always made him work harder. She'd listened to countless diatribes on it and could probably still quote them word for word.

"I own the bookstore," Everly said and wished she hadn't. There was no use defending herself to Nancy, and there never had been. Everly may have her master's degree and own a business, but she'd never be good enough for the golden boy Jackson Law in her mother-in-law's eyes. She'd lived with that fact for years and usually ignored it. Today, apparently, she couldn't keep her mouth shut. "And books are the building blocks for everything in life. So I get to be part of a little bit of everything."

"Hmm." Nancy narrowed her eyes before putting her attention back on the boys. They handed her their book, and she looked it over before beginning to read to them. She was usually a wonderful grandmother, and Everly clung to that fact. Peter had sat down on her couch and pulled out his tablet, reading something like usual. Everly would usually be on board with that, but the man more often than not looked down on her reading choices since she tended to prefer fiction to what he read. After all, she lived a non-fiction life that didn't have a happily ever after. She wanted to escape into a world where she could find that peace.

And that was enough of that.

She said her goodbyes and headed into the bookstore to take the afternoon and evening shifts. Freddie had classes that day, and her other part-time worker had called in sick—something unusual for him—so she would be on her own for the day. While it wouldn't be easy, she could handle it. It wasn't as if she had a choice.

Her hands trailed over her books as she walked the shelves, putting things that had been moved as customers browsed in their correct places. She dusted as she went, answering questions and leading others to the section they were on the lookout for. As she went from genre to genre, she made a mental note of areas where she could improve, or decorations that might need to be changed. She liked keeping things fresh throughout the months so people were never bored when they walked into her shop. Though how anyone could be bored in a bookstore, she didn't know. There were entire worlds in each of her books, volumes filled to the brim with characters people could fall in love with or loathe with every fiber of their being. They could be a warrior for the day, or a maiden in a distant land. There were self-help books and non-fiction historicals waiting for someone to open their pages. Her children's section had endless stories and bright colors that could bring a smile to even the poutiest of babies.

Everly held back a happy sigh as she filled a bag with books for a customer at the cash register. She was always a little jealous that people got to walk out with new books, knowing that new adventures were on the way. It was a silly thing to feel, but in some instances, she was the dreamer Jackson never fully understood. She might be competent—or maybe more than proficient at owning a business and the critical thinking that came with the responsibilities—but in her heart, she was a book lover. A reader. A dreamer.

The sun began to set as she nibbled on the sandwich she'd brought in from home. She could have gone to Taboo and picked up something far more appetizing than a creamy peanut butter and grape jelly sandwich, but she'd known she wouldn't have time today. It didn't really help that she was a crunchy peanut butter and strawberry jam fan, but since her boys liked what they liked, she saved money and went with their tastes for this particular item.

Maybe if Jackson were alive, she could have gone with something different—he'd been a crunchy peanut butter fan, as well—but she couldn't justify having two jars in her pantry when she was on a budget.

And how sad was that thought. If only she had a husband who had lived so she could have the sandwich spread she desired?

Everly set her meager meal down and grimaced. She missed Jackson for more than just his tastes in peanut butter. She missed him with every fiber of her being as evidenced by the ache in her heart, even if the pain wasn't as agonizing as it once had been. Time had healed that. Time and necessity. She couldn't raise her children and work as hard as she did if she wallowed for too long. She'd come to terms long ago with the fact that her husband was never coming back and he'd never meet his children. She might not have moved on in the sense that she'd been on a date in the past three years, but she'd at least stopped crying herself to sleep a while ago.

She frowned, rolled up her garbage, and disposed of it in the bin under her desk. She needed to remember to clear that before she closed up shop for the night. Had she seriously not been on a date at *all* since Jackson?

Of course, the answer was no. She hadn't wanted anything to do with another man when she'd been home alone, breastfeeding the twins and trying not to cry. Storm had been a tremendous help at the time, making sure she had groceries and watching the babies so she could shower the three-day-old dried milk out of her hair. And by the time she'd found her rhythm at being a mom and had healed just a little bit more every day from the loss of her husband, she hadn't had time to look for a man. Hell, she barely had time to put on makeup in the morning now.

Maybe she *should* start thinking of dating again. Hell, it had been over ten years since she'd been on a first date, and she wasn't even sure she could remember how to do it. Her heart didn't hurt as much as it had before when she thought about meeting someone else, though, so maybe that was a sign.

She let out a breath, not sure what to do, but she couldn't focus on that right now. Or the fact that the first image that came to mind when she thought of a man to date was the one man she shouldn't.

Nope. Not going to think of that man or his muscled body beneath those soft flannel shirts of his.

She closed her book and went to the back to pick up the mail the postwoman had dropped off earlier when Everly had been in the middle of a rush. She looked through the stack of bills, flyers, and notes from publishers as she made her way back to the front in case a customer came in. Though she doubted it since it was getting late and a storm was coming in. She only had another hour or so until she closed up shop anyway, and she figured she'd be bringing paperwork home with her so she wouldn't have to deal with her in-laws' patronizing looks.

As she set most of the mail on the desk, she looked down at one envelope in her hand and froze.

It was addressed to Jackson.

She swallowed hard, noticing that while there was postage on the envelope and a Fort Collins stamp, there wasn't a return address. He'd never gotten mail here. Even the stereotypical patriarchy-filled letters that were sent generically were usually addressed to *Mr. Everly Law.* As if she couldn't be a female business owner.

She hesitantly opened the letter and froze once again.

I'm still waiting.

What on *earth* could that mean?

Who was waiting? And for what? She looked on the back, but it was blank. That made no sense, and honestly, it creeped her out probably more than it should have. She set the letter on top of the others and looked through the windows at the darkening clouds. The storm was coming in earlier than expected, which wasn't that uncommon for Denver so she decided to close up shop a bit early and take care of the cash on hand and everything else.

She was just finishing up putting her deposit in her cash bag for the safe in the back room when she noticed a particular scent in the air.

Smoke.

She looked to her left in horror as smoke billowed out from the back room, flames dancing along the window frames and below the shelves. Her hands shook as she grabbed the cash bag, her purse, and whatever she could from the top of the desk and tried to decide if she could take care of this with her fire extinguisher.

The flames moved far faster than she thought possible, taking out books and curtains, engulfing sections in a single breath. Her whole world was on those shelves. Her memories. Her past. Her present. Her future. And yet the flames didn't discriminate. It burned them all.

She coughed, the smoke burning her lungs, and knew that whatever had started the fire might have happened quickly, but her store was a box of tinder, waiting to burn. If she called the fire department now, there still might be a chance. This was far, far too much for her.

Her eyes watering and her throat burning, she ran out of the front and tried to press the keypad on her phone, tears stinging her eyes along with the ash.

"Everly!"

She looked up, her hands shaking so hard she dropped her phone. "It's on fire," she gasped. "My store. I...how is it on fire?"

Storm hurried to her, his face pale, and ran his hands over her face and down her arms. "Are you hurt? Talk to me, Ev."

"I...I...I need to call the fire department."

"Austin is already on that." He bent to pick up her phone and stuffed it into his pocket. "I was at Montgomery Ink hanging out when we saw the smoke. I don't hear your fire alarms, Ev. Why aren't they going off?"

She frowned, not turning to look at her store. She couldn't. Not yet. "I don't know. We just had an inspection last week. Everything should be fine." She repeated the latter twice more, knowing it was all a lie.

Storm took her bag from her hand and stuffed her mail, cash bag, and whatever else she'd grabbed from inside before putting the purse over his shoulder. He should have looked ridiculous, yet all she could do was try not to cry.

Sirens sounded in the distance, echoing off the tall buildings of downtown Denver. She knew they were for her, and that just made it more real. Storm gripped her chin and, somehow, she found the strength to pull away and turn.

Flames poured out of her windows, her door. Smoke billowed, and people shouted as they tried to protect their own businesses and vehicles. The storm that had been coming in wouldn't make it in time. Any rain it would bring would be far too late to douse the flames and save anything of hers.

She'd lost it all.

Storm wrapped his arms around her, and she leaned into him, her head resting on his chest as she watched her hopes and dreams literally burst into flames.

Once again, she was witnessing her life altering forever on its course. And once again, she was with Storm.

She wasn't alone.

But she wasn't whole.

CHAPTER SIX

Storm tightened his arms around Everly's small body and tried to control his erratic pulse. He figured she'd be able to feel the rapid staccato of his heartbeat beneath her ear, but he couldn't put much thought into that, not when he could barely think at all. Holy hell, when he'd seen the smoke billowing from Beneath the Cover's windows, he'd thought part of him had died.

He didn't know what to do with that reaction or why he'd felt so strongly, but he didn't have time to dwell on it. No, he had to keep Everly close and make sure she was still there.

He'd almost lost her.

Letting out a shaky breath, he slid his hands through her disheveled hair and hugged her tightly again before pulling her back so he could look into her eyes.

"You're okay? Was anyone else in there with you?"

"I was alone." Everly shook her head and started to speak again before coughing. He cursed. She needed medical attention, and he'd been standing there like a selfish idiot, needing to touch her to ensure that she was real. Before he could think about his back and the consequences of what he was about to do, he bent down and scooped her up, searching for a paramedic or someone to help.

Everly wrapped her arms around his neck and let out a coughing squeal. "Storm! What are you doing?"

"Finding you a doctor," he growled out, a sharp pain shooting up his spine, shocking him.

Austin, Jax, Storm, and Derek—who had been at the shop with him when they'd seen the smoke— rallied around him. They'd dropped everything to run toward Beneath the Cover to see if they could help, but it looked as if they'd be too late to save the building.

But he'd be damned if he'd be too late to save Everly. He wouldn't lose anyone else. Not if he could help it.

"What's going on? She hurt?" Austin asked, his voice gruff.

"Let me find someone," Jax said quickly before hurrying off. Jax was Montgomery Ink's newest artist, and Storm didn't really know the man, so he looked over at Derek, another artist from the shop, and gave the man a nod. Derek ran after Jax to help him find someone, but Storm couldn't focus on anything but the woman in his arms. It wasn't that he didn't trust Jax, it was that he needed someone he *knew* looking, too. Storm knew Derek would have understood that even without words, knowing the other man's past.

"You're going to hurt yourself," Everly said before coughing again. "I'm too heavy for you."

Storm tightened his grip. "I'm not going to drop you. Stop fidgeting so we can get you help." His back gave a twinge, but he ignored the pain. He'd deal with it later like he always did. What worried him more were all the sounds and shouts around them. If he weren't careful, he'd have another damn panic attack because of the sirens. He just had to keep breathing and keep Everly safe. That was all that mattered.

The paramedics arrived moments later, Jax and Derek by their sides, and Storm set Everly on her feet. She leaned into him, her back to his front, and he knew if she'd been in her right mind and not clearly in shock, she wouldn't have done it. Since Jackson's death, the two of them had done their best to not touch each other. It was as if the idea of them hugging like they used to would bring back the pain in full force. So they'd remained distant.

But not that evening.

The EMTs put an oxygen mask over her face as a precaution and had her sit down on one of the benches that lined their street, but Storm couldn't sit down next to her. Instead, he stood behind her, keeping his hands on her shoulders so she wouldn't get the crazy idea to get up and walk back to see what had happened to her store.

A bookstore on fire would have gone up quickly, and everyone knew it.

"You should be fine, but we're just making sure," one of the paramedics said. "You weren't in there long, but we're not taking any chances."

"Keep the mask on," Storm warned.

Everly shot him a look even as she pressed the mask to her face. He knew she didn't like taking orders, and he rarely gave them, but he was all out of patience right then.

The fire marshal and police showed up next to talk to Everly, and Storm was glad he and his family were there to stand by her side.

"Mrs. Law?" the older man who had to be the fire marshal asked. "I know you told the paramedics you were the only one in the building, but can you be a hundred percent sure of that?"

Everly nodded and lowered the mask from her face.

"She's supposed to keep that on," Storm growled.

The older man raised a brow. "Mr. Law?"

For some reason, that punched Storm right in the gut, and he shook his head. "Just a friend."

Everly blew out a breath and thankfully didn't cough. "I was alone." Storm reached down and lifted the mask to her face again, giving her an intense look. She glared but inhaled a few times before lowering the mask once more. "I was about to close up shop because we had no customers and I was working on my own."

Her throat worked as she swallowed hard, and he heard the tears in her voice. Damn it, that bookstore had meant almost everything to her. The twins and her books were her life, and now part of that had gone up in flames. And there was nothing Storm could do about it.

"Tell me exactly what happened." The marshal had his notepad out, and the cops were staring down at her with questions in their gazes.

Storm frowned and looked over at Austin, who came to stand on his other side, making sure Everly knew she wasn't alone. Jax and Derek joined the circle, showing their support. The four of them weren't small guys, and there were enough tattoos and piercings showing that they made for an intimidating force. Everly wouldn't be alone through this, and if it looked as if there would be an issue, they'd call the Montgomery lawyers right away. It's what they did for family.

Once again, he put the direction of those thoughts from his brain and focused on Everly as she told everyone what had happened.

"You didn't see anything out of the ordinary? Smell anything?"

Everly shook her head. "Nothing. I don't know what happened." This time, a tear slid down her cheek, and Storm let out a curse.

"She already told you what happened. She needs to rest."

One of the cops glared at him, and Storm glared right back. He wasn't in the mood for a pissing contest.

"We can't go inside yet, but from we can tell from the outside, it looks as if an accelerant was used and the fire alarms were disarmed. I need to know everything."

Everly let out a choked sob. "What?"

Storm's whole body froze. He'd assumed it had been faulty wiring or an accident. The building wasn't that new, and he'd never been inside the walls to make sure everything was up to code. He should have, damn it. But if it looked like *arson* it wouldn't have made a damn difference.

"Do you know anyone who would do this?"

She shook her head. "Arson? How...how can that be? The alarms?" She looked over at Storm, her eyes wide with a glassy sheen. They asked her a few more questions, and Storm knew they were just fishing at this point. No one knew what was going on, and he needed to get Everly home.

He looked over at Austin, who gave him a nod. He had backup in case no one listened to him. It was good to have family, and right then, Everly was part of theirs because she didn't have anyone else.

"She needs to get warm and indoors." As soon as he said it, lightning cracked overhead, and he held back another curse. "It's about to pour here, and I don't want her out in it."

"I can speak for myself," Everly said softly, though there was no emotion behind the words. He knew she was in shock, and he needed to get her home.

The fire marshal looked up before letting out a sigh. "I'll be in contact soon." He gave her a frown. "We'll need to do an investigation, so you can't enter the building until we give the go ahead. I'm sorry this happened, but I'm going to do all that I can to see *why* it happened."

Though it didn't sound like a threat, Storm was still a little worried. "Th-thank you," Everly said softly. "I...my store." She whispered the last two words, and Storm wanted to punch something. He wasn't the violent one in his family—if *any* of them were truly violent—but he tried to use words or pointed silence to get his point across rather than his fists. Yet right then, he wanted to punch someone. Anyone who put that look in her eyes.

Everly was the strongest person he knew. So strong that she pushed him away every time he tried to help her. And yet she looked so small just then. Small and helpless.

He'd be damned if he let her stay that way because someone dared to take part of her happiness.

Eventually, the authorities got her information, and she took their cards. Since Storm still had her purse over his shoulder, he stuffed the cards inside along with whatever she'd saved from her place and zipped it closed.

"I'm driving you home," Storm said after a moment. "I don't want you on the road right now."

She let out a long breath, and he was relieved that she didn't cough when she did so. "But what about my car?"

Storm looked past her to the still-smoking building even as raindrops began to fall. "You're parked behind the building I would assume, and now you're blocked in by all the emergency vehicles. We'll get your car tomorrow. I promise. But it's already raining, and you need to lie down."

She pressed her lips together before turning to look at Beneath the Cover. "I don't know what I'm going to do."

Storm put his hand on her shoulder, at a loss for what to say. "You won't be alone."

She looked over her shoulder, sadness in her eyes that he couldn't quite name. "I already am." With a sigh, she looked back at the smoke as the rain began to fall in earnest.

"We need to go," he said as he took her hand. "Come on."

Everly slid her hand away from his as she turned and nodded. "Thank you for the ride."

She was so polite, and yet there wasn't anything behind her words. No emotion. Once he got her home and with her boys, maybe that would change, but he was out of his depth here. He waved at the others, who all went back to Montgomery Ink, but Everly didn't seem to notice. Instead, she quickly walked by his side as they made their way behind the tattoo shop where he'd parked. He helped her into the cab of his truck and tried to buckle her in, but she waved him off.

"I'm okay, Storm." She shook her head. "Well, not okay, but I'll find a way to be. I always do." There was such bleakness to her voice that he wanted to shake someone, but there was nothing he could do. There wasn't ever anything he could do when things got out of hand. "Can I have my bag?" she asked.

He slid it over his shoulder, once again ignoring the searing pain in his back. He'd screwed up something when he lifted her, but he hadn't listened to the warning in his head telling him not to do something stupid with his body. Getting Everly safe had been more important than a few aches and pains.

"Thank you," she whispered.

"Don't thank me," he said gruffly. "I couldn't do much."

She met his gaze. "You did everything." She blinked away tears before looking forward, and he closed the door to the truck. He didn't know what she'd meant exactly, and they were both too off-kilter for him to ask. So he did what he did best when it came to Everly and ignored what he was feeling. Instead, he walked around to get into the driver's side of the truck.

As they drove to her place, they didn't speak to each other, but she'd pulled her phone out of her purse so she could call Jackson's parents, who were apparently watching the twins. The windshield wipers moved back and forth quickly as the downpour came in earnest.

At least the last of the flames would be out of the store. And what a horribly sad thought that was.

When they pulled into her driveway, no one came out of the house—even to the awning-covered porch— to greet them. If they'd been going to his parents or any of his siblings' homes after a fire like that, his family would have run out into the rain to greet them by their car. They wouldn't have waited a single moment to ensure that everyone was safe and whole.

And yet, no one came out to greet Everly.

She'd taken her keys out of her purse before they'd gotten out of the truck so she easily unlocked the door on her own, but Storm was still right behind her as they entered the house.

"Mommy!" James shouted as he ran to her, Nathan right behind him. Everly dropped her bag on the floor and went to her knees, holding her boys close as they hugged her. They pulled away for a moment to hug him too before going back to their mother. He loved those two boys like his own, even if most of the time he felt as if he had no idea what he was doing. He looked up to see Everly's in-laws glaring at him.

Storm stuffed his hands into his pockets, awkwardness settling over his shoulders as he looked up at Nancy and Peter. Jackson's parents stood stiffly a few feet away, clear disdain on their faces. He'd never understood why Everly let the two of them get away with so much, but he figured it had to do with Jackson himself. The older couple had never approved of the match and had always been a little stiff toward Everly. Hell, they hadn't liked Storm either since he was considered a blue-collar worker with a master's degree rather than their academic son. But when Jackson was alive, they'd been much warmer to Ev. Storm remembered that much. When their son died, they'd put Jackson on a pedestal where no one could bring him down, completely ignoring his faults and errors. And as they did that, they needled their daughter-in-law. If their son had been perfect, then Everly should be, as well.

And that coldness just looked starker against the contrast of what *should* have occurred when they heard that Everly had lost not only her shop but also almost her life.

If she hadn't left the building when she did...

No, he couldn't think about that right then and stay sane.

Everly kissed her boys once more before standing up. "Thank you for watching them later than what we agreed on."

"They're our grandsons." That was all Nancy said. She didn't ask if Everly was okay. Didn't make a comment about the fact that Storm was there when he normally wasn't. It was just so...off.

Everly put her hands on the top of her boys' heads, her chin high. She still had a smudge on her cheek, and her hair was out of place, and he knew she needed to sit down. Heck, *he* needed to sit down, or his back was going to lock up soon.

"Thank you again."

Jackson's parents gave them one last look before gathering up their things and leaving. They said goodbye to the boys, but didn't bother speaking to Storm at all, and didn't say another word to Everly. He knew they had to still be hurting over the loss of their only son, but hell, he barely recognized the people who had just been in the room.

"Grandma make sketti," Nathan said with a grin. "It was okay."

Everly smiled sadly and ran a hand through his pale hair. "I'm glad you ate, baby."

Storm cleared his throat, and then everyone looked over at him. "How about you jump in the shower, Ev? I'll hang out with the boys while you get cleaned up." He gave her smoky clothes a pointed look, and she let out a sigh. They hadn't discussed it, but since the boys hadn't looked worried at all and he'd overheard her conversation with Nancy on the phone, he figured Everly didn't want the kids to know about the fire yet—something he totally agreed with. But kids were observant, even as young as the twins were, and they would catch on that something was wrong soon if he and Everly weren't careful.

"Oh," she said after a moment before looking down again. "I...you don't have to stay, Storm."

He waited for her to lift her head and meet his gaze. "Yeah, I do."

"Oh, well, thank you." She cleared her throat. "The boys need to get in their PJs and get ready for bed. We'll do baths in the morning."

"I can do that. Go clean yourself up, Ev." He said it with kindness, but he still heard the order in his voice.

She gave him a look but still left to go shower while he dealt with the boys. The two of them were so excited about having Storm over that it took extra time to get them into their PJs since all they wanted to do was run around the room with their pants over their heads. Despite the way the evening had gone, he still laughed with them and helped them get ready for bed.

By the time Everly came into the room in sweats, a tank, and one of those cotton wraps she owned, the boys had their teeth brushed, their pajamas on, and were gearing up for story time.

"Thank you, Storm," she said softly. He nodded and kissed the tops of the boys' heads before heading back into the kitchen. He knew Everly probably wanted alone time with her kids after everything that had happened, and he didn't blame her.

Instead of heading home like he probably should, he went to her kitchen and got out a couple of mugs and packets for hot cocoa she kept around for the boys. This late, he knew Everly liked chocolate with extra marshmallows rather than coffee, and he wanted to get something warm in her before he left.

By the time she came into the kitchen, he had two steaming mugs of hot cocoa on the counter and a can of tomato soup on the stove. It sounded like a gross combination, but it was the only soup he could find that didn't have pasta shapes.

"You didn't have to do all of this," Everly said, her arms wrapped around her middle.

"I know, but I wanted to." He didn't know what else to say, so he handed her a mug.

"Thank you." She took the hot cocoa from him and wrapped her hands around the warm ceramic. "I don't think I'm fully processing yet."

"You don't have to process yet. You need to get warm and get some sleep. You can deal with things and figure out what you need to do tomorrow." He let out a breath. "I'm just so fucking sorry, Ev."

She met his gaze, her eyes filling with tears. "I hate to cry. I *hate* it. And yet all I seem to be doing lately is crying."

Storm cursed and set down his mug then pulled hers from her hands. He cupped her face, and she stiffened. "Your store just burned to the ground, and it looks like arson. Cry, Everly. That's okay. You're allowed to."

She pressed her lips together, a single tear falling down her cheek. He brushed it away with his thumb, and her eyes widened. When she took a step back, he knew it was for the best.

Before he could say anything else, she frowned and picked up her purse from where she'd set it on the kitchen table. "There was a note."

He froze. "A note?"

She pulled a piece of crumpled paper out of her bag. "I don't know if I picked up the envelope since I just threw things in my bag as I ran out, but I got this letter today. It was addressed to Jackson, so it's not connected to this I don't think, but it's still weird."

She handed it over to Storm, and he frowned. *I'm still waiting.*

"Huh. We should show this to the cops just in case."

Everly blew out a breath. "I have no idea what I'm going to do."

He set the note down on the table and pulled her close. "You don't have to know yet. But I'm not letting you do it alone." He'd promised himself he'd always be there for her, and yet he hadn't been enough. He still wasn't enough.

She wrapped her arms around his middle, and he slid his hand up and down her back, calming himself as much as her. When they pulled away from each other a few moments later, their faces were only a few short breaths apart.

Almost as if he were someone else, as if he didn't know the consequences, he lowered his head, brushing his mouth along hers. She froze for the barest moment before pressing her lips against his, the pressure a sweet agony he couldn't comprehend until it was too late.

When his tongue slid along the seam of her lips, she opened for him, their breaths mingling, their bodies pressed tightly together. He almost deepened the kiss until he realized what the fuck he was doing and pulled away, his body shaking.

"Fuck. I'm sorry, Ev. I'm so fucking sorry."

She blinked up at him, confusion clear on her face.

He didn't let her speak, didn't let him say another thing. Instead, he brushed past her, trying to get himself under control and fled from her house.

He'd kissed his best friend's wife.

His *dead* best friend's wife.

There wasn't a level in hell good enough for him. He'd burn, and he'd deserve it. And yet...and yet he knew he'd never forget the softness of her lips, the taste of her tongue.

Yeah, he would burn.

CHAPTER SEVEN

Everly gripped her phone as she checked the time once again. It had been over an hour since the nurse had checked in on them in the waiting room, and she was about to crawl out of her skin.

That had been a familiar feeling for the past three days.

Since the fire that had taken her bookstore three days ago, she'd gone through what had happened countless times, had spoken to a dozen officials about what she could do, and now she could only wait and see what the next step would be. She hadn't been able to walk inside to see the remnants of her place of business, but she *did* know that her place had been burned down on purpose.

Arson, the fire marshal had said. Arson. And, thankfully, they believed someone other than she had done it, or she'd be an even worse wreck. They were still waiting on the report, and she still didn't have a job or a place of business, but she couldn't think about that.

Because today was not about her or her store.

It was about James.

Her baby boy was in the middle of surgery, and she couldn't be there for him. She could only sit or pace in the small waiting room with the lumpy couches and stiff chairs. Thankfully, though, she wasn't alone. Nancy and Peter sat on the loveseat across from her, a book in Peter's hand and a stern expression on Nancy's face. And it was because of times like these that Everly never pushed Jackson's parents away. They might make Everly feel unwanted or like a bad mother sometimes, but they loved their grandchildren with all their hearts.

They weren't the only ones who had shown up, though. Storm sat in the chair next to her, a sleeping Nathan in his lap. She hadn't known if he'd come since they hadn't spoken since the *incident* in her kitchen that night. But he'd known the time of the surgery and had arrived with coffee and sweets and had hung out with Nathan to keep her little boy entertained for most of the time he'd been there. Storm had only spoken a few words to Everly, and she was kind of glad for it. This wasn't the time or place and, frankly, she had no idea what she'd say anyway.

Storm's parents had even shown up, and she'd almost cried. Marie and Harry Montgomery were two of the most amazing people in the world. They'd also been to this hospital too many times to count recently with their grown children and their own issues, but she was so honored they'd come. The two elder Montgomerys had gone to the hospital cafeteria to get coffee for the rest of the group a few moments ago, and she missed their presence. They'd kept Jackson's parents at bay, and now there were no blockers.

"Jackson wouldn't have let this happen," Nancy said suddenly.

Everly froze. "Excuse me?" she clipped.

"The store. He wouldn't have let you keep the store so long with the children at home. If he'd been here, you wouldn't have let it burn to the ground. Now you have no income for his children, and you're far too stressed to take proper care of the boys."

Everly couldn't quite believe what she was hearing. Of all the far-fetched ideas Nancy could have come up with, this topped anything Everly could have imagined.

"Nancy," Storm growled out. "That's ridiculous, and you know it." He kept his voice low and rubbed his hand over Nathan's back as if to keep him asleep. And while Everly was grateful, she did *not* need him defending her.

"I've got this, Storm," she said quietly, her voice calm. She stood up and walked over to Nancy, leaning forward so the woman could hear her as she whispered. "I know you're hurting. I know you're scared. I am, too. But—"

She didn't get to finish her statement because the door opened at that moment, and James's doctor walked in, a calm expression on his face. She turned on her heel immediately and moved toward him.

"How is James?"

"He's doing just fine," the older man said softly.

Jackson's parents, as well as Storm's, circled around her, and she saw Storm out of the corner of her eye stand up with a sleeping Nathan in his arms, rocking the boy even as he rose.

"The surgery went well, and he's in post-op. We'll get him settled into his room in a moment, but you can come back with me now so we can talk. He's waking up slowing from the anesthesia, but he's still groggy and will be in and out for a few hours. He's calling for you and someone named Storm, though. I thought he was talking about *a* storm for a bit, but I think he wants a person or a stuffed animal or something along those lines. We can go over the details of the surgery and his recovery as we walk. Do you have a Storm?" the man asked, a gentle smile on his face.

Everly stiffened, refusing to look behind her so she could gather her thoughts. Nancy huffed out a breath beside her, but Everly was not in the mood to deal with that woman and her attitude.

"I'm Storm," the man in question said softly. "Ev, you okay with me going with you? Just so he can go to sleep if that's the problem."

She finally turned and nodded. "I think James would like that, even if he's really groggy."

Storm nodded, and instead of laying Nathan down on the couch, he handed her son over to Marie, who cooed and rocked the baby boy. The older woman looked as if she held a three-year-old in her arms without looking strained every day. With how many Montgomerys there were, though, Everly figured that might be true.

Everly continued to ignore Jackson's parents, still hurt and annoyed about Nancy's comments, and followed the doctor to James's room, Storm by her side. Her nerves were shot, but when he reached out and gripped her hand, she tangled her fingers with his and calmed ever so slightly. She refused to even think about what any of that meant, instead focusing on what the doctor was saying. Everything had gone well during the procedure, and the implant had been inserted. They still had many hurdles to overcome, but the biggest part was done. She felt like she wanted to break down in tears from relief, but held it in. She'd done far too much crying lately and couldn't focus on her kids if she was a blubbering mess.

The fact that she held Storm's hand during it all was not lost on her. The fact that it steadied her, however, worried her.

When they made it to James's room, her little baby looked so small on the bed, tubes running in and out of his body. They'd decided to shave his entire head, instead of just the side because he'd wanted to look cool. Nathan had also wanted to buzz-cut his hair, but there had only been so much Everly could take, and she'd talked him out of it.

Nathan had been quiet and still in his hospital bed less than a month ago, and here she was, once again, looking at one of her babies in pain.

How much more could her soul take?

"You can stay here for as long as you need," her doctor said softly. "We're in the wing where we can bring in a cot for you to sleep if needed, as well."

She nodded, her voice not quite strong enough to speak.

"Thank you," Storm said quietly. "We appreciate it."

The doctor left, and Everly went to James's side. He had an IV in his hand, so she gripped his tiny wrist, holding back tears. This wasn't his first surgery, but that didn't make it any easier. And she never wanted seeing her children in pain to become rote.

"Hey, buddy," Storm said softly as James's eyes fluttered open.

James smiled but didn't say anything. Everly figured he wasn't really awake and wouldn't remember this, but she'd talk to him just like Storm was.

"You're such a strong boy," Everly said softly. "I love you, baby."

She and Storm talked to him for a few more minutes before he went back to sleep, his chest rising and falling steadily in his slumber. She let out a shaky breath and stood up, needing to collect her thoughts.

Storm followed her out toward the waiting room and stood like a silent protector at her side. Before they made it though, they stopped in the hallway, as if both of them needed a moment to collect themselves before seeing the others.

"Thank you," she said after a moment. "I've been saying that often recently, but thank you."

"They're Jackson's kids, Ev. Of course, I'm going to be here."

She refused to let the hurt in at that statement, but before she could say anything, he mumbled a curse under his breath.

"That's a lie. I'm not here because of Jackson. That's part of it, but not all of it. I love those kids, Ev. And I'm here because of you, too." He let out a breath. "I'm not sure what that means, but I'm still here." He reached up to cup her face, but stopped, lowering his hand before he touched her.

She had no idea what was going on, but she knew something had changed.

His phone rang at that instant, and the nurse at the counter glared. "You're going to have to take that outside in the waiting room. No phones in here."

Everly frowned at him as his face closed off. He turned off the ringer, a new tension in his shoulders that hadn't been there before. "I have to leave anyway," he said after a moment, his voice gruff. "Tell the kid I'll be back."

"What's going on?" His attitude had changed in a blink, and she couldn't keep up with it all.

"I need to go. I'm glad he's out of surgery, and hell, I'm just happy to see him awake for even those few minutes. Do you want me to send Nancy and Peter back? I'm sure my parents can watch Nathan while they're back here so you three can be with him. You said Nathan was staying with Jackson's parents tonight anyway, so you three probably need to talk."

He was rambling, and she didn't know why. She didn't seem to know anything these days.

"I...yes, send them back." She paused, concern filling her. "What's wrong, Storm?"

His jaw tightened. "Nothing new. I've just got to go."

And with that, he turned and left her standing like a fool in the hallway, confused, a little hurt, and knowing that she needed to put that all away and put her children first.

Because that was what she always did. She was a mom first, Everly second.

And that was the only way she knew how to be. The only way she *should* be.

CHAPTER EIGHT

"Where does this go?" Storm asked, the light box in his hand almost too heavy after so much lifting that day. He swore to himself that he wouldn't lift more than a pen for the next week after everything he'd done to himself recently.

"Over in the living room," Clay said, a frown on his face. "Wait. No, the family room." The kid ran a hand through his hair and gave Storm an embarrassed smile. "I keep forgetting what I'm calling each room in the house. I've never had so much space, you know?"

Storm just shook his head, a smile playing on his face. "You've earned the space, though, kid. So call the rooms what you want. Just stick to it."

Clay rolled his eyes and lifted a much heavier box. He was almost fifteen years younger than Storm and didn't have back issues so he could do all the heavy lifting he wanted.

"You know, I'm twenty-four now. Not so much a kid."

Storm set the box down with the others and rubbed his lower back. "I'm looking at forty, Clay. Pretty sure you'll always be a kid to me."

The younger man snorted. "Okay, old and wise one. Whatever you say. You want to take a break? Your back has got to be killing you after all that lifting."

Storm shook his head. "I'm fine."

"But—"

"Let's finish up," Storm interrupted, not in the mood to rehash the past. Of course, that was an inevitability since that was what they'd always done. The only reason he was even at Clay's new home helping him out was because their pasts had crossed that fateful night twenty years ago.

Shit, had it really been twenty years?

Two decades of secrets, pain, and nightmares. And yet he was sure that it wouldn't end anytime soon. Clay would always be on the periphery of Storm's life. Always a symbol of everything that had been lost. A reminder of his penance.

Storm had been helping out Clay and the kid's grandparents for the past two decades. They'd formed a bond on a rainy night when the world had gone to hell and the sound of screeching metal echoed...a memory that still kept him up at night.

Clay blew out a breath. "Fine, old man. But then you're sitting down and helping me unpack a few boxes instead of lugging everything around. It's been a couple hours already. I didn't figure you'd be helping me for so long."

Storm shrugged. "You're moving into your first home. One that you own rather than rent, and you're only twenty-four. I'm proud of you and wanted to make sure you had everything you needed."

Clay smiled, looking more like the kid he'd been rather than the man he'd become. "I'm just glad the loan assist went through. Rent around here is even more expensive than a mortgage."

Storm nodded. "The market right now is off-kilter for sure. We're doing more rehabs than new builds these days. Though I have a feeling that's going to change soon. It's all cyclical."

Clay picked up another box. "Do you like doing rehabs? I know you're the architect of the company. Wouldn't you rather work on something from scratch?"

"Not necessarily."

The two of them set down their boxes in the kitchen before moving to the living room and taking a seat on the couch. His back thanked him, and he let out a slow breath before cutting open the top of a box to start making piles for Clay.

"What does that mean?" Clay asked, working on his own box.

He thought about how to answer since he hadn't really thought about it before. He just loved what he did, even if it stressed him out most days. Though that might come from working with family day in and day out. "Both aspects of what I do appeal to different parts of my creativity, I guess. It's not always about making something new. Sometimes, I get more out of seeing what I can do with something already there. Time takes its toll on homes and buildings, even if we do everything in our power to make sure it doesn't do too much. I like going into what's already there and seeing how I can make it work for what's needed now. There's something interesting in finding a layout and design that not only brings in part of the past but blends it into what's happening around us. Function and features."

Clay grinned at him when Storm looked over. "What?"

Clay shrugged. "You sound like you love your job and you believe in what you do. I've always admired that."

Uncomfortable, Storm waved it off. "And that's why you decided to go into applied mathematics rather than architecture? Not going to follow in my footsteps?"

"Well, I had dreamed of being a rocket scientist, so I found something that works for me. I like watching things being built, but I'm better at figuring out *why* it works rather than making it work. My dad was a welder, you know. He was like you, good with his hands *and* his brain." Clay gave Storm a sad smile. "I tend to cut myself with safety scissors."

Storm had stiffened at the mention of Clay's father and forced himself to relax. The mention of the ghost in the room always sent that reaction through Storm's system. The two of them had talked about the other man numerous times as part of their therapy, but it still never made it any easier for Storm to hear a memory like that tossed into casual conversation.

The fact that Clay could so easily mention his father, however, allowed Storm to calm. There would always be that unspoken pain between the two of them, but the idea that Clay could remember his father with a smile told Storm the other man had healed. Had grown.

Storm wasn't sure he could ever heal the way others thought he should. It wasn't as if he deserved to *not* feel the guilt, the pain. He'd ruined lives with one night of screeching metal and screams. He shouldn't be allowed to move on like Clay had. The kid deserved peace. Storm, did not.

Clay seemed to notice Storm's lack of verbal response and cleared his throat. "I wish you'd have brought Randy with you. I like when you bring your dogs in training."

Grateful for the subject change, Storm grinned. "He's a little too small to have around underfoot with all these boxes and moving parts. Randy, by the way, will stay with me permanently. I'm not training him for another family or patient."

Clay's eyes brightened. "Really? It's been a while since you had a dog of your own."

Storm shrugged and moved on to another box. "I thought it was time."

There was a beat of silence before Clay spoke, his voice soft. "The dreams getting bad, then?"

Storm let out a slow breath. He hadn't shared all of his secrets with Clay, but anything having to do with why they were connected was fair game. It was what he'd told himself twenty years ago when he'd first come around to make sure four-year-old Clay was okay.

"Sometimes. I tried meds for a while thanks to my therapist, but those didn't help either."

"Having a dog in the house might help, then?"

"Maybe." He swallowed hard. "And if not, the damn pup is cute as hell, and his feet are far too big for his body. Ears, too. Makes me smile, so that has to count for something."

"You got a picture?" Clay asked.

Storm reached into his pocket and shuffled through his photos on his phone until he came up with one where Randy sat on his butt, his head tilted and his floppy ears at a funky angle. He had his mouth open, and his tongue lolled out. Seriously, the puppy was too adorable for his own good, and it made training him to be a therapy dog hard as hell.

Storm lifted bubble wrap from the box in front of him and frowned when he noticed a photo on top of a frame. It wasn't inside the frame like the rest of them, but rather, haphazardly placed in the box. But it wasn't the setting that made him frown; it was the *very* familiar face in the photo. A face he hadn't seen in three years. And there were dozens more photos in the box underneath that one. Dozens of photos of this woman and a man Storm thought he knew—with children surrounding them.

Storm's throat went dry as he shakily took the photo out of the box, trying to comprehend what he was seeing.

The man stood with his arms around a younger woman, smiles on their faces as the man rested his hand on the woman's round stomach. In any other situation, it would look like a normal pregnancy shot with a loving couple.

Yet there was nothing normal about this.

Jackson. That was Jackson's face. Jackson's body. Jackson's arm around a pregnant woman that was *not* Everly. Who the hell was this woman, and why did Clay have a photo of Jackson—or a man that looked *exactly* like his dead best friend—in a box in his new home?

"What's wrong, Storm? You look like you've seen a ghost."

He gripped the photo hard, bending it, and let out a curse before forcing his hand to relax. "I think I have," he whispered, his voice coarse. He held out the photo so Clay could see what he held in his hand. "Who is this?"

Clay frowned before his eyes went dark. "Oh. Him. Don't you know him? You brought him by that one time, right? I totally forgot. That was the douche—

may he rest in peace—who knocked up my aunt and never actually stayed with her. Jackson or whatever."

Storm's ears rang, his pulse racing. "I...I...I brought him around?"

Clay ran a hand through his hair. "Yeah. Once when you were on your way to a camping trip or something and wanted to stop by. It was a while ago, but my aunt Rachel was at my grandparents' and she met Jackson. Apparently, they hit it off." Clay scowled. "You never brought the guy back around and never mentioned him, so I figured you weren't that close. And since even thinking about him pisses me off, I didn't talk about him either. Why? What's wrong?"

Storm took in deep breaths, trying to wrap his mind around what Clay was saying. He tried to remember when he'd brought Jackson up to Fort Collins and blanked for a moment until he remembered a long weekend about ten years ago. Jackson had been with Everly then, and Storm had been dating some woman named Susan. Both women had wanted to come with them but ended up having school or work get in the way, so he and Jackson had made it a guys' weekend. Storm had wanted to stop by Clay's to drop off his birthday present in person, and since Jackson was one of the only people who knew about *why* Storm hung out with Clay, he'd brought his friend along.

There had been a woman at the house, he remembered. Clay's grandparents and aunt had been there to do an early birthday celebration. Rachel, Clay's aunt, had been Everly's age—young, pretty, with fiery red hair and smoky eyes. He hadn't thought anything of it. Jackson had been dating Everly and had married her only a short time later.

"Are you saying Jackson is the father of your cousins?" he asked, his voice low.

Clay frowned. "Were you and Jackson still friends, then? I figured you weren't since you never mentioned his kids."

Because Storm hadn't known Jackson had any beyond the twins. Holy shit. "Answer the question," he barked.

Clay's eyes widened. "I don't know much since I don't talk to Rachel. She's a bitch." He winced. "Sorry. But it's true. She's not nice, and never got along with my dad. But, yeah, she and Jackson dated off and on. They never lived together, but they had three kids together. The youngest is three, born a week or so before Jackson died." He paused. "What's going on, Storm?"

Three kids. Jackson had *three* kids with this other woman. And the entire time, he'd been dating or married to Everly. The youngest child was the same damn age as the twins. Holy hell. Storm didn't know the man he'd called his friend at all. He couldn't think, and he had no idea what he was going to do, but he knew he couldn't do anything sitting on the couch next to Clay.

"I need to go."

Clay stood up with him. "Hold on, man. Talk to me."

Storm shook his head but held onto the photo. "I can't. Not yet. I'll tell you everything soon. I need to take this with me." He held up the photo.

Clay waved it away. "Take it. I didn't even realize the damn thing was in there. Are you okay to drive?" The younger man's face paled as he said it, and Storm cursed.

He moved forward and gripped the other man's shoulder. "I'm okay to drive. I promise. I just need to go. I'll tell you everything soon." But he had to tell someone else first.

If he could.

"Text me when you get home," Clay ordered, and Storm nodded before leaving. He had over an hour drive to think about what the hell he would do, and he knew he'd need even more time than that.

On the way down south, he kept his attention on the road, never one to simply think and let his mind wander when driving—not anymore. But even as he focused on the drive, he couldn't quite comprehend what he'd just learned.

Jackson had another family? That just didn't make sense. His friend had been a good man. A little scatterbrained at times when it came to doing household things or remembering bills, but he had always been so focused on his studies and research that Storm had forgiven him. Everly had done much of the same for Jackson, Storm remembered. She had taken care of the house and the bills. She'd done most of the preparation for the twins, though Storm remembered Jackson being excited—if a little lost—at the thought of becoming a father.

He gripped the steering wheel harder. But, in reality, it looked as though Jackson had already been a father three times over by the time he died and the twins were born. Shit. Rachel's youngest was the same damn age as Everly's boys.

How on earth had Jackson found the energy to keep two families?

Bile coated his tongue as the answer came to him.

Business trips. Jackson had taken countless trips for work, and though some of those must have been real since Jackson had died coming back from one, it was obvious not all of them were. There was no way he could have been out of town so much and *not* have been with Rachel some of those times. The idea that Storm had been the one to introduce them made him physically ill. He hadn't known that that one meeting would forever alter not only his reality but Everly's, as well.

He pulled into his driveway, sweat forming a sheen on his brow. He'd have to tell Everly. There was no way around it. He'd have to find a way to tell her, show her the photo, tell her his part in it.

Break her world wide open.

He couldn't lie to her, and there was no way he'd be able to keep a secret this big from her, but he had no idea how he would find the right words. Were there *right words* for something like this? He didn't know. And things had been awkward as hell since their kiss in her kitchen. He still didn't know what he was going to do about it, but now it seemed all for naught. She'd want nothing to do with him once he told her what he knew. The ache that echoed in his chest at that thought told him more about what he felt for Everly than he dared admit.

He shut off the engine and looked to the right, frowning when he noticed Wes's truck parked next to his. He'd been focused on parking without giving himself a headache and he'd missed the fact that his twin was probably in his house right now. Just what he didn't need. More questions. More stares. More reasons for Wes to hate him because Storm couldn't open up.

This, however, wasn't his secret to tell.

He stiffly got out of the cab of the truck, his back aching something fierce, and closed the door behind him before gingerly making his way up to his front door. As soon as he opened it, he let out a sigh.

Wes lay in the middle of his living room, his arms up as he tossed a ball in the air so Randy could run around him and jump awkwardly to catch it. It wouldn't have been an issue, but the puppy kept jumping on Wes's belly and chest and probably other more sensitive areas to get the ball. That wasn't the kind of training Randy needed, and Wes knew that—or at least Storm thought his twin did. That's what happened when you kept secrets, you forgot what other people knew.

"Is there a reason you're in my living room and letting my dog run wild?" Storm asked, throwing his key in the bowl by his door.

Wes grinned as Randy licked his ear and he sat up, his arms full of wiggling puppy. "I had a few things to go over with you, and since you weren't here, I figured I'd hang out with my main man." He rubbed Randy's belly to the puppy's obvious delight.

"You could have called," Storm said before taking a seat on the couch. It took all his strength not to show the pain radiating down his spine. Hell, he needed a long bath tonight. He'd been terrible on his body for the past couple of weeks.

"I could have, but I wanted to see you anyway. See if you wanted dinner later or something." Wes stood, setting Randy down at his feet.

Storm held out his hand, and Randy trotted over before sitting down on his rump at Storm's command. He gave the puppy some love before Randy went back to Wes to play.

"What did you need to talk to me about?" Storm asked, pinching the bridge of his nose. "I'm exhausted. Can it wait until tomorrow?"

Wes blew out a breath. "What is up with you, man? You've been getting surlier recently, and retreating more and more into your own world. What's going on?"

Storm shook his head. "Nothing," he lied. "I'm just tired and had a long-ass day." And needed time to himself to go over the ramifications of what he'd learned today.

"We need to talk about this project since Tabby is taking vacation with Alex, and Harper is on his honeymoon with Arianna. I need you to step in at the construction site. I can't do it all on my own, and Tabby *needs* this time off with Alex because she hasn't taken a break in years."

That much is true, Storm thought. And she'd just gotten engaged to their brother, Alex, who had been through his own hell. They deserved time together away from the rest of the Montgomerys. He didn't relish the idea of staying out of the office and hurting his back more, but he couldn't blame everyone for needing time away to live. It wasn't as if Storm had a family of his own.

"I'll see what I can do," he said finally.

Wes glared. "That's it? You'll *see what you can do*? First, you hire your girlfriend; now, you're backing out? I thought we were partners, Storm, but you're keeping secrets. We're twins, remember? I can tell. But, apparently, I'm not good enough for you to confide in. Just make sure you don't fuck up the business and our family as you're trying to figure out what the hell is wrong with you." Hurt filled his twin's eyes, and Storm desperately wanted to tell him everything. But he hadn't twenty years ago because of shame, and he couldn't tonight either. Not after what he'd just discovered.

Wes pressed his lips together at Storm's silence before letting out a long breath. "I wish you'd tell me, Storm. I'm still your twin." And with that, his brother walked out, leaving Storm alone with his thoughts and his demons.

He was fucking everything up, and yet Storm knew the worst was yet to come.

It always was.

CHAPTER NINE

Everly ran her hand over Nathan's hair and bent down to kiss his forehead. She'd already done the same to James, though she'd had to be careful thanks to his bandages. This was the first day they were home in their beds after the surgery, and it was their naptime. James needed more rest than usual as he healed, and Nathan had wanted to take a nap in solidarity. Her boys were breaking her heart, and she'd never loved them more than she did right then.

When her phone buzzed in her pocket, she frowned, wondering who it could be. She checked the screen, only to find it listed as *Unknown*. Normally, she'd let it go to voicemail, but since she was waiting on calls from her insurance company as well as the authorities, she answered quickly once she was out of earshot of the boys.

"Hello?"

No one answered.

"Hello?" she asked again.

There was a moment of silence before the call disconnected. She frowned.

That was weird. With a sigh, she put her phone back into her pocket and went back to what she was doing. She had a list as long as her arm to get through and no energy to do it.

Her back ached, and she hadn't slept more than a couple of hours each night for the past few days, but sadly, she wouldn't be allowed to join the boys in their nap. There just wasn't time for that. Since she'd been in and out of the hospital with the kids, she'd gotten behind on household chores and other things on her to-do list. Not to mention the fact that James's hearing tests and therapy were going to begin soon, and she needed to get the whole family prepared for that, as well. They were also taking ASL classes as a family because even if James's surgery gave him the gift of hearing out of both ears, she wanted them all to be well rounded and have another skill to communicate with the world.

Of course, she also had to deal with paperwork and the fire marshal about her property since they still hadn't let her inside to see the damage. That was a dark cloud hanging over her home, and she knew it might break her if she truly gave in to her worry.

She pressed her hand against her belly, her stomach roiling at the thought of everything she'd lost. She'd seen the outside of Beneath the Cover and knew there wouldn't be much—if anything—to salvage. She'd spent years making that place another home for her, a refuge for those in need of books and new worlds, and now it was gone. She had no idea who could have burned her place to the ground, who hated her enough to do so. And if it weren't for that note to Jackson she'd found in the mail, she might have thought it was just a random vandal. But now, she wasn't so sure.

Someone knocked on the front door, and she winced, looking down at her sleeping babies and letting out a sigh of relief that they hadn't woken up. She hurried to answer whoever it was so they wouldn't ring the doorbell instead and truly wake everyone up.

She looked through the peephole, nervous energy coursing through her as she opened the door. "Storm," she said softly. "I didn't know you were stopping by."

He had his hands in his pockets and a frown on his face. That wasn't an entirely new look for him since he usually frowned around her—or didn't show any emotion at all. Since Jackson's death, the days when Storm smiled for her were rare. She let out a shaky breath, annoyed with herself for thinking about that right then.

She'd *kissed* the man in front of her, and now all she could do was think about her husband? Storm had been Jackson's best friend, and yet she couldn't stop picturing that kiss...and wondering what else Storm could do with that mouth of his.

And that was enough of that.

"Can I come in?" he asked, his voice that low growl that she always liked but never admitted to liking.

She moved back, and he took a few steps into her home so she could close the door behind him. "What's wrong?" she asked. There had to be something wrong. For a brief moment, she wondered if it was about their kiss, but for some reason, she knew it had to be about something else. He wouldn't look as tortured as he did right then if it was just about what had happened between them.

"I need to tell you something," he said softly, his gaze boring into hers. "And you're not going to like it."

She blew out a breath. "Well, if I'm not going to like it, you might as well tell me since I'm doing laundry and I don't like that either. Make it a two for one."

Storm reached out for her but then, apparently, thought better of it and let his hand drop. She tried not to let that hurt. "I'll help," he said quietly.

"If that's what you want to do." She was stalling, and they both knew it. She had no idea what he was about to say, but she didn't want to hear it. Yet she was an adult, so she'd listen even if she had to keep her hands busy since she was so nervous around him these days. "The boys are napping, so we'll have to keep it quiet."

He nodded as he fell into step beside her. "I figured they'd be tired after the long week they've had. That's why I knocked instead of ringing the doorbell."

Not everyone would have been that thoughtful and considerate, and that just showed her that there were far more layers to Storm than others saw on a daily basis. "Thanks."

She set about pulling the wet clothes out of the washer, throwing some in the dryer and hanging most of her clothes to air dry. Storm helped in silence, tossing the boys' clothes in the dryer since they were mostly cotton and could handle the heat. Her clothes tended to fall apart since, apparently, no one could make sturdy women's clothes look cute these days. And now she was thinking about clothes and dryer settings rather than what Storm had to say. This was a whole new level of her burying her head in the sand.

"Tell me, Storm. Just get it out. It's obviously bothering you." She paused. "Is it about the kiss?" she blurted then immediately regretted it. "I mean, never mind. Forget I said anything." She started the dryer and went to move more clothes to the washer, but Storm gripped her wrist lightly, halting her. She let him turn her around so she faced him, her back to the moving dryer and her front so close to his.

"It's not about the kiss," he said softly. "I don't regret it." He blew out a breath, and she pressed her lips together, not sure where he was going with the conversation. "I have something to tell you that might make you hate me, but you have to know."

She frowned. "What on earth could make me hate you?"

He pulled back slightly and reached into his pocket, taking out a photo. She froze, somehow knowing that whatever was on that photo was something she didn't want to see.

"I was visiting a friend," he said. "Helping him move into his new place, and when I unpacked a box, I found this." He handed her the photo upside down, and she refused to take it.

"What is it?" she asked, her voice hollow. There was something wrong, something she couldn't quite name.

He flipped the photo over, and she glanced down, her world shattering. "Clay, the guy I know, is this woman's nephew. Apparently, Jackson was with her for years." His voice broke. "They have three kids, Ev. Three goddamn kids and I didn't know."

She swallowed hard, her eyes filling with tears, but instead of breaking, instead of sadness, she only felt rage. "Why are you showing this to me? It's not him." She refused to look at it again, pushing his hand away. "It's just someone who looks like him or whatever. My husband wouldn't have cheated on me. He *loved* me. He's the father of my children, not hers. I don't know what lies someone told you, but you don't get to come in here and spread them to me. Jackson was *mine*." Even as she said the words, doubt crawled into her mind. He'd always flirted with waitresses and other women around her, but he was so smooth about it, it always felt like kindness rather than flirting. And he'd gone on so many business trips, had *died* because of one...

But, no. That couldn't be true. Her husband didn't have another family.

"Ev..."

"No. Don't talk. Don't say anything else. Whatever this Clay told you was a lie. It has to be. Jackson wasn't like that. He was a good man. A wonderful man. He's dead, Storm. Nothing will bring him back, and tarnishing his memory like this only makes things worse."

Hands shaking, Everly pushed at Storm's chest, needing air. He staggered back, pain in his eyes. For a moment, she thought it was because of what he'd just said, but no, that was *physical* pain.

"What's wrong?" she asked. "Did I hurt you?"

He gritted his teeth. "I'm fine."

He didn't sound fine. So she lifted up his shirt, putting her hands on the tense muscles of his side and back. There were faint scars under her fingertips, scars she hadn't noticed before because he tended to hide his back from her. She frowned. "What did you do to your back? Oh my God, did I hurt you?"

She ran her hands up and down his sides, and he tensed. When she looked up, she froze, the heat in his gaze singing her where she stood.

He slid his hand over her cheek slowly, his thumb brushing her skin oh so softly. The rough pad of his thumb from where he held his pencil when he worked scraped her skin just right. Too right. "You're not hurting me, Ev."

She swallowed hard, her brain going in a thousand different directions, yet each of them ended with her in his arms. She didn't want to think, didn't want to do anything except *be* right there in his arms, with his body so close to hers she could feel the heat of him through the thin blouse she wore.

She needed to think about what he'd just said, needed to remember that her children were sleeping on the other side of her home and that her place of business had just burned down, but she didn't. Instead, she pushed those thoughts from her mind just this once and decided to do something for herself.

"Kiss me," she whispered. "I need you to kiss me." Need. Such a small word for something so big. She never let herself need, not anymore. It had always been about others—something she didn't regret. But right then, in her laundry room with the world pressing down on her shoulders with so much weight she could barely breathe, she didn't want to think about anything.

Just her. Just Storm. Just *them*.

His hand shifted to tighten around the back of her neck, pulling her hair ever so slightly as he did so. Her mouth parted, and he lowered his head. "I shouldn't be doing this."

She arched her back. "Then do it anyway." She needed to forget, to lose herself. She might regret it later, bur right then, she only needed to be in this moment, be in his arms, be with *him*.

From the way Storm looked at her, she knew she wasn't alone in her thinking. Then he lowered his head and *kissed* her. Their mouths met in a tangle of need and moans, his hand tightening even more in her hair, and the other sliding up her side. She ran her hands up and down his back, the ridge of scars so faint she would have missed them if she hadn't been keenly aware of the feel of his skin. She wanted to know what had happened, wanted to know his secrets, but she didn't ask. This wasn't the time for secrets, wasn't the time for anything except their need, their mouths, their hands. She'd worry about everything else later.

He moved her a step so her back rested along the dryer, the heat and rumbling sensation sending shockwaves through her system. She'd never kissed like this, never made out in her laundry room as the vibrations did wonderful things to her body. Jackson had always made sure they made love in bed with the lights off so they could "explore" one another softly. Before him, she'd only slept with one other man, and it had never amounted to much. She'd never come with her first boyfriend and rarely came with Jackson. It just took her forever to get into that headspace, and by the time she was there, her partner was already done. She knew she wasn't the only woman in the world with that issue so it didn't matter all that much.

But from the way Storm pressed the hard length of his erection against her belly, she had a feeling she might miss out if she *didn't* come with him. However, there was no such thing as a magic penis, and she knew it would take more than that very nice hard length for her to get off.

Storm tugged on her hair again, this time pulling away so he could look into her eyes. "I lost you," he said with a growl. "Are you regretting this already?"

She shook her head. "My mind wandered." That was her problem in bed. She kept thinking about what she was missing or forgetting, so much so that she couldn't just enjoy the moment. It wasn't anyone's fault, it was just the way she was wired.

He tilted his head. "Then I'm not doing my job." His hands went to her waist, and she widened her eyes. "Gonna need you to jump a bit, Ev. As you saw, my back isn't what it used to be." He lowered his head and kissed her quickly. "No questions. Not right now. I don't think either of us wants those at the moment."

Since she agreed with him on that part, she didn't ask about his back. Instead, she put her hands behind her on the dryer and jumped up with his help so she ended up sitting on top of the moving machine. The heat and vibrations went straight to her clit, and she gasped, surprising herself.

Storm grinned then, making him look even more handsome. She'd be lying if she said she'd never noticed how attractive he was. The damn man was far too good-looking for his own good, but never in her wildest dreams would she have imagined her legs wrapped around his waist as she sat on her dryer.

"Feel good?" he asked, rocking into her.

Her eyes crossed, and she tightened her hold on him. "Uh-huh."

He nipped at her chin before kissing her again, this time a little harder, a little longer. "Tell me when to stop," he whispered in her ear before gently biting down on her earlobe. That sent shivers through her body, and she pressed her breasts to his chest.

"Don't stop." This was crazy. She knew this. He knew it. And yet neither of them was going to stop. She honestly couldn't believe she was doing this, and yet as soon as he ran his hand down her belly and under her leggings, she arched, all thoughts of what they shouldn't be doing fleeing her mind in an instant.

The rough pad of his thumb went over her panties, proving to both of them how wet she was. She had to curve her back ever so slightly so he could slide his hand underneath the damp cotton to reach her heat. Their eyes met, and he worked his finger between her folds and up to her clit.

She shuddered, biting her lip as he started to move his hand, bringing her closer and closer to the edge. They didn't say anything, and she was glad because she wasn't sure she would be able to speak at all. His fingers speared her, and her body shuddered. It had been so long since she'd been with anyone that she gasped, her body tightening around him. She also didn't use internal vibrators these days since, usually, she could only come by clitoral stimulation.

He continued to work her on top of the dryer, and the vibrations under her butt just pushed her closer and closer to the edge. But even as that happened, she backed away without meaning to, her mind going to what might happen instead of what *was* happening. This was how she always ended up in bed, and she hated it. If only she could actually focus, she might be able to orgasm.

Storm took his other hand at that instant and tugged up her shirt, exposing her bra. He kissed her over the lace, leaving a wet mark as he went to the other breast. She leaned her head back, her body warming from the dryer and the power of his touch.

"More fingers, Ev?" he growled. "Or do you want my fingers on your clit and breasts?"

She blinked up at him, her body shaking. "Huh?" she asked, her mind hazy.

"You keep getting close and backing away. Tell me what you like, and I'll make sure you get there. I can read your body, but there's nothing better than hearing your words. You know yourself. Tell me what you do to make yourself come."

No one had ever asked her that. Hell, she was pretty sure she'd never even asked herself that. "Um, I don't usually come with penetration." Though his fingers were *inside* her at that moment, she still blushed. There was something far more intimate in talking about how he could please her than him actually pleasing her.

"Usually." He nodded. "Okay, we can work with that." He reached around her and changed the setting on the dryer before grinning down at her. "We'll go for the faster tumble dry."

She smiled but let out a moan as the vibrations under her increased, and she found herself rocking on his hand. He kept kissing her mouth, her neck, her breasts, even as his fingers worked their magic on her clit. She found herself on the edge once again, but before she could think herself off of it, he pressed down on her clit at the same time he pinched her nipple and kissed her.

She came with a gasp, her body shaking, her hips arching on his hand and the hot dryer. He kept kissing her, taking in her moans as she came down from her high. As the cycle on the dryer ended, she leaned back, her body hot and heavy. He removed his hand from her pants, kept his eyes on hers, and licked each and every finger. Slowly.

She almost came again.

"I...I've never orgasmed that fast. Ever. Like I don't orgasm enough to know if I do it right most days and..." She snapped her mouth shut, appalled she'd been so honest.

Storm's eyes softened, and he leaned down to take her lips in a soft, lingering kiss. "You're beautiful when you come," he said, his voice gruff. "And I'm going to have to see you do that again."

She licked her lips and looked down at the straining budge behind his zipper. "What about you?"

"What about me?" he teased, his eyes dancing.

But before she could reach between them, the doorbell rang, and reality stepped in. She sighed, and he let out a curse.

"Next time," he said quickly, and she froze. Would there be a next time? Damn it. She couldn't think about that right then. Everything she'd tried not to think about when she was in Storm's arms slammed into her and she grew cold. "Fuck." He helped her right herself, and she slid off the dryer.

When the doorbell rang again, she let out a curse of her own. "Damn it. I'm coming." She blushed at that thought but moved past Storm. "Can you make sure the boys are still sleeping?" she asked. "I'll get the door."

Storm nodded and walked to the back of the house without another word. She could still feel him inside her, the echo of memory so intense she knew it may not ever fade away completely. But now she had no idea what they were going to do because life wasn't just about feeling good for a single instant, it was about so much more, and they had more baggage than most—and she didn't even know all of his secrets.

She pushed those thoughts from her mind as she opened the door to reveal a familiar redheaded woman.

A woman Everly had just seen in a photo she'd vowed couldn't be real.

It *couldn't*.

The woman raised her chin. "I hear Clay spilled the beans. I think it's time we talked."

Everly blinked, wondering why everything seemed to be moving so slowly, as if she couldn't quite make coherent thoughts. This was the woman who had apparently been with Everly's husband and had three kids with him.

That can't be her, she thought.

This was all a dream.

A nightmare.

Because even though Everly had lost almost everything she held dear, this couldn't be her life. It couldn't be this bad.

And yet she knew, it not only could be. It was.

CHAPTER TEN

S torm heard a female voice that seemed to be from a distant memory as he left the boys' room. They were still conked out from a stressful week and, thankfully, hadn't woken up during the laundry room interlude or from the doorbell. But based on who he thought that voice belonged to, he knew the worst of things was yet to come.

"We can have this conversation on your porch so your neighbors can hear everything, or I can come in, and we can talk about this like adults."

Storm hurried to the front of the house, his hands fisting. He could not believe Rachel had the nerve to show up at Everly's house after all this time. Because that's exactly who this woman had to be. As soon as he saw her in the doorway, he recognized her. He had no idea what she could be doing here, but he knew nothing good could come of it. Hell, he still smelled of Everly, and his dick ached something fierce. Yet all of that and the questions that had whirled in his mind after the dryer session slid away as soon as he saw the redhead at the door.

Fuck.

He went right to Everly and put his hand on her shoulder, making sure she knew she wasn't alone. From the way Rachel's eyes narrowed on his hand, he knew that might have been a mistake, but he didn't care. Everly needed him right then even if she didn't want to admit it.

Rachel smiled, her eyes going wide. "Oh, Storm. You're here. You can help me explain to Everly what happened."

Everly stiffened, and he tightened his jaw. "Not sure what you want me to say, Rachel. I just found out yesterday and came over this morning."

"You can come in," Everly said calmly, but he knew she was anything but calm right then. "But only because I'm tired of the vagueness. You *will* leave when I tell you to. Do you understand?"

Rachel gave Everly a sad smile and nodded. "Of course. This must be trying for you."

Storm was ready to kick this woman out right now, but Everly stood back, pushing him back, as well. Rachel strode in, her chin high as she surveyed the house. Jesus, this woman was some piece of work if everything Clay had said was true. But if Everly needed answers, then they'd get them. And Storm would do everything in his power to protect Ev and the twins as they did.

They took their seats in the living room, Rachel in the high-backed chair, Everly on one side of the couch, him on the other. He gave Ev space only because she seemed to need it. He'd move closer the minute it looked as if she needed him. He didn't know how this conversation would go, but he knew it probably wouldn't be good.

Rachel opened her mouth to speak, but Everly held up her hand. She was so stoic, so freaking stiff that he was afraid she might break. Others might not see the emotion rippling beneath the icy exterior, but he didn't know how anyone could miss it.

"Before you begin with what must be a fascinating tale, I'm going to tell you what I know, and you will nod or shake your head with what is true or false." Rachel narrowed her eyes but thankfully didn't speak. "If this is all a misunderstanding, then I'm sure we can move forward, but from the way you walked in here with a smile instead of fear, I have a feeling you will be walking back through that door quite quickly."

"You think you know everything?" Rachel spat. "You don't know anything."

It took everything he had not to speak up, but Everly didn't need him taking control of the situation. She had it firmly in hand and would do what she had to do. If she needed him, he'd be there. Right now, he was just her visible support.

"I said you could nod or shake your head. I didn't say you could speak. You are in *my* home. A home I shared with my husband. A husband, I fear, *we* might have shared."

Storm almost reached out to grip Everly's hand but stopped himself just in time.

"I hear you had an affair with my husband, perhaps even when Jackson and I were merely dating at first. Is that correct?"

Rachel glared but nodded.

Everly's fisted hands tightened on her lap, the only visible evidence she was breaking inside. He wanted to fix this. Wanted to kick Rachel out. Wanted to go back in time and kick Jackson's ass. Yet he couldn't do anything except watch Everly take matters into her own hands and find the only control she could. He refused to take that away from her.

"You slept with Jackson Law, my legal husband, for years."

Rachel nodded.

"How many? And yes, you can speak for this answer."

Storm didn't know why Rachel was allowing Everly to control the conversation, but he had a feeling she saw what he did: Everly meant business.

"Ten years," Rachel bit out. "We were together for ten years. He loved me. Had a *life* with me. I understood that he needed to marry you for one reason or another, but he was *mine* for ten years."

Jesus Christ. Storm knew the timeline since he'd been the one to bring Jackson up to Fort Collins, but hearing it from Rachel's lips just made it that much more real. What the hell had Jackson been thinking? And how had they all been so blind to what the other man was doing?

"Ten years," Everly repeated. She paused for a moment, and Storm once again forced himself not to go to her. It would only make her resent him for coddling her in front of Rachel. "And you have children?" The last word was whispered, and he *knew* she was on the verge of breaking.

Rachel nodded. "Three. Jackson is nine. Holden is seven. And Mariah is three."

Jackson. They'd named their fucking son, *Jackson*. Storm's hands shook, and he tried to remember if the man he'd called his friend had slipped up at any point. Had Storm really been so in his head that he'd missed all the lies? Missed the fact that Jackson was a horrible person who could even hurt Everly from the grave?

Everly blinked. "Three years old."

Rachel smiled, and he saw the bitterness in it. "Yes, the same age as your kids. He wasn't with me as much during the last pregnancy because you were taking up so much of his time." Rachel wiped a tear he couldn't see, and he figured she was probably faking it. "We loved each other. No, he wasn't with us as much as he should have been, but I understood. He had responsibilities with you and with work. He'd made promises, and he wouldn't break them. I found that noble. He loved me, you see. Loved me so much that he kept coming back. He was such a good father." Rachel smiled again, this time her eyes going dreamy. "I miss him so much. He's missing his children growing up."

"Yes, he is." Everly's voice was so sharp it could cut steel. "He's missing *my* boys growing up. He never met his children."

"He met mine," Rachel bit out.

"What do you want?" Everly asked after a moment, and Storm's head pulsated at the temples.

"I want us to know each other," Rachel said simply, but Storm knew there had to be more to it. Hell, from the way Ev's back straightened, she knew, as well.

"What do you want?" Everly repeated, her hands appearing stiff as she unclenched her fists.

The other woman sighed. "Fine. Raising three children is hard. Raising *Jackson's* three children without him is hard. You have help. He left everything to you, but he couldn't do the same for me."

He knew it. It was all about money. It had to be. Rachel hadn't gotten a penny in the will, but she'd had a part of Jackson Everly had never laid claim to.

"I had nothing to do with the will, Rachel." Storm wanted to wrap his arms around Everly and make this all go away, but he knew there was nothing he could do.

Rachel's eyes narrowed for the barest moment before she visibly fought to look a little more innocent. "I deserve it, Everly. My *children* deserve it. If you won't listen to me now, I'll make *sure* you listen to me soon. Damn sure."

"That's enough," Everly said calmly, but she was anything but calm. "That's more than enough."

Rachel narrowed her eyes, and Storm opened his mouth to speak before rethinking. This was Everly's choice, but he'd forcibly make Rachel leave if he had to.

"Get out," Everly said calmly.

"We're not done," Rachel cried.

"Yes. We are. Get out before I throw you out. Before I let Storm do what he's wanted to do from the moment you walked in—force you out of my home."

Everly stood, and Storm did the same. He was beyond ready to get this woman out of Ev's home so they could talk. He couldn't believe Rachel would just show up after all this time and think everything would be okay. He *knew* there was something more going on, but he couldn't figure out what it was.

"I can't go. We're not done yet."

"Yeah, you are. Now get out." He hadn't meant to chime in, but he was beyond done. And from the way Everly kept so, *so* still, he knew she was, too.

"You knew!" Rachel screamed. "You knew. You introduced us."

One of the boys made a noise from the back of the house, and Storm held back a curse at the look of manic glee in Rachel's eyes. There was seriously something wrong with this woman.

"Get out," Everly said a little bit firmer. "Get out before I call the police." She made a step toward Rachel, and the other woman got out of her chair quickly.

"This isn't over," Rachel said as she stormed away.

"I fear it's not, but right now, I don't really care. Now get out of my home."

Rachel stomped through the front door, her hair flowing behind her, and Everly closed the slab of thick wood behind her and then locked it.

"I'll go check on the boys," Storm said softly. "Be right back."

Everly turned to look at him, her eyes full of anger. "I need a moment to think, so thank you."

He bent down to kiss her, thought better of it since he had no idea what the hell he was doing, and jogged to the boys' bedroom. James was still sleeping, his stuffed bear tucked in his arms, but Nathan was sitting up and looking around, wide-awake.

"Uncle Storm?" Nathan asked, rubbing his eyes.

"Hey, buddy," Storm said softly so as not to wake up James. "You doing okay?" He knelt by the bed and ran a hand over Nathan's blond hair.

"Uh-huh. I heard loud people."

Damn it, Rachel.

"It was just someone at the door. They're gone now. You want to play with your trucks in the playroom so James can sleep?"

Nathan nodded and held up his hands to be picked up. Storm's heart ached as he picked up the little boy who had never known his father. But now that Storm had learned more about who the man truly was, he wasn't sure that was a bad thing.

He turned with Nathan in his arms to see Everly in the doorway, her arms wrapped around her middle. "Hey," he said softly.

"Hey," she said back before looking at Nathan, her mouth forming into a small smile. "I'll bring you a snack in a bit if you play like a good boy. How's that?"

Nathan snuggled into Storm's neck and nodded. "Okay."

"How are your lungs?" she asked her son as Storm moved closer.

"Good." Nathan let out a loud, wet breath on Storm's neck, and Storm did his best to keep from cringing. Kids were constantly leaving slime and grime on him, even though he didn't have any of his own. He just happened to have tons of nieces and nephews, as well as the twins around. He didn't mind it, though. Unlike some, he *liked* kids.

Everly grimaced, her eyes dancing with laughter for a bare moment before the reality of everything that had already occurred that day settled in. Storm swallowed hard and followed Everly to the playroom where they let Nathan get out his toys. Everly picked up the video monitor so she could watch him while she and Storm talked in the living room. He knew she usually kept the twins in her sights as much as possible, but this wasn't a conversation they needed to have in front of the boys.

They made their way back to the living room, and he ran a hand over his scruff, figuring he might need to shave soon. "I...I don't know what to say."

"Did you know?" Everly asked immediately. "I mean, you knew enough to tell me today, but Rachel said you introduced her to Jackson. And as much as I don't want to believe a word that came out of that woman's mouth, it all seems like too much of a coincidence for you to know her and Jackson and for all of this to come to light."

Storm reached out and gripped her hand. She let him, though they didn't sit. He knew they each had too much nervous energy to do so.

"I didn't know Jackson had another family until last night. I spent the night tossing and turning, figuring out how to tell you. I know I probably should have driven right here once I found out, but I needed time to process and make sure that it made sense

111

timeline-wise before I did something stupid like tell you what Clay told me, only to find out it wasn't true."

"Who is Clay? And you still haven't answered my question."

Storm took his hand back and ran it through his hair. "It all goes together. Yes, I did introduce the two of them." Everly sucked in a sharp breath, and he cursed. "But I didn't know what I had done at the time. I know Rachel's nephew, Clay. The guy I got the photo from." He tried to order his thoughts and couldn't quite do it, so he just went with what was in his head. "Remember that camping trip Jackson and I took ten years or so ago? The one you wanted to go on but couldn't?"

Everly's eyes narrowed, but she nodded. "I remember."

"Well, on the way to that trip, we stopped by Clay's house so I could drop off his birthday present. Rachel was there, and I guess that's how she met Jackson. I don't know more than that. I didn't know they ever saw each other again. Hell, I'm pretty sure I only met her once or twice after that, and only in passing. I knew she had kids, but didn't know the father. I didn't even know the kids' names. Nothing ever pointed to the fact that the man I thought I knew, the man I called my best friend, was a fucking liar and a cheat."

Everly hugged herself, and Storm moved toward her. He held open his arms, and she sank into his embrace. When he tightened his hold, she let out a sob, her tears soaking his shirt. She cried, and he hated himself. Hated that he had been part of this, even if he hadn't been aware.

"How do you know Clay?" Everly asked after a few minutes, her voice hoarse. "There's a story there."

He ran his hands down her back and sighed. "I haven't told many people about him."

"Is he your son?" Everly asked suddenly.

Storm shook his head, but she couldn't see him. "No," he said after a moment. "It would be easier if that were the case. Clay isn't my son, but I've been in his life since he was four years old."

He pulled back so he could look into Everly's eyes as he told her a tale only a few people in his life knew. *She deserves to know*, he thought. She deserved so much more than him.

"When I was twenty, I was in college with Jackson—as you know. I visited my family here in Denver, and Wes at his college often—I went to a different college than Wes because our scholarships ended up that way. We figured it would be good because we had always been the twins and were attached at the hip. Plus, Jackson and Wes didn't get along, so it was easier for everyone if my brother and I learned to be our own people as well as Montgomerys."

Everly took his hand and pulled him to the couch. "I think we both need to be sitting for this."

Storm nodded and took a seat next to her, his hand still over hers. "I was driving back home after visiting Wes, and it was raining. I was tired but still alert." He could still hear the sound of raindrops hitting his windshield. Still feel the wind on his face when that windshield shattered. "A man fell asleep at the wheel and went across the median. Since it was raining, I hadn't been driving that fast, but fast enough. He hit me head-on. Totaled the car. It didn't break my spine, but nearly." He blew out a breath as Everly squeezed his hand. "The doctors said I screwed up enough in my back that a broken vertebra would have been easier to deal with. That's why I have so many back issues and why I don't work at the sites as much as the rest of my family. I just can't handle the manual labor anymore. I worked through the pain when I was younger, but I can't now."

He was rambling about himself and not what had happened, and he needed to stop.

"I was lucky," he rasped. "I lived. The man driving didn't. He died on impact. His four-year-old son, Clay, didn't get a scratch on him because he'd been in the back and properly strapped into his booster, but he lost his father. He'd already lost his mom when she died during childbirth, and because of me, he lost his dad, too." Storm blinked back tears, his throat raw with that familiar burn. "I killed a man, Everly."

Everly shook her head, tears falling down her cheeks. "No, you didn't. It wasn't your fault."

"Yeah, it was. At least, part of it. Maybe I could have slowed down. Maybe it was too dangerous to be on the road. It doesn't matter. A man died, and I was driving." He blew out a breath. "Only my dad and Austin know. They were the ones at home when the hospital called." He pressed his lips together, trying to gather his thoughts. "I never told Wes." How could he? How could he let others know his shame?

"Oh, Storm." She leaned closer to him on the couch, and he moved his arm so she could sit right by his side. He needed that warmth, yet he hadn't known it until just now.

"I never told Wes because I couldn't. Not at the time. And as the years passed, it got harder and harder. He's always known something is up, but we moved past it. At least, I thought we had. Now, he's even wearier, and I know I need to tell him or I'm going to break something so inherent between us that we won't be able to fix it."

She kissed his jaw, surprising both of them. "But you told Jackson?"

He swallowed hard, tightening his grip around her. "Yeah. We were roommates in college, so he knew I'd had surgery and needed time to recover. Austin came up and rented an apartment, so I ended up staying with him while I healed. I could walk, but it hurt like a bitch, you know?"

"Why didn't you come back down to Denver? To your family?"

Storm hung his head, trying to come up with words. "I couldn't. I couldn't let them see me like that, and I couldn't tell them what I'd done."

"It wasn't your fault, Storm."

"It still feels it, even if I wasn't the one who fell asleep. There were so many what-ifs, and yet there was nothing I could do in the end. Jackson knew, though. He was there when I came back to school after missing a semester. He slept in the same apartment with me when I screamed in my sleep or when I had episodes." He looked down at her. "I still have PTSD, though therapy helps. I had a dog named Ben for a while who was a certified therapy dog that helped me calm down when things got too loud, or stuff reminded me of the accident. When he passed away, I didn't get another dog, but I helped train others in the program."

Everly set her hand on his chest, and he let out a breath. "Is that what you're doing with Randy?"

He kissed the top of her head, needing the touch. "Yes, though I'm going to keep him," he said with a smile. "I'll train other dogs in the future, but Randy will be mine."

"I still need to meet this puppy," she said after a moment.

"You will."

They were silent for a while, their breaths evening out. He hadn't told another soul about what had happened that rainy night after he told his father, Austin, and Jackson, and yet he'd told Everly without breaking down. That had to mean something. Actually, it meant more than something. He could tell her things...but he knew he also needed to tell his family. He couldn't keep this secret any longer without hurting them more than he already had.

"What am I going to do?" she asked, her voice low.

"I don't know, Ev," he answered honestly. "But I'm not going to let you do it alone."

He held her for a few minutes longer before getting up and checking on the children. He'd been honest when he said he didn't know what the next step would be, but no matter what, he couldn't let her face it on her own. He'd be there—for her, for the boys...for whatever came from what they were becoming. Always.

CHAPTER ELEVEN

Even though Everly didn't have a place to work, she still had bills to pay and forms to go over. The authorities hadn't let her into Beneath the Cover yet, and she was getting antsy. They kept telling her they needed to collect more evidence and that their investigation wasn't over. And while she wanted to get inside and start seeing what she could salvage, she also knew that this waiting time was good for her. Or at least that's what she told herself since she knew that once she stepped inside her home away from home, she wouldn't be able to pretend that everything was okay anymore.

Because nothing would ever truly be okay again.

The note that she'd gotten the evening of the fire kept coming back to her. If it hadn't been postmarked, she might have thought it was connected to the fire, but the more she thought about it, the more she figured it had to be from Rachel. The other woman was the secret Jackson had been keeping from her, so the note could have been from her. Or it was just another skeleton in the closet the man she'd thought was her husband and love of her life had been keeping. It didn't make sense to her that the note and the fire were related, not after finding out about Rachel.

The fire was probably just some person who wanted to make things burn and had nothing to do with her or her store in particular.

Everly sighed, annoyed with herself for going down yet another avenue of thought that led to the fire. The authorities weren't telling her anything except that they were still looking, and all she could do was sit on her hands and pretend as if she knew what she was doing. Her sanctuary was gone, and nothing would bring it back. She could rebuild, but it wouldn't be the same.

Her phone rang, and she answered without bothering to look at the readout. It rang every thirty seconds it seemed these days, and she wanted to hide the darn thing in her desk.

"Hello?"

No answer.

She frowned and looked at the readout again.

"Unknown? Again?" she mumbled, her brain exhausted but remembering the other time she'd had a hang-up call.

"Hello?"

The call disconnected, and she set the phone down. She hoped whoever it was got over their fixation with calling her soon because this was getting freaking annoying. Hopefully, it was just a wrong number, but an uneasy feeling settled into her stomach. It was all just a little too much, and she was jumpy.

She finished up her paperwork and set it in the drawer on her desk, shutting down her computer as she stood up to go check on the boys. They'd been playing with their blocks in their playroom for the past twenty minutes, and though she could see them on the monitor, that was more than enough time for them to get into trouble.

As she made her way into the playroom, she looked down at her watch and held back a curse. She had less than an hour until Alex and Tabby came by to watch the boys. They'd volunteered tonight since Everly had plans.

In fact, Everly had a date.

With Storm.

Their first date.

She tried not to let the panic set in, but it wasn't easy. Somehow, she'd gone from being Storm's friend who always seemed to set him on edge, to a woman he'd made come on her dryer, to one he now wanted to date in public. She was so far out of her depth it wasn't even funny.

"Mommy!" Nathan said with a grin. "Blocks!"

She smiled as she sat down between then. "Yes, blocks! Can you build me a tower?" Between the hospital visits and aftercare, they hadn't been able to attend nursery school as regularly as she'd have liked lately, so she was doing her best to make sure she helped with their fine motor skills as much as possible. She ran her hand over James's knee. "Can you build one together?"

"Hmm," James answered, his attention on the blocks in front of him. He studied them quietly before giving her a nod. Her boys took turns as to who would be the loud one for the day, and sometimes, the days overlapped and her ears would ring. They were becoming little men with unique personalities, and she couldn't wait to see how they grew up. She'd taken what Storm had said a couple of nights before to heart, about how he and Wes had to become their own people as well as who they were as twins and family.

She might be guilty of referring to her sons as "the twins" more often than not, but she also made sure to talk about their individual accomplishments and needs. And now that she was aware of it even more, she'd be sure to keep that up.

They played with blocks until the doorbell rang, and she held back another curse when she looked at the clock. An hour had passed since she'd sat down, and now not only would her knees hate her for sitting in this position for so long, she wouldn't have that much time to get ready for her date.

"Door!" Nathan yelled and got up quickly to run to the living room. He and James loved to get the door with her, but she didn't want them to do it on their own.

Thankfully, Everly was faster than they were and picked Nathan up with one arm before bending and picking up James with her other. Her biceps strained under their weight, and she held back a sigh. Her babies weren't babies anymore, and lugging around twins kept getting harder as they grew up.

Somehow, she held them and got the door open once she'd looked through the peephole to see her babysitters on the porch.

"Alex!" James squealed.

"Tabby!" Nathan shouted at the same time.

Everly snorted at their delight and moved back to let the couple in. Alex reached for James, and Tabby reached for Nathan. Everly let the two take her twins and closed the door behind them.

Her boys were so happy and giggly as they said their hellos to Tabby and Alex. They'd known Tabby since birth, and though Alex was relatively new to them, they'd clung on to him quickly. Everly figured it was because Alex looked so much like Storm, if a little more worn. Alex had gone through his own hell but had crawled his way out of it, and for that, Everly admired him.

"You aren't dressed," Tabby teased as she set the boys down to play with Alex in the living room. They *had* to show him their toys one by one. Again.

Everly looked down at her leggings and tunic and winced. "No, and I don't have any makeup on either." She blew out a breath and glanced at the boys.

"Alexander, can you watch them for a minute? I'm going to help Everly."

Alex looked up and winked at his fiancée. "No problem, baby. We've got this. Don't we, boys." He flexed his very nicely muscled arm and growled. Everly held back a laugh as her boys mimicked him. They were all just so stinking cute.

When she and Tabby walked into Everly's bedroom, she noticed Tabby wiping a tear from her face and she frowned. "What's wrong?"

Tabby shook her head. "Nothing. Really." She smiled, and there was real warmth behind it. "I just get emotional when I see Alexander with kids." She didn't elaborate, and Everly figured there was a private story there.

Everly hugged her friend, leaning her head on the other woman's shoulder. They'd been there for each other since they first met, and yet they each had secrets they hadn't told the other. She hadn't told Tabby about Rachel or Jackson's other family and honestly had no idea how to bring it up. She knew she needed to share soon or it would rot within her, but for now, she needed to think about what she was going to do. Storm knew, she thought. Storm knew and would be there for her.

She let out a breath.

And tonight, they were going on a date.

She still didn't quite know how that had happened. It had come out almost casually that he wanted to take her to dinner so they could just breathe after their conversation on the couch that night. At first, she'd thought he meant her and the boys, but she saw the heat in his gaze. And while she knew for a fact that he'd welcome the twins if they went out to dinner, she also wanted tonight to be just about them.

So here she was, totally not ready, and holding her best friend because she had no idea what she was doing.

"This is your first date since Jackson, right?" Tabby asked, her voice careful.

Everly held back the wince at his name. It hurt so much to think of him now, and not because of the pain of loss. How could she lose something that she evidently never had?

"Yes, but it's Storm."

"Yeah, it's *Storm*." Tabby blew out a breath. "Those Montgomerys just come at you full tilt, don't they?"

Everly rubbed her temples. "I don't know how we got here, but now I have to find something to wear that isn't for work or playing with the kids and do something with my hair." She tugged on her ponytail. "I think I've forgotten how to use a curling iron."

Tabby rolled her eyes and tugged on the hairband in Everly's hair. Her long, honey-blond hair was in need of a cut, but she just didn't have time. She always wore it back. Sometimes, she died it darker using a home kit, but it faded after only a few short weeks.

"Did you wash it this morning?" Tabby asked.

Everly tried to think and came up blank.

Her friend snorted. "Well, if you have to think about it that long, then probably not. Go take a shower and I'll pick out an outfit for you."

"I don't have that kind of time. It takes me forever to do my hair."

"Not with the hair dryer I brought. It does it in like three minutes. It's the glory of hair dryers."

Everly raised her brows. "Tell me you didn't buy the Dyson."

Tabby reached into the satchel she wore that Everly had thought was just a large purse. "I bought the Dyson."

Everly swore she heard angels sing as her friend pulled out the very expensive yet amazing hair dryer. It was on her wish list for when she made a million dollars—not that it cost that much, but it sure seemed like it.

"Alex got it for me as a gift." Tabby blushed. "His latest commission did really well, and I think he was tired of me complaining about my hair. Now I will let you use it tonight so you can have wonderful hair for your date. You won't even need to straighten it or anything if you use the attachments." Everly must have looked skeptical because Tabby beamed. "I'll even help. I promise. Now get going, woman."

Everly scampered to the shower and tossed off her clothes, trusting Tabby to figure out something for her to wear. It was nice having girlfriends and feeling like a woman for once—not just a mom or a business owner. It had been far too long since she'd felt anything like that.

She soaped, washed, shaved, and did her best not to slip and fall since she was working fast, and got out of the shower in record time. She ran a comb through her hair, slapped on some product, and started rubbing lotion her skin with her favorite orange blossom scent. Hopefully, Storm would like it.

She paused.

She'd *shaved* and was now worrying about the scent of her skin.

She was going to have sex with Storm Montgomery tonight.

Very dirty and very steamy sex from the glimpse she'd gotten from their tryst in her laundry room.

She blew out a breath and ignored the butterflies in her stomach. She could do this. This was Storm. He wasn't someone new, he was someone she trusted and cared for. And that was totally the problem.

"Stop thinking so hard," Tabby said as she walked into the master bath. "I set out that blue dress with the black shrug you had in the back of your closet. You don't need hose or anything since it's hot as heck right now and I'm letting you borrow my open-toed wedges. The blue dress swings out so you're going to look adorable. Now let's get your hair done and then we can pick jewelry while you're doing your makeup."

"You sound like a drill sergeant."

"Thanks," Tabby said with a wink. "Now, hand me your brush and let me show you the glory that is Dyson. Not just the Dyson, but actually Dyson. He's been named."

In less than ten minutes, Everly had her hair blown out, her makeup on, and was putting on her shoes when Tabby walked back in with a grin.

"Amazing, right?" Tabby asked. "The hairdryer. I mean, you *look*...oh my God, so hot right now, and Storm is going to pass out when he sees you, but I was talking about my hair dryer."

Everly laughed, feeling a little more at ease with Tabby's love for an inanimate object. "If I weren't sure you could take me since you're taking boxing lessons from Alex, I'd fight you for it."

Tabby narrowed her eyes, though her lips twitched. "I'd win, Everly. Don't fight me for Dyson."

"I think she'd pick him over me," Alex said from the doorway.

Tabby blew him a kiss. "It would be a tough choice, that's for sure."

Alex put his hand over his heart and took a step back. "Ouch, baby."

Everly smiled for a moment before frowning and picking up her bag. "Wait. Where are the boys?"

"I let them play outside with the chainsaw. Is that bad?"

She let out a mock growl. "Alex Montgomery."

He held up his hands, a smile playing on his face. It was so good to see since he hadn't smiled much until he found Tabby. "Storm knocked instead of ringing the doorbell, so he's letting James and Nathan show him their blocks again."

Everly froze. "Storm's here?"

Alex nodded. "Yeah, and you're going to knock him dead, Everly. You look hot."

"If I weren't so secure in our relationship and if I didn't agree with you, I'd hit you right now," Tabby said with a mock scowl.

Everly's heart thudded, but she wasn't sure if it was because of how they acted, or the fact that Storm was in her house.

"Go get your man," Tabby said. "He's waiting."

Everly let out a breath. "Okay, then."

She moved past the couple and made her way into the living room, praying she didn't fall in her heels. The wedges made it easier to walk, but it had been a while since she'd been in anything but flats.

Storm looked up when she walked into the living room and froze. He wore a coal-grey shirt and even darker pants. He hadn't worn a tie or jacket, but that was just fine. He looked edible. Lickable. So freaking sexy.

And he was *hers*—if only for the night.

Storm stood slowly, his gaze going over her body. "You look amazing." His voice had gone husky, and she almost pressed her legs together to keep the throbbing at bay.

"I was thinking the same thing about you."

"Mommy's pretty," James said with a grin.

Nathan blushed and came over to pet the bottom of her skirt. "Blue."

She squatted down to hug them both. "Thank you, boys. You have no idea how much I love hearing that." She loved them so much and would do anything for them, but tonight was about her and Storm. She could do this. She just had to take that chance.

Storm held out a hand to help her up, and she blew out a breath. "Ready to go?"

She nodded. "As ready as I'll ever be."

He snorted but squeezed her hand. "Sounds about right." They said their goodbyes, and she ignored the knowing looks from the other adults in the room as they made their way to Storm's truck.

"Let me help you up," he said as he went to her side.

"What about your back?"

He shrugged. "As long as you help me, we're good. I probably won't be carrying you too much since I don't want to hurt us both."

She frowned as he helped her into the cab of the truck. "You picked me up on the day of the fire."

His face went serious, and he cupped her cheek. "You were hurt. I'd have done anything for you."

She swallowed hard, her hands shaking. *We're going on a date*, she told herself again. This was Storm. *Her* Storm. Though when he'd become hers, she didn't know. She'd just have to live in the moment, just this once.

Just this once.

They'd gone to a steakhouse they both loved, ate far too much and laughed during their meal. She hadn't thought it was possible to feel so relaxed around him, but once they'd gotten over the initial awkwardness that came from the fact that it was their first date, it had been wonderful.

Now they were on their way back to his place so she could meet the puppy. And while that was a legitimate excuse, it was also just that, an excuse.

They were going to his place to make love, have sex, do very dirty things. They both knew it, though they hadn't said it. And though she was nervous, she couldn't wait.

He pulled into the driveway and turned off the engine. "You ready to meet Randy? He's in his crate, but I'm pretty sure that thing is bigger than my bed."

She let out a light laugh. "I love puppies. I want to get one for the boys, but I just don't have that kind of time."

Storm nodded and got out of the truck, and she did the same, just slower, and they met in front of the grill. He took her hand, and she squeezed his back. "They are time-consuming. Once he's a little bigger, I'm taking him in to work with me. He's just in the yipping phase that will annoy the clients to no end right now. I wouldn't really care if they were annoyed, but Wes and Tabby would, so we're waiting." He opened the house door and let her in. From where they stood, she could hear the loud yipping, and Storm rolled his eyes. "His bark will get lower as he gets bigger and older. It's not as bad as it was, so I'll probably take him in this week anyway. I hate leaving him here."

She leaned into his arm for a moment as they walked to the back. She'd been to his place before, though it had been years, so he didn't need to give her a tour. They had so much history, and yet it wasn't the same now as it had once been. Nothing was.

"You're a good guy, Storm Montgomery."

He wrapped his arm around her shoulders and kissed the top of her head. "If you say so. Now, be ready to be attacked and kissed." He winked. "Not by me. Yet."

He opened the crate, and Randy bounded out, his ears and feet far too big for his body.

"Sit, Randy," Storm said, his voice that low command that made Everly want to perk up.

The puppy sat down quickly but wiggled so much in excitement that he fell over. She saw Storm's mouth twitch, but he didn't grin. Randy was in training after all, so she put her hand over her mouth so she wouldn't end up laughing at how adorable the two of them were.

"Good boy," Storm said and rubbed the top of his head. "Now, let's go out back."

That must have been code for something because Randy bounced up and ran toward the back, his little feet sliding on the tile.

"He's not using his claws," she said as they stood out on the porch so Randy could take care of his business.

"He does sometimes, but he's learning not to scratch up my floor. Smart dog," Storm said then groaned as Randy tripped head over feet on his way back to him. "And once he grows into those feet of his, he'll be a giant with hopefully a little more grace." He patted his thigh. "Come on, boy. Come meet Everly."

Even in a dress and heels, she knelt down so she was at Randy's level. "Hello, Randy."

The puppy held out a paw, and she fell in love. When she reached to shake it, his whole body began to shake with her. She laughed and ran her hand down his soft back. "You're so pretty." She looked up at storm. "Don't get on me for calling a boy dog *pretty*. Look at his coat. He's gorgeous."

"Not going to fight with you on that one," Storm said with a shrug. "He *is* pretty. And cute. And all those adorable words men pretend they don't think. You can pick him up if you want so we can go back inside." He winced. "Unless you don't want to get your dress dirty."

She immediately reached out and lifted Randy to her chest and stood. The puppy licked her face, and she nuzzled into him. "He's so soft."

Storm reached out and cupped her face. "So are you."

She let out a breath. "Storm."

He leaned over the dog and kissed her softly, though Randy barged in, demanding kisses, as well. Thankfully, both of them moved out of the way in time to avoid the puppy's tongue.

They laughed, and Storm shook his head. "Silly dog. How about we go wash up and then I'll see just how soft you are." He slid his hand down her waist and she moved into him. Wanting more.

"I want you, Ev. All of you. I want to taste you. Lick you. Eat you. Then pound into you as you take my cock. I'll be hard and rough, then soft and sweet. Anything you need, Ev. Anything."

She clamped her legs together, but before she could say anything, her phone rang. "Crap. That's Tabby's ring."

Storm took the puppy, and she grabbed her phone, answering it on the next ring. "Tabby? What's wrong?"

"Nathan has some tummy issues. We separated them, but if it's a stomach bug, James might already have it. Alex is hanging with Nathan right now, and I'll be with James, but I figured you might want to come home and be with your boys. They want their mom."

Everly let out a sigh, her heart hurting for her babies. Kids got sick, she knew, but she hated it when it was *her* kids.

"I'll be right there," she said. "Give the boys my love." She hung up and gave Storm a sad look.

"I heard," he said quickly. "The volume was up. We'll take Randy with us, so he doesn't have to stay in the crate for long."

"I'm sorry."

Storm cupped the back of her head and kissed her hard. "Never be sorry. Those boys are everything, and you're one of the best moms I know. Let's get you home, and if you want, I can stay and relieve Tabby and Alex. That is, if you're okay with that and if you don't mind Randy."

She ran a hand over the puppy's head. "I think we'd all like that." She sighed. "Thank you, Storm."

"You don't have to thank me for caring for those boys."

She knew that. He'd always been there for her and the boys, even when they'd had that weird tension between them. And as much as she wanted to jump into bed with him right then, she knew that maybe this grace period was a good thing. It would give them both more time to think and figure out if this was what they truly wanted.

Because as much as she wanted to live in the moment, she couldn't. Everything was much more complicated than them just having a quick fling, and as they drove back to her house, she knew they were both letting that sink in.

Her choices when it came to Storm would never be easy, but maybe, just maybe, complications would be worth it.

She just didn't know.

CHAPTER TWELVE

Storm had a headache, and he'd slept for shit the night before, but that was his own fault for sleeping on Everly's couch. The boys hadn't wanted him to go after he'd helped tuck them in, and frankly, he hadn't wanted to go either. Now, he was at his desk at work, chugging coffee and trying to get his brain to work.

"Did you get to look at the file I sent you?" Wes asked. "And why do you look like shit."

Storm flipped his brother off. "We're twins, you know. Maybe you should stop commenting on my looks."

"We're fraternal twins, so that doesn't count. What's wrong, Storm?" Wes's voice went low at the end, and Storm felt like a heel. He needed to tell his brother what had been grating on him for years, and he would, but sitting at his desk right then wasn't the place to do it. He'd been a coward for far too long, and now he just needed to figure out how to explain to Wes what had happened and why he hadn't told him.

It was the latter that made him worry. He didn't have a good reason for not telling Wes other than that he'd been ashamed. And in retrospect, that wasn't a damn good reason at all.

"Storm?"

He shook himself out of his thoughts. "Sorry. I was at Everly's all night and didn't sleep well."

Wes's brows rose. "Does that mean what I think it does?"

As they were alone in the office for now, Storm didn't mind explaining. He'd told Alex about his date with Everly since his other brother would be babysitting the kids, but he hadn't told the others. And he should have, damn it. He'd spent so much of his life keeping things to himself, he kept forgetting to tell the people he loved the important stuff.

"Not exactly." Storm blew out a breath. "I was over there with Randy last night because Nathan got sick and Ev needed help."

Wes stiffened. "Asthma attack? Is he okay?"

Though Wes hadn't known Storm had kept in contact with Everly and the boys as much as he had after Jackson's death, once Alex and Tabby had started dating, the entire Montgomery family had brought Everly into their fold. The fact that Wes cared so much about the boys told Storm how great a man Wes was.

And damn it, Storm needed to rise up and be the kind of man his twin was—even if Wes was annoying as hell most days.

"Just a stomach bug that he seemed to get over this morning. But since James just had the surgery, we were worried that he'd get sick as well so we had to separate them. You remember us as kids, we hated being in different rooms most of the time, so my job was to distract James."

"I'm glad they're okay now." Wes paused and seemed to collect his thoughts as he sank down into the chair in front of Storm's desk. "So are you and Everly a thing now?"

Storm nodded. "Yes?"

"That was a question, not an answer."

Storm blew out a breath. "Yes, we're a thing, but I don't know what kind of thing we are. Our first date was last night, and it ended with us taking care of the kids." He didn't mention the laundry room incident. That was just for him and Everly.

"That's what happens when you date a woman with kids, but you can handle it. You guys have a history, though. Are you going to be okay?"

Saying they had history wasn't the half of it. He hadn't told Wes about Jackson's other family, and he wouldn't until Everly gave him the go ahead. That wasn't his story to tell, though he was part of it.

"We're still working it out," Storm said honestly. "I don't know. But I wouldn't have risked my friendship with her if it weren't something important. You know what I mean?"

Wes nodded. "Yeah. I do." He opened his mouth to say something else but stopped when Jillian walked in, a frown on her face and a stain on her shirt. He *really* didn't want to know what that stain was considering she was their plumber.

"You're late," Wes clipped out, and Storm held back a sigh. He honestly didn't know why these two didn't get along, but it wasn't his problem. They were adults and would have to figure out their issues on their own. He had enough to deal with.

Jillian put her hands on her hips and scowled. "One of my previous contracts had an issue with her sink this morning. When I signed on to the company, it was with the understanding that I might need to finish out with some clients along the way. I called Tabby and let her know since that *is* her job, after all.

And I don't have a scheduled appointment for another two hours. I might be behind on paperwork right now, but that just means I'll stay late or bring it home. Don't worry, Mr. Montgomery, my work will get done." She blew out a breath and looked up at Storm. "I heard the twins were sick. They okay?"

Storm nodded and assumed Tabby had told her. They were all becoming friends, after all. "Yeah. They should be. You could call Everly if you want and talk to them."

She raised a brow. "Not sure that's a good idea yet."

"What's with the cryptic remarks?" he asked with a frown.

Wes huffed. "What she's saying is that maybe your ex-girlfriend shouldn't be calling your new girlfriend when things are so new, and they haven't figured out their places in your life yet. And for the love of God, don't say anything about anyone not being your girlfriend. There is only so much of that I can take."

Jillian's jaw dropped, and Storm pinched the bridge of his nose. Wes could be annoyingly insightful when he wanted to be, but Jillian didn't know that.

Wes stood up and brushed by Jillian, and Storm had a feeling the contact had been accidental. They both stiffened before quickly moving away from each other. Hell. He'd known having them work together might be hard, but he hadn't known it would be *this* bad. They'd just have to find a way to work it out, though because both Jillian and Wes were the best at what they did. Montgomery Inc. would be better with both of them. They just had to realize that.

"Did you get that file?" Wes asked suddenly. "The one I asked you about?"

Storm nodded. "Yeah, it's on my list. I need more coffee and then I can get on it."

Wes waved it away. "You were up with a sick kid. That's all you needed to say." And with that, he walked back to his desk as if he hadn't just been quizzing Storm and Jillian. His brother made his head hurt, but at least Wes's heart was in the right place.

Jillian went back to her desk that was next to Luc's in the back and went to work. As the lead plumber and electrician in the company respectively, they didn't tend to work in the office that much, so they shared a space. Decker and Harper also shared space in the other corner since they were usually on jobsites, as well. Storm figured they'd have to add on to the office eventually or get another building because the company—and the family as a whole—was growing at a rapid pace.

Rubbing the back of his neck, he opened the file Wes had sent and scanned over it just as the door opened again, but this time, Everly walked through it, her teeth biting into her lip.

Storm stood quickly and rushed to her. "What's wrong?" She'd never come into his work before, even when they'd just been friends. It worried him.

Everly shook her head. "Everything's fine. I mean, as fine as it can be since I can't work right now and my employees are without jobs and pay. You just left your wallet last night, and you didn't answer your phone." She whispered that last part, and he figured it was because he'd stayed over.

He kissed her softly, aware his brother was staring at them. Jillian wouldn't be able to see them from where she was since the stairs blocked them, so he didn't mind showing off his new relationship with Everly. He wouldn't shove it in Jillian's face, but he would find a way to make everything work.

"Hi," he said after a moment.

Everly pulled back when he did, her cheeks pink. "Hi."

"Thanks for bringing me my wallet. And I had my phone on vibrate since I had a meeting earlier. I must not have felt it. Sorry about that."

She shrugged and looked around the office. He could see the tension in her shoulders, and he knew he had to make her feel less awkward about standing in the middle of his place of work after their kiss.

"It's not a problem," she said after a moment.

"Where are the kids?" he asked, wondering why they weren't there.

Everly's eyes narrowed. "They're with Nancy and Peter. Jackson's parents are spending more and more time with them these days, and I just don't know what that means."

They are fucking assholes, who want control over everything Everly does, he thought, but he didn't say it. Instead, he tugged on her hand and led her to one of the back rooms where they could talk, and Everly wouldn't feel like she was on stage. He knew he probably shouldn't have kissed her like that in public, but he hadn't been able to hold himself back. He'd have to do better next time.

Jillian waved at them as they made their way back, and Everly stiffened, her gaze going between him and the other woman. Well, wasn't this just awkward.

"What are you doing today?" he asked. He knew she still had tons of things to do even if she couldn't walk into her store, and he wanted to shift the attention off the fact that he worked with Jillian.

"Paperwork and scheduling," Everly answered. "I knew you'd hired Jillian, but isn't it awkward for you?" she blurted. "I mean, I don't know if I could work with my ex." Pain slashed across her face, and he knew she was thinking about Jackson.

Damn it, everything was just so damn complicated. "It's only awkward when people keep mentioning it," he said with a snort. "We work in two different areas of the company, so we really only see each other in times like this when she has paperwork to do." He let out a breath. "She's still my friend, Ev. Is that going to be a problem?"

Everly frowned but shook her head. "No, I mean, it shouldn't." She pinched the bridge of her nose. "You know, just a few short days ago, I would have said it wouldn't be a problem at all. And it *isn't*. It's just..."

"That you're still processing what happened with Jackson." He fisted his hands at his sides and took in a deep breath. "Me, too. Hell, if I could, I'd find a way to kick his fucking ass for daring to betray you like that."

Everly put her hand on his chest. "He betrayed you, too. He has another *family* out there, and he's not here to make excuses for it. I don't know what I'm going to do or how I'm going to tell his parents—because I'm going to have to tell them—but I do know that this isn't going away just because I want it to."

And Storm knew it would make it harder for her to trust him. He knew that, and hell, he understood it, but it didn't make it any easier to swallow.

"We're taking it one day at a time." He tucked a piece of her hair behind her ear. "I don't know what the right answer is when it comes to Jackson, but I'll be here if and when you need me. As for Jillian, we're friends. It might be a little awkward right now because we're all figuring out how things will go, but I want to say that we'll still be friends. If that's going to be a problem for you, then I need to know."

She shook her head. "I don't know what you and I are, but what I do know is that you wouldn't cheat. You *couldn't* cheat. You always put everyone else ahead of yourself—something Jackson never did, and we let him get away with it. So maybe that's on us."

Storm slid his hands down her arms. "No, that's on him. Always." He hugged her because he couldn't *not* touch her right then, and she wrapped her arms around his waist. He had no idea what they were doing, but he knew this was important, so he wasn't going to mess it up. And because it was getting far too serious and confused in his mind, he reached around and patted her ass, laughing when she stiffened for a minute before going up on her toes to bite his chin.

"Hands, Storm. You're at work."

He winked, bringing levity into the room. "I own the place."

She rolled her eyes, so he kissed her.

"A few of us are grabbing lunch at Taboo in a couple of hours. Want to join? I mean, if you didn't already have plans. I don't think Tabby can come, though, so you won't know everyone as well as you do her."

She bit her lip. "I don't have plans," she said slowly. "And since I don't have a job, I guess lunch would be okay."

"Damn it. I wish the police would be able to tell you more. I hate that you can't do anything about the store yet."

"You'd think they'd at least let me do a walkthrough to survey the damage, but they want me so far away from it, it's not even funny." She frowned. "Taboo is just across the street, so I'm still going to be able to at least see the outside again. God, it looked so bad the last time I saw it, Storm. I don't think we're going to be able to save anything. *Anything.*"

He hugged her tight. "I'm so fucking sorry, Ev. I hope they catch the goddamn person soon and let you into your store. Yeah, it's going to be hard, but you won't be alone." She wouldn't have been even before they started this new aspect of their relationship. Things might have changed between them, but he'd always tried to be there for her before, as well. "And, Ev? You know people who can help you rebuild, you won't be alone," he repeated.

She sighed into him. "I know." Her voice was small, and he wanted to kick something for making her sound so defeated. "It's just all too much. I want to be able to face it head-on, but I'm *tired*."

He ran a hand down her back. "You have a right to be, Ev. You're so damn strong all the time. If you need to rest, that's what my shoulder's for."

She nuzzled into him, and he held her close, knowing that this was only the beginning. He didn't know where they would end up or if he'd made a horrible mistake by taking a different step in the direction of who they were together, but right then, all that mattered was the woman in his arms.

And he'd fight the world for her.

Even if she could do it on her own.

WES

Wes had never felt more out of place than he did right then, and he had no idea how it had happened. They sat in his favorite café, the one he'd been to countless times. Taboo shared a side door with his family's tattoo shop, Montgomery Ink, so he was there weekly, if not daily for coffee and food. The place wasn't local to where he lived or worked, but he liked what he liked and wanted to spend time with his family. So it wasn't the setting that was off.

Nor was it the people—not really. They didn't get to have lunches during the week with family like this since they all had to work, but sometimes, they could schedule a get together. Not all the Montgomerys were present since there were like forty of them in the area, but enough were there that it should have felt familiar to him. His brother-in-law and lead contractor, Decker sat across from him. Decker's wife, Miranda, was a schoolteacher, so she was at work in the middle of the day, or she'd have been there, too. Meghan and Luc were there, cuddling close as they laughed over a story about one of their kids. They both worked at and owned part of Montgomery Inc. so it made sense they could be there. Maya and Austin owned the tattoo shop, so they had walked over to eat with them, though none of their significant others could join in. Maya's husbands were in the middle of projects themselves, and Austin's wife, Sierra, had a random rush at the boutique she owned across the street.

It wasn't even that the owner of Taboo, Hailey, wasn't there that seemed off. She usually served them and would end up eating with them and her husband and tattoo artist, Sloane, but she'd caught a bad cold and was at home resting with Sloane by her side, most likely making soup. The others had smiled sweetly when Hailey's staff had mentioned it, but Wes had only grinned, knowing it didn't reach his eyes.

He just felt...off. Maybe it was because he and Storm were the final two Montgomerys who weren't married off or on their way to being so. He hadn't meant to be one of the last ones still single, but everyone else had fallen around him, and he'd been left standing with Storm.

But from the way Storm leaned into Everly as they shared a secret conversation with one another, Wes had a feeling his brother would fall soon, as well—if he hadn't already—and Wes would be alone. It was a tricky situation all around since Everly had been married to Storm's best friend—a man Wes had hated, even though he told himself it hadn't been jealousy. He'd just disliked Jackson in general. And now Storm was with the man's widow. Complicated didn't even begin to cover it.

And the main complication sat on the other side of the damn table.

Jillian.

Storm's ex. Or not really an ex. Just his friend. Or his fuck buddy. The woman who had led his brother around by the balls and let him waste so much time of his life on a relationship that hadn't been serious. Yeah, Wes had his own issues and reasons for why he was still single, but it hadn't been because of an on-again, off-again relationship that amounted to nothing.

And, somehow, she'd ended up working with them.

The fact that she was the best goddamn plumber he'd ever seen just made him more annoyed. For some reason, Jillian rubbed him the wrong way, and he couldn't figure out exactly why. Some people were just like that, and yet Wes usually wasn't such an asshole from the get-go.

Apparently, things with Jillian were different.

He *knew* he needed to grow up and act like a professional. He'd heard himself when he ranted about her to Storm and had tried to stop it, but there was just *something* about her that made him act like an idiot.

And that just pissed him off more.

Of course, it didn't help that she acted just like he did. She looked up and over at him and scowled before giving him a wink and continuing her conversation with Maya.

Jesus, he needed to get a grip. Because he didn't like the man he was becoming. And if was indeed the last single Montgomery, then he'd better get his life in order. Soon.

CHAPTER THIRTEEN

Everly would rather take an ice bath and almost freeze to death than do what she was about to do. She would rather wax her entire body than answer her front door when they got to her house. She would rather eat only Brussels sprouts for a week—and not the good kind that was pan fried in a wok with oil and soy sauce. No, the stinky steamed kind with no salt or pepper. *That* was what she wanted to do rather than deal with the situation at hand.

But because she was an adult and knew what needed to be done, she'd do it. But she didn't have to like it.

"I have James and Nathan watching a movie in the playroom, and I'm going to hang out with them like you asked when you're talking to your in-laws, but if you need me for more, I'm here," Storm said as he walked into the living room. He wrapped his arms around her waist, and she leaned into him, closing her eyes so she could focus on his touch and not on what needed to happen. The two of them hadn't slept together, though they'd gotten closer and closer over the past few days. She knew that they would soon, and their relationship would hit a new level. But she couldn't think about that at the moment, not when she had to focus on one of the other thousand things going on in her life right then.

"I think I'll be okay," Everly said as she pulled away, turning so she could face him. "This isn't a conversation I want to have with them, and frankly, if I could have found a way around it, I would have. But they need to know that this woman is out there and what might become of it." She pinched the bridge of her nose, that familiar ache in her brain making her dizzy. "I need to talk to Rachel again. I need to figure out if what she's saying is even true, even though the evidence is piling up. I need to figure out if and when I'll tell the boys and how I'm going to deal with the fact that they have half-siblings. I also don't know what Rachel wants, but I have a feeling since she clearly wasn't named in the will *at all,* it must have something to do with money—something I don't really have other than the house and the boys' college funds." She blew out a breath. "So, yes, I have all of that to worry about, and I have no idea what I'm doing, but keeping this a secret from Nancy and Peter will only make everything worse in the end. Even if it all ends up a lie and I've spread this horribleness to Jackson's parents, at least I didn't hide it from them."

Storm's eyes widened just a bit as she spoke, and she winced. She'd rambled a bit there, but honestly, everything was so far out of her realm of knowledge that she couldn't quite keep her thoughts in order. She'd tried to practice what she planned to say to her in-laws in the mirror, and all she'd come out with was that their son was a worthless piece of shit. A *potential* worthless piece of shit.

Not exactly helpful.

"Like I said, I want to hit Jackson. And I know that violence doesn't solve anything but..."

"It would at least be a little helpful right about now," Everly finished for him.

He ran his hand down her back, and though she didn't want to, she let him take care of her, just this little bit. "I'll be in the back with the boys so they don't have to hear what's going on or deal with this. And so you won't have to worry about them. But I'll be out here if you need me. You know that."

"I do, but..." She didn't know how to say this without putting her foot in her mouth, but since that was how the whole night would probably go, she just went with it. "I don't know if this is the right time to also let them know that you and I are together. I mean, if we *are* together. Or whatever we are."

Foot in mouth.

Again.

Storm stiffened before looking down at her. She thought she saw hurt flash in his eyes but she couldn't be sure. He touched her face, and she wanted to lean into him again, so she didn't. "We *are* together. Let's get that out there in the open. I don't know what it means beyond that, but you and me? We *are* a you and me. As for not telling Nancy and Peter? I get it. I don't like it. But I get it. So I'll stay in the back with the kids, and if you need me, I'll be here, but I won't let the others know what's going on between us."

She closed her eyes and leaned forward to rest her head on his chest. He slid his hands down her back, and she sighed. "It's keeping secrets. The one thing I *didn't* want to do but I can't tell them everything all at once. And they are *Jackson's* parents. Not mine. They don't get a say in who I'm with, so they will just have to deal with that. However, right now, I don't want to give them any more stress since I'm about to tell them their perfect son wasn't so perfect."

And her perfect husband wasn't the man she'd thought he was.

No, she thought. He'd never been perfect in her eyes, and that had been fine. She'd thought he was *hers*. That was the issue. But he'd been Rachel's, as well...and maybe even others', since if he could cheat on her with one woman, he could probably do it with more. Apparently, that's the kind of man he was, and she hadn't seen it. Maybe she'd chosen not to see it, but she wouldn't blame herself. She didn't have the time or energy for that.

Storm kissed her softly, bringing her out of her thoughts, and for that she was grateful. "They aren't going to be happy, but they've been giving you hell for so long because they don't know how to grieve without lashing out. I know they aren't going to take it well, but I have to have hope that they aren't going to make it messy."

"From your lips to God's ears," she said quietly. The doorbell rang at that instant, and she sighed. "I'd better get this over with."

Storm kissed her again and gave her a tight hug. She didn't know how she felt about the fact that his support made her feel better. Yes, she was thinking far too much about what he meant to her, but in reality, she had to keep herself from falling in love with him. If she leaned on him too much or let herself feel something she shouldn't, she'd end up getting hurt again. Her world falling down around her once because of a man was more than enough.

Storm went back to the kids' playroom, and Everly straightened her cotton dress before going to open the door.

"Here goes nothing," she whispered to herself as she turned the doorknob. The older couple stood on her porch, their standard slightly elitist looks on their faces. "Nancy, Peter, thank you for coming by on such short notice." She'd asked the day before, so it really wasn't that short notice, but she didn't want to annoy Nancy right out of the gate.

Peter gave her a nod before following Nancy into the house. Nancy didn't say a thing, but gave Everly her critical eye before looking around the living room. Everly had cleaned up the house well before they had shown up and had kept the kids out of the area so it would *stay* clean for longer than twenty minutes. Normally, Everly wouldn't care as much as she did, but she didn't want to start off fighting. She had to pick her battles.

"Can I get you both some tea? Soda? Water?"

Peter shook his head and sat down, his book in his hand. The man seriously didn't talk much since Nancy could speak enough for both of them.

Nancy sat down next to her husband and put her purse in her lap. "No, thank you. What is it you wanted to speak to us about? Is it because we want to take care of the children's needs more and more? I'm sure you understand that with your life in such...disarray with the fire, and even when you were working full-time, young boys need guidance and care. Peter and I are ready and able to help make that happen." She held up her hand as if to ward off any discussion and gave Everly a small smile.

Dear God, this was going to be harder than she thought. If Nancy thought she was going to take over parenting because of whatever crazy reason she had, she was going to be in for a rude awakening when she realized just how hard Everly would fight for her boys.

"We aren't talking custody, of course. They *are* your children. But they were also Jackson's. And since Jackson is no longer with us"—she paused and wiped a tear Everly knew was real—"we want to ensure his legacy lives on."

Everly blinked, an odd rage filling her. She'd spent most of her marriage trying to live up to Nancy's expectations—and failing. She'd learned to live with that even if she tried to make things easier in some cases, but Nancy was off her rocker if she thought that what she was saying was anywhere near the realm of appropriate.

"Are you going to ensure Jackson's other children are also taken care of?" Everly blurted, her hands fisted in her lap.

Peter stared at her, but Nancy's face went red. "What on earth are you talking about, Everly?"

Well, she hadn't meant to say it quite like that, but now she couldn't seem to stop herself. "Jackson has three other children. Did you know that? He might even have more since I didn't know about these three, so who knows, he could have twenty more kids out there in different cities waiting for their daddy to come home."

Everly stood as she spoke, and Nancy did, as well. Peter looked shell-shocked from his seat, as if he couldn't even gather up the energy to stand.

"Stop your *lying*, Everly," Nancy bit out. "I don't know why you think making up lies about my son will help you in any way, but you're only hurting yourself." Nancy's mouth went thin, and her eyebrows pinched. "You shut your mouth. Our son would never have done what you're saying. He was *perfect*. He died far too young, and I will not have you tarnishing his name. You weren't good enough for him when you married him, and you're clearly not good enough to raise his children now."

Everly pulled out the photo of Jackson and Rachel, her hands steady, though her stomach revolted. This was going far worse than she'd expected, but she couldn't stop now. "This is your perfect son with his arms around a very pregnant woman and his lips on her cheek. This is the man you claim can do no wrong."

Everly should have figured that Nancy would lash out, but she didn't register the slap until the sting in her cheek burned. She put her hand to her face and blinked.

"Shut your mouth," Nancy spat.

"Did you just *hit* me?" Everly asked slowly, patting her cheek. It was warm to the touch, and she knew there would be a red mark once she lowered her hand.

"I'll do it again if I have to. How *dare* you accuse Jackson of having other children with this *woman*?"

"You're going to want to keep your hands off her," Storm said from the hallway, and Everly resisted closing her eyes with a groan. This wasn't going to end well.

Peter had stood when Nancy slapped Everly and now put his hand on his wife's arm. "Nancy, calm yourself. I'm sure there is a reasonable explanation."

Nancy rounded on her husband. "Oh? She's a liar. A liar who thinks she can tarnish my son's legacy." She turned to Storm. "And just what are you doing here at this time of night? You did nothing but hold our son back when he was alive, and now you're here, thinking you can tell me what to do? You think you can try and *replace* him. You wouldn't even amount to half of what my son was."

Everly was done. "Nancy. Shut up and sit down or get out of my home."

Nancy turned back to Everly, her eyes wide for a moment before narrowing to slits. "Excuse me?"

Storm moved closer, but Everly held up her hand to stop him before turning back to her mother-in-law. "This is *my* house. *My* family. How dare you speak to me this way? How dare you *hit* me? You've treated me like crap for over ten years, and I took it because it was the easier way out, but no more. If you think you can continue to treat me this way, I will make sure you *never* see your grandsons again." Everly's chest heaved, but she wasn't done. "And I'm not telling you about Jackson's other family to hurt you. I'm telling you because you need to know what is out there and what is going on with your son's past. I don't know what I'm going to do about the fact that he has three kids outside of our marriage, but what I do know is that I can't ignore it forever. And you know what? It could all be a lie anyway." She blew out a breath, still angry. "I don't think it is, not with my gut feeling, but it could all be a lie. I'm going to find out because I have to, but I thought tonight I'd give you the courtesy of telling you the truth. But you clearly can't listen to anything that might fracture the perfect image you have of your golden son. Well, guess what, Nancy. He wasn't perfect. I never thought he was, even before this came to light. But I thought he was mine. I guess I was wrong. Because even if he isn't the father of those children, he still has his arm around another woman, and the picture was taken *after* we were together. I remember that shirt," she whispered. "I remember buying it for him. I remember when he had that ugly goatee. And that was all *after* we were together."

"You're lying," Nancy growled out. "You're just a low-class whore who seduced my son, and now you're trying to tarnish his good name for his sons."

"Get out." Storm's voice was low, full of authority, and Everly was *not* happy. She could handle this herself and didn't need a man coming in and taking over. Jackson had done that enough. She didn't need Storm to do it, as well.

Peter tugged on Nancy's arm before looking between Storm and Everly. "We'll leave for now," he said softly.

"Excuse me?" Nancy asked, her voice shrill.

He bent and handed his wife her purse. "We need to talk this out and let it sink in. Once we're a bit calmer,"—he gave a pointed look to his wife—"we'll be in touch." He paused for a moment as Nancy glared at him, muttering things under her breath that Everly knew weren't kind. "I...I hope it's not true."

And with that, he pulled his wife out of the house while she screamed and ranted, with Storm following them as if to make sure they didn't make a run for it in the opposite direction.

He locked the door behind them and turned, his face set in stone. "I cannot believe she fucking hit you. Let me get you some ice."

"I'm fine," Everly bit out.

"No, you're not." He moved forward, his hand out. "Your cheek is all red."

Everly moved back, not wanting his touch right then. Hurt shadowed his features, and he lowered his hand.

"I wasn't going to hit you, Ev," he said, his voice gruff.

She shook her head. "I know that."

"Then why are you moving away from me?"

She raised her chin. "I was handling it, Storm."

His eyes narrowed. "She *hit* you."

"And she wasn't going to do it again. She surprised me with the first one, but I wouldn't have let her hit me a second time." She blew out a breath, not as angry anymore but beyond tired. "You can't just take over, Storm. You can't just come into my life and think that you can fix everything. You can't. You aren't my husband, and apparently, my husband wasn't truly my husband either." Her voice broke at that last part, and she hated herself for it. She was handling this all wrong, but at some point, it had become too much to deal with.

"Everly," he whispered. "I'm not trying to take over."

"You did. You are. Just...just don't try to fill his shoes, Storm." She closed her eyes, holding back the tears. "Just go. I need you to go. I need to be alone with my sons tonight."

"Ev—"

"Just go."

She opened her eyes and watched him stand there for a few moments before turning and leaving without another word. When the door clicked shut behind him, she wanted to fall to her knees and curse Jackson and break down into sobs. Instead, she rolled back her shoulders and locked the door before going back to the playroom where her boys were peacefully watching a movie. She'd tuck them into their little beds and read them a story, and when they were asleep, she'd sink into her tub and cry.

Because with each passing day, she was losing more and more of her past, losing more of the dream she'd thought she had with the man she loved, and she was so afraid if she didn't stop moving, didn't stop trying to be strong, she'd lose even more.

She'd lost herself when she lost her husband, and she hadn't even realized it.

She couldn't do it again.

Not even for Storm.

Her phone rang and she looked down at the screen.

Unknown.

Tears slid down her face as she answered. "Hello?"

No answer.

"Who is this?" she screamed. "Why won't you leave me alone?" Her hands shook, and when the call disconnected, she threw her phone on the couch. She slid to the floor, bile filling her throat.

She couldn't do this. It was all too much.

Everything was just too much.

CHAPTER FOURTEEN

Storm had made some mistakes in his life, but last night was a doozy. He'd been friends with Everly long enough to know that she did *not* like it when anyone spoke for her. Hell, that was the case with any woman he knew. And what did he do? He'd walked right in and spoken over her, demanding that Jackson's parents leave her home. Then he growled around the living room, stalking the older couple out the door like a Neanderthal.

No wonder Everly had kicked him out, as well.

"You're here late," Jillian said as she walked by his desk.

He shook himself out of his thoughts and looked up. "So are you."

She shrugged and tucked her hair behind her ear. She wasn't wearing her normal ponytail, which surprised him. In fact, she wasn't wearing her normal work outfit at all. Instead, she looked ready for a date in a slim black dress and heels.

"Are you going out?" he asked and leaned in his chair to stretch his back. He'd been bent over his table most of the day since he'd wanted to get his side project on paper as quickly as it had appeared in his mind.

Jillian gave him a small smile before rolling her eyes. "Yeah, it's a Friday night, and I have a date. I just forgot my phone on my desk because I'm an idiot. Thankfully, I'm meeting the guy at the restaurant, so hopefully, I haven't missed his call."

"Don't let him pick you up at your house until you reach a few dates. You never know with people these days."

Jillian laughed and went back to her desk to pick up her phone. She looked through it, and he raised a brow at her.

"Why are you laughing?"

"Because you're being all overprotective. It's cute."

He frowned. "It's not cute."

Jillian patted his cheek before moving back again. "Yeah, it is. I don't have brothers, so it's kind of nice to have you being all growly about who I date."

"Since we've slept together, I hope to hell you don't think of me as your brother."

"Now who's being gross? I just meant that it's nice to have someone care, you know?"

Storm leaned back in his seat. "I've always cared, Jilly."

"I know. I cared, too. I *care*. But not the right way. And this thing between you and Everly? That's exactly what you should have, not whatever you and I kept trying to make work because we were lonely. So now I'm going out on dates and trying to find my Mr. Right."

That was a lot to process all at once now that his brain was working a little bit better, and something she'd said triggered a conversation they'd had. "You saw this coming," he said after a moment. "You saw Everly and me together."

Jillian blushed, though she shrugged as if it weren't a big deal. "I thought I saw something between you that could be amazing, and I didn't want to stand in the way. I didn't know what exactly, but I saw potential."

"And I didn't for too long."

"She needed time to heal, and you guys weren't ready yet. Now, you are. Plus, no one ever sees true potential when they're so close."

He wasn't quite sure what to make of that, but he pushed it to the side for now since he had other things on his mind. "I never felt lonely with you, Jillian. We were friends. We still are."

She gave him a sad smile. "We might not have been lonely together, but it still wasn't what we both truly needed. I'm never going to regret what we had, but I'm glad we're both finding ways to move on and yet still be in each other's lives." She paused. "That is if Everly doesn't mind. Not all women would be happy with an ex, even if I'm not technically that with you, hanging around."

He didn't disagree. "She and I have talked about you some, and I think she's fine with it, but maybe once the dust settles, we'll find a way to make it so the *three* of us are friends. I don't want to lose you, Jilly, but Ev? She's..."

"She's everything. Or at least she will be. Now, are you going to tell me why you're working so late when you could be hanging out with your woman? I mean, I'm pretty sure you haven't slept with her yet so why aren't you doing that instead of hanging out in a dark office."

"How the hell do you know whether I've slept with Everly or not?"

"I see all. I know all."

He flipped her off, and she laughed. "I'm headed to her place in a few, if you really care. I just had to finish up a few things, and I'm pretty sure she needed time away from me anyway."

She narrowed her eyes. "What did you do?"

He held up his hands. "Something stupid that I'm going to fix. Or at least try. We're both still testing out the waters, and I made a mistake. One that I regret and will atone for."

"I don't want to have to hurt you."

"I thought you were my friend, not hers."

Jillian shrugged. "I like her, and her boys. And Tabby is a little busy right now, so Everly needs more girl power behind her."

Storm smiled despite himself. "I think she'd like that." He blew out a breath. "You better head out for real, or you're going to miss your date. I'm here if you need to talk, Jillian. Remember that."

She smiled at him, though it didn't reach her eyes. "You're a good man, Storm Montgomery. Just make sure you don't screw everything up because you're so in your head."

He picked up his things and walked her out to her car. She could handle herself, and they had security cameras, but they'd had issues recently, and he wasn't going to risk it after dark. They each went their separate ways, and he headed to Everly's house, hoping she'd let him in and not slam the door in his face. He hadn't called or texted that day because he knew she needed space and he didn't want to smother her, but damn it, he missed her.

She opened the door after the first knock, and he took in the image of her. She wore cotton pants and a tank top and had her hair piled on top of her head. She smelled of the soap she used during the boys' bath time, and he had to hold himself back from bringing her into his arms and never letting go.

"I saw your lights when you drove up. Thanks for not using the doorbell since I just got the boys down."

He held his tablet under his arm, or he'd have stuffed his hands into his pockets so he didn't accidently reach out and touch her. "I figured. Do you think I can come in? I promise not to stay longer than you want me to."

She stepped back and gestured him inside. "I'm glad you're here. I was going to call you tonight, actually. I'm so sorry, Storm. I didn't mean to take everything out on you, but I guess it was all too much and I just blew up at everyone."

He frowned and set his tablet on the table by the door. "Don't apologize. I'm the one who should say I'm sorry. I took over because I hated seeing you hurt, but it wasn't my place. Hell, you can take care of yourself, and I should have just been there as support, not the one taking over. I'm sorry, Ev. You don't need me acting like an asshole and making you feel like you can't do things on your own."

She shook her head and wrapped her arms around his middle. When he slid his arms around her, holding her tight, she rested her head on his chest.

"Things got a little out of hand. Just...just with everything." She sighed into him, and he ran his hand down her back.

"Yeah, they did. And I'm sorry for coming in and trying to take over. You just...you just mean so much to me, and when she hit you, I lost it."

She looked up, her eyes widening. "You mean a lot to me, too, Storm."

He cupped her face and leaned down to brush his lips over hers. "So, I did something that you might not like or think I'm crazy for even attempting, but..." He pulled away from her and reached for his tablet.

Everly frowned. "You're worrying me."

"I didn't know what to do with myself, so I played around with what we could do with Beneath the Cover."

Her face paled, and her eyes widened, and he wanted to kick himself. "You did what?"

"Shit. I knew this was probably a bad idea." He brought up the blueprints he'd been working on and turned the screen so she could see. "We had the specs from when the company did work on it, remember? Some things would have to change, but I figured I could get a feel for it. You had mentioned before that you wanted a better flow in the back from the seating areas to the shelves, so I played around with built-ins rather than things that take up more space."

She looked down at the screen, her hand hovering over it before looking up at him. "You did all this?"

He nodded, swiping through a few different ideas. "And you can hate them all, and that will be okay. When I get stressed, I work. And since designing is one of the things that calms me, I worked on this for you. I know you didn't have any input, so these are really just from a launching-point perspective, and I can throw them away. It can also be too soon, and I get that. Hell, we don't even know what the place looks like right now, but my brain couldn't stop working, so I just did it."

She blinked rapidly, and he knew he'd messed up. The bookstore was *her* place, and he'd stepped in and taken over. Again.

"Shit shit shit. I'm sorry. I shouldn't have done anything. I just took over and did the exact thing that I did wrong before."

She reached up and put her hand over his mouth. "Stop talking, Storm."

He kissed her fingertips, unable to hold himself back. When she sighed, he kept his mouth shut, hoping she'd let him stay and give him another chance.

"I can't believe you did this," she whispered.

"I'm sorry."

She shook her head. "I can't believe you did this because it's *amazing*. You have such talent. I know you did a few sketches, but I love each of them for different reasons, and I didn't even get a chance to study them in-depth. I know you didn't do these thinking your way would be the only way, you did it because you wanted to try and do something to clear your mind and make me happy. I get that. I *love* that." She blew out a breath. "And I'm not saying it right, but Storm? Thank you. Thank you for thinking of me, and thank you for listening to the little things I've said over the years and using that to make your designs. You're right in that we don't know what we're in for with the store." Her words got a little shaky, and she sucked in a breath. "But in the end, that doesn't matter. I mean it does, but I *know* you'll be able to help me when the time comes."

She cupped his face, and he finally let out the breath he'd been holding. "You like them?" he asked, his voice hoarse.

"I do."

He smiled then. "When the time comes, and you're ready to rebuild, you can do whatever you need to do, and I'll do it with you. Not *for* you. I hope you get that."

"I do." Her fingers traced his lips. "The boys are sleeping," she whispered.

He swallowed hard, his dick filling and pressing against his jeans. "Yeah?"

"Come to bed with me." She bit her lip, looking a little shy. "Please?"

He set down the tablet again so he could cup her face. "Are you sure you're ready?"

"I've been ready for far longer than I want to admit," she said with a blush.

"Now that's something a guy wants to hear." He smiled as he said it, then kissed her. First, it was just a soft brush of lips; then, it deepened, his body pressing against hers as she wrapped her arms around his waist. They moaned into each other, exploring each other's mouths, her taste a delicious dessert on his tongue.

They kept kissing, their hands exploring as they walked back to the bedroom. He'd have liked to have swept her up into his arms and carried her back there, but they both knew he'd end up hurting himself if he did. She *knew* why he ached—and not just for her. That fact just made him want her more. He'd trusted her with the most secret part of himself, and now she was about to do the same.

He tugged on her hair tie, and her tresses cascaded down her back, long enough for him to wrap around his hand and tug if he wanted. Only he didn't know how she liked to be touched, how she liked to be loved. They might have gotten closer to this moment before and she'd come on his hand, but he still didn't fully know what she liked.

And he couldn't wait to find out.

Her hands slid up underneath his shirt, her fingernails raking down his back as he rocked into her, his length pressing against her belly. They both groaned, their bodies practically shaking.

"Soft or hard?" he asked, a smile playing on his lips.

"Both?" Everly asked, her eyes bright. "Maybe a little soft, then a whole lot of hard, then soft again?"

He snorted before taking her lips again. "I'm not twenty anymore, so I might need some time in between all those to rest."

She laughed and bit his chin. "I can find ways." Her hand trailed down in between them before cupping him through his jeans.

"Oh, yeah?" He tilted his hips so he filled her hand even more. "Why don't you show me?"

"We'll have to be quiet," she said softly, running her hand slowly over him. "The boys are sleeping, but they could still wake up."

He kissed her slowly, craving her taste. "You'll have to bite down on a pillow or something to hold back your cries, then."

She raised her brow. "You think you can make me scream?"

He lowered his hands to her butt and squeezed. When she moaned and grinned, he said, "I know it."

He ran his hands over her, loving the way she felt under his touch. He helped her out of her shirt, and then her bra, and while she blushed slightly, she didn't hold back when he cupped her breasts with his hands. They didn't overfill his hands, but they were perfect for his large palms. When he brushed his fingers over her nipples, her head fell back, and she arched into him. Needing more, he lowered his face and licked the tight buds before taking turns sucking each into his mouth.

"Storm."

He lapped at her, wanting to bury himself between her breasts, but knowing that would be for later. Right now, he needed to get her naked and under him. He reached between them to pull down her leggings and let out a curse.

"What is it?" she asked, her eyes clearing.

"I don't have any condoms with me."

She shook her head. "I have some. I bought a box." She blushed before shrugging it off. "I knew we were headed this direction, so I bought some. I can't be on birth control thanks to blood clot issues, so I wanted to be prepared." She cupped his face and kissed him softly. "As much as I'd love to feel you without the condom, we both need to be checked out, and I don't want to get pregnant." She frowned. "I...I really need to get tested fully. I didn't think about that." Her eyes filled. "Because of Jackson. What if...?"

He kissed her hard, trying to push away those thoughts from both of them. "We'll both get tested as soon as possible. And because you're worried and it's a smart idea, we'll use condoms *and* resist going down on each other until we're sure." He lowered his forehead to hers and sighed. "Though I'm going to continue having dreams of you riding my face until you come, sadly."

She sighed. "And I really wanted to go down on you since you've made me come *twice* and I haven't had the pleasure."

He kissed her again. "*You* had the pleasure," he said low. "I thought that was the point."

"Ha ha." Her eyes danced. And though they were smiling now, the weight of what lay between them and the past that kept coming back to haunt them was still there. But they'd make love tonight, and maybe the next day, as well. He'd have her in his arms, and continue to fall deeper and deeper. Just because they had to live with their pasts and other people's mistakes didn't mean they couldn't live for the now.

When they started kissing again, their hands sliding over one another, Storm let her strip him down. He toed out of his shoes and pants before going down to his knees to strip off her leggings and panties.

"I *really* want to kiss you there, but I'll refrain."

She pressed her thighs together as he slid his hands down the soft skin. "Stop being so tempting."

"I could say the same to you." He kissed her knees, then her thighs, before standing back up so he wouldn't do something stupid like lick her until she came. He'd made a promise, and he'd keep it—even if it killed him just a little to do so.

Naked, they wrapped their arms around each other and took turns licking up each other's necks before their mouths met. Their bodies rocked into one another, and soon he was on his back with her on top of him, a condom in her hand as they sucked and kissed and bit. They hadn't discussed it, but he figured she'd made sure he was on the bottom for their first time to help his back. He didn't mind because it gave him more access to her breasts, her mouth, and her hips, and yeah, he'd be less likely to hurt himself.

"Slide it on me," he ordered, his voice a growl.

She opened the packet and slid the condom over his length. When she squeezed the base of him, his eyes crossed, and he steadied her hand. "You'll make me come that way, and then I won't get to have my fun."

She bit her lip as she rose above him. "We wouldn't want that," she breathed.

He had his hands on her hips, steadying her as she slid over him. They both moaned as one, her tight sheath squeezing his dick, warm and ready for him.

"Jesus, you're big," she said with a groan.

"And I didn't even have to ask you to say that."

She laughed before her eyes rolled back as he moved.

"Cup your breasts, Ev. Play with your nipples as I fuck you."

She didn't say anything as she did as she was told. He thrust in and out of her, planting his feet on the bed so he could get a better angle. When she began to rock her hips, meeting him thrust for thrust, he sped up, his body aching for her.

His balls tightened, and he knew he was close, so he reached up and brushed his thumb over her already swollen clit. It had peeked out from under its hood and his mouth watered. Soon, he decided. Soon he'd taste her and have that swollen nub in his mouth. For now, he'd use his hands.

And when she came, she fell forward, her hands on his shoulders as she called his name. He wasn't far behind her, his body sweat-slick and shaking with his release.

They wrapped their arms around each other, his cock still inside her as they fought to catch their breaths. He'd known finally making love to Everly would mean something, but he hadn't known it would be this. This overwhelming need to hold her and never let her go; to protect her and, all the while, watch her continue to grow into the confident and amazing woman she was.

He'd gone and done the one thing he'd once promised himself he would never do.

He'd fallen for his best friend's girl.

And yet...that wasn't who she was anymore. She was *Everly*.

And, Storm thought, she was *his*.

At least, he hoped.

JILLIAN

Her heart hurt, and yet there was nothing she could do. No matter how many times she told herself she was stronger than what people thought of her, she knew she was only lying to herself.

"And that's enough of a pity party for you." She rolled her shoulders and got out of her truck. The door screeched closed, and she knew the damn thing was on its last leg. Just one more thing to add to her ever-growing list of things to do. Her list was longer than her truck at this point, but now that she was working for Montgomery Inc., she could actually start checking some things off.

Working with her ex that wasn't an ex had its perks. She had healthcare, a salary, and people who respected her, even if she were a woman in a so-called man's job. Of course, with that came the one thing she didn't want to do...working with *him*.

Wes Montgomery.

Storm's twin and general pain in the ass. He'd hated her for as long as she'd known Storm and hadn't minded letting the world know it. It didn't matter, though, she loved her job, and Wes could just suck it.

She blew out a breath and tried to ignore the tears stinging her eyes. She was *not* going to cry. She just needed sleep or coffee or both. She hadn't gotten much of either with everything that had happened the night before.

"Ignore it," she muttered to herself. "Everything is fine. You will be fine. Get over it."

"Talking to yourself in the parking lot?"

Of course, he'd see her trying to give herself a pep talk. Of course. Why wouldn't it be Wes who came up behind her? It could have been Godzilla or something, but no, it had to be Wes Montgomery.

"I couldn't find anyone with a decent brain to talk to so, of course, I spoke to myself." When she got flustered, she got mean, and she hated that about herself.

"Uh-huh." Wes gave her a once over before going to the door and opening it, gesturing for her to walk in. "After you."

She gave him a bright smile, though she knew it was false. "Thanks."

As soon as she walked into the office, Storm looked at her and frowned. "What's wrong?"

She held up her hand. "Nothing."

"You're lying."

Everly, who had been standing next to Storm, looking over some paperwork frowned, as well. "Storm, stop badgering her. But, Jillian? What's wrong?"

While most people might think that Everly and Jillian slowly becoming friends was a weird thing, those people didn't know them. Jillian loved Storm, just not in the right way, and she had a feeling Everly was falling in love with Storm in the best way possible.

If the two of them couldn't get along, then there would be issues. Thankfully, they seemed to get one another, and there weren't any cat fighting issues.

No, that only went on between her and Wes.

She'd told Storm that she wanted to find her own happiness and a man who deserved her, but really, she'd broken their connection because she'd seen the sparks between Storm and his best friend's widow. There was no way she could have stood in the way of that.

The two of them stared at her long enough that she knew it would be futile to hold back. "Dad fell yesterday cleaning the gutters and broke his leg. Plus, there was some bruising on his chest they were worried about." She blew out a breath, and tears filled her eyes. She blinked them angrily away. "He's still in the hospital but stable."

"Fuck," Storm growled and went right up to her and hugged her hard. Storm always gave wonderful hugs. When he pulled back, Everly was there, hugging her, as well. And then Tabby was hugging her, and Jillian ended up a blubbering mess.

She didn't know what was going to happen with her father, but having people around her that wanted to comfort her helped. And even though Wes didn't hug her, he still stood near, giving her a sympathetic look. That counted for something, even if he still annoyed her to no end.

Her life wasn't going exactly how she'd planned it, but she could find a way to make it work. She always had before, and she'd be damned if she let anything break her down now.

Not again.

CHAPTER FIFTEEN

Everly tried not to get her hopes up, but she couldn't help it. This *had* to work. They were at speech therapy that morning, and today they'd work with the implants to see if James could fully hear. It was just the first step of many in this new phase of their lives, but she could *feel* the intensity of the day.

Her baby was on a new path, and she was right there with him.

Thank God Storm was in the waiting room with Nathan, so she didn't also have that on her shoulders. She knew she'd have to keep an eye on that as she couldn't always have Storm take care of one of the twins or even both of them when the need arose. He wasn't their father, and they were still new in this part of their relationship. Boundaries had to be made and monitored. Boundaries were important.

It was weird to have someone to rely on for situations where it would be easier if she had help. She'd never had that. Jackson hadn't been around for a single day of his children's lives, and she'd done everything on her own.

No, she amended; Jackson hadn't been around for the twin's lives. Apparently, he'd been around for his two older children, and perhaps even for a few days of his third child with Rachel.

Bile coated her tongue, and she pushed those thoughts away. She still hadn't decided how she would handle that particular situation. It was almost as if she were ignoring it, but she had so many other things on her mind and schedule that it was easy to pretend it didn't exist.

For now.

She let out a breath and ran a hand down James's back. Her baby smiled up at her, and she fell in love with that sweet little face all over again.

"Are you ready?" the doctor asked. James's speech therapist, as well as two nurses stood around them.

"Yes," she said firmly as James put his tiny hand in hers. "We're ready."

"Ready," James said, his eyes on her lips as if he were reading them. She knew he could hear out of one ear, but there were a lot of times he missed things because he wasn't looking at who spoke, or someone started talking to the wrong side of him or too quickly. Hopefully, after all the pain and nervousness that had gone into the decision-making for the surgery, this would all be worth it.

It was times like these that she wanted someone to lean on and to talk to. Storm's face came to mind, and she pushed that thought out. They were nowhere near that point in their relationship, and she wasn't sure they ever would be. Nor was she sure she *wanted* a partner like that. She'd never had one, after all. What if it didn't work out? What about her boys?"

She let out another breath and focused on what was going on around her instead of the thoughts in her head. Today wouldn't be like one of those videos

171

on YouTube where a baby heard their mother's voice for the first time, and everyone ended up sobbing. James already knew her voice as well as his own, but now he might be able to hear a little better out of his other ear. Even if it didn't work completely, the doctors were hopeful it would help his balance and his self-awareness.

They started the setup, attaching different things to James's head and ear, as well as plugging things into the computer. She knew what each thing was and why it was used as she'd researched every part thoroughly on the internet and in her many books, but right then, it all went out the window. All she could see was her little boy and his bright eyes.

Then the nurse patted Everly on the arm and nodded. This was her cue to speak. They'd wanted Everly to be the first one, and now tears stung the backs of her eyes. Apparently, this might end up one of those videos after all since the other nurse had Everly's phone and was recording just in case.

"James? Can you hear Mommy?"

James's eyes widened, and he reached up to where the implant was. Tears fully fell down Everly's cheeks, and she slid her finger down James's nose.

"James?"

"Mommy! You sound strange." Tears filled her baby's eyes, and she held back from hugging him too close since there were still a few wires in the way.

"You sound perfect," she said once she caught her breath. "Just perfect."

"You're perfect, too, Mommy," he said with a smile, rubbing under his ear. "I love you."

Now she was openly sobbing along with two of the nurses. Why she'd put on mascara that morning, she'd never know. "I love you, too."

Then they let her hold her son, and someone ushered Storm and Nathan into the room. She met Storm's eyes, and he looked down at the boy in her arms before smiling so brightly she knew she'd fallen head over heels in love with him.

And she prayed she wasn't making a mistake.

Later that afternoon, they sat at an outdoor café that let in dogs, and she couldn't quite believe how she'd gotten to this point. Both her boys were in their boosters sitting across from one another and in between her and Storm. Randy had curled up in Storm's lap about half an hour ago after a wild and crazy time in the park and his lunch. Right now, the puppy lay sprawled over Storm's lap with his tummy big and full. The boys had wanted to feed Randy some of their food, as well, but Storm had been firm that Randy didn't eat people food and was in training.

Both James and Nathan had nodded sagely and promised not to hurt the "twain." They were seriously adorable.

And when the waitress had remarked at how well behaved the boys were and how they were such a gorgeous family, the boys hadn't noticed, and Storm hadn't seemed freaked out. In fact, he'd just gone with it and continued to help Nathan with his sandwich. Apparently, Everly would be the only one freaking out today. The man had even taken the day off from a busy schedule to help her and the kids. Wes had understood, even though it meant there were more things on his schedule. Storm had told them that things would get crazy soon with Tabby on vacation, but Everly knew he could handle it. It just meant that he might not be able to spend as many afternoons with her on weekends or nights like they had been doing.

The waitress had thought them a family.

Everly swallowed hard, trying to relieve the emotion clogging her throat. What emotion it was exactly, she didn't know.

Storm gave him a weird look. "You okay?" he mouthed.

She swallowed hard and nodded before reaching over to help James wipe his face. Storm did the same to Nathan, and she held back the sting behind her eyes. She didn't know why she was acting this way, but she needed to get a grip. Storm had always been amazing around her children, and that hadn't changed. It was that he was always with *her* that had made everything go haywire. She didn't know how to act around him when it wasn't just the two of them anymore. That was her problem, though, and she had to get over it.

If it weren't for the fact that she had her place of business and the whole Rachel thing on her mind, as well, she might have been able to function. As it was, she felt like she was always a few steps behind.

Once they were done eating, Storm paid— something she tried to prevent since she still had money even if her job had literally gone up in flames, but he'd given her a look—and they drove back to her place in her SUV. He'd left his truck at her place since she had the car seats and he didn't.

He'd driven since she had to take a phone call with the fire marshal and didn't want to put it on Bluetooth through the car while the boys were there. Unfortunately, there hadn't been any other news, and she *still* couldn't walk through the place since it was still under investigation. The marshal had just wanted to update her with what little they had.

Yes, it was arson.

No, they weren't sure if the note was connected, but they were still investigating.

No, they didn't think it was her.

Yes, they were still looking for the culprit.

She had no idea what she would do if she couldn't start rebuilding soon—if that was what she wanted anyway. There might not be enough to salvage, but damn it, it had been her dream and income. Now, it was nothing.

She swallowed hard, ignoring the pain in her belly at that thought.

Storm tapped on the steering wheel, and she looked over at him. When he smiled at her quickly before turning his attention back to the road, her heart did that pitter patter thing that worried her.

"I'm thinking about getting car seats for the truck. It would be easier in case we ever want to take my vehicle, though I don't mind taking yours."

She frowned. "You want to buy car seats for the boys?"

He shot her a glance before turning back to the road. She knew why he was so vigilant now about focusing on driving rather than looking at her, and she didn't blame him. It hurt her to think that he still carried all this guilt. And though others might have been a little uneasy about how that all connected to Jackson and Rachel, she wasn't in the slightest. Storm had spent his life atoning for sins that weren't truly his to carry, and him feeling as if he had any part of Jackson's adultery shouldn't be part of that weight.

"Ev? You there?"

She blinked, pulling herself out of that mental side trip. She couldn't quite seem to focus on anything today.

"Sorry, uh...why would you want to buy car seats?"

He frowned at her before once again turning his head to the front. "Because I'm spending more time with you, and you never know when you might need me. If that's going to be a problem, though, just let me know."

She heard the hurt in his voice and hated herself for it. Just because she was being cautious didn't mean she had to be a jerk about it. He was trying to help, and she needed to figure out what to do about it.

"I think that would be sweet of you," she said after a moment, thinking through her words.

"We can talk about it more," Storm said after a moment. "No need to rush."

"The boys *do* like your truck," Everly said, trying—and failing—not to sound like an idiot.

Storm grinned at her, and she held back a sigh of relief when it reached his eyes. "That's because my truck is amazing."

She laughed quietly, trying not to wake the two sleeping boys in the back. They'd conked out with Randy between them soon after they'd gotten into the SUV.

By the time they got the boys into bed for an afternoon nap, and Randy secured in the laundry room with a chew toy, Everly's nerves were shot. She kept saying the wrong thing and didn't know what to think, but hell, she couldn't really blame herself with everything that was going on. Of course, that wasn't quite who she was, so she blamed herself a little...but still.

"Now that the boys are napping and we have a few minutes, why don't you tell me what's going on?" Storm asked as he walked into the kitchen. She'd just pulled down two glasses for water, and she turned, her back to the counter and Storm right in front of her.

"What do you mean?"

He sighed and took the glasses from her hand and set them down. "Come on, Ev. You're acting weird. Was it what the waitress said? Or the fact that I've been with you all day when you normally have the boys to yourself? They don't know what's going on between us or they would have said something. That's who they are. But if my being around is going to mess things up, I need to know. Are we moving too fast for you?" He cupped her cheek, his thumb softly caressing her skin.

"I'm just feeling a little overwhelmed," she said honestly. "And not just because you and I are finding our way together."

He blew out a breath. "You're going through so much, and I hate that I can't help."

"But you are," she said quickly. "The fact that you're here with me is helping."

"Even though my being here is causing you to freak out a bit?"

She winced. "I'm not sure how to act around you. We're friends. We *were* friends. Then we were a little off after Jackson died. And now we're more than friends. *Way* more than friends. And you're so amazing. But you also know so much about me and are connected to everything going on even as you're going through your own list of problems. It's all just a little much if I think about it all at once."

He lowered his head to hers and sighed. "Then think about it in steps. That's how I've learned to live the past twenty years. Going through it all at once will just bear down on you until you can't breathe."

She put her hands on his chest and leaned into him instead of pushing him away. All day, she'd slowly been doing that, pushing him away ever so slightly so she could find her control, but that hadn't been the right way to go about it. She couldn't keep putting her past with Jackson on Storm's shoulders. Yes, she was afraid to trust and lean on someone fully, but Storm wasn't Jackson, and she knew that.

"You're not Jackson," she whispered, and Storm stiffened.

"I know I'm not," he said carefully as he leaned back to look her in the face. "Are you sure *you* know that?"

She swallowed hard and nodded. "Yes, I do. My brain gets a little confused at times, but I *know* you aren't him. He wasn't ever really all the way there throughout most, if not all, of our relationship. I'd always thought it was because he loved his work and dove into it full steam ahead, but now I'm not so sure."

"He was an asshole," Storm bit out.

"Yeah, he was. He fucked me over, and damn it, he fucked Rachel over too, but I don't know if that woman thinks of it that way. He screwed me up, Storm, and I didn't even realize how much until recently."

"If I could hurt him, I would."

"But you can't. He's gone, and he left his mess for us to deal with. I'm just surprised it took this long to come out."

"If I hadn't found that photo...hell, if I hadn't introduced the two of them, nothing like this would have happened."

She shook her head, glaring. "Don't blame yourself. He would have found another way. Another woman. That's how men like that are, right?" She blew out a breath. "But anyway, yes, he messed me up, and I've spent the past three years learning how to be a single mom. I can't change that overnight with you. And I know that sucks, and I'm being hard, but I have to think of my kids first."

"I won't hurt them. They've always mattered to me."

Tears filled her eyes, and she angrily wiped them away. It seemed she was always crying these days and she hated it. "I know they do. And that's one of the reasons I'm with you. You *care*. You put everyone else before yourself, even if it hurts. You're my friend, Storm. My friend and my lover. And I don't know how to put those together with the man I know. I just need time to figure it all out."

He cupped her face before taking her lips without another word. When he pulled back, they were both breathless. "You don't have to figure it out right now, nor do you have to do it on your own. You can't do anything about your store right now, and you will figure out what you're going to do with Rachel soon. I know it. But as for me? I'm here. I'm not going anywhere. Yeah, I might be a little busy in the next few weeks with Montgomery Inc.'s workload, but I'm not staying away. I want you in my arms, Everly. I just want to be there. We'll figure everything else out. Together if you want, or you can do it on our own if that's what you think you need. I won't force you to make decisions or make them for you. I'm not that guy, even though the growly part of me wants to be that guy."

She laughed since he winked as he said it, and she reached up and kissed his chin. "You're amazing, Storm Montgomery."

"My mom thinks so. Speaking of my mom..."

She frowned. "That was an odd nonsequitur."

He winced. "My mom wants you and the boys to come to the family barbeque at their house next weekend. And I should warn you, there will be many, many Montgomerys. All eight of us local kids, and I think she invited my cousins from Colorado Springs since it's their turn. There are far too many of us do to a whole event with all four sets of cousins in one place. We'd overrun Denver with Montgomerys."

Her brain hurt. "Your mom wants us to come?"

He nodded. "She'd want you to come even if you weren't with me. You and the boys are in her web now, so that means you *will* be taken care of."

"She and your dad came to the hospital for James's surgery," she said absently.

"Yeah, my parents are pretty great like that. I should warn you that she knows you and I are together and will probably say something and want to get to know you more, but you're tough. You can handle her. Mostly." He smiled as he said it, and she leaned into him, laughing.

"Just what have I gotten into with you and the Montgomerys?"

Storm grinned. "A whole lot of trouble. It's one of our mottos."

"You have more than one?"

"We even have a tattoo. Once you're a Montgomery, you're always a Montgomery."

She couldn't quite comprehend having that kind of family. She'd never had it, and Jackson's parents had never warmed to her. Hell, they weren't even speaking to her right now. But the Montgomerys? They were a whole new kettle of fish.

And she had no idea what she was doing.

"What should I bring?" she asked, blowing out a breath.

Storm smiled, his eyes dancing. "Just you and the boys. That's all she'll need." His voice lowered. "That's all I need."

She leaned into him, and he kissed her. "The boys are asleep, you know."

He kissed her again. "So I hear." A kiss on her neck. Behind her ear. Then a bite on her jaw. She practically swooned into him. He slid his hands over her and she kissed his shoulder, needing more.

He pulled her into her room and ground against her, sending shivers down her spin. "I want to taste you." They'd been tested and finally got their all-clean results back.

She shook her head. "I need to taste you first." Before he could say anything, she went to her knees in front of him. Thankfully, he didn't protest as she unded his belt and lowered his zipper before she pulled his cock out of his pants. He slid his hand through her hair, letting out a groan.

When she gripped the base of his cock and squeezed, he let out a raspy chuckle. "I'm going to come too quick for you, babe. I want to come *inside* you."

"If you come in my mouth, it'll still be inside me." She winked before licking up his length. "And if I make you come now, that'll give you more time to lick up every inch of me while you recover before you fuck me hard into the mattress." She *knew* her face was bright red as she spoke but she didn't care. She might be only slightly embarrassed, but it was sexy to dirty talk with Storm, and from the way his eyes practically rolled to the back of his head as she spoke, he liked it, too.

"That sounds like a challenge." He gave her a feral grin. "I like it."

Before he could somehow convince her otherwise, she sucked on the tip of his cock and flicked him with her tongue.

"Jesus Christ."

In answer, she hummed against him while bobbing her head and working what she couldn't get into her mouth with her hands. She cupped his balls, rolling them in her hand while sucking on the side of his dick with wet, loud kisses. She knew from the way he tightened in her hold that he liked it when she licked up the vein running along his shaft.

When she wrapped her mouth around him again and slid her free hand along the strip of skin behind his balls, he groaned, tugging on her hair even more. She relaxed her tongue and swallowed every drop of him as he came, his legs shaking against her.

As soon as he slid out of her mouth, he brought her up to kiss the breath from her. Their bodies shaking and their breaths coming in pants, they stripped out of the rest of their clothes.

"On your knees in front of me," Storm ordered, giving her ass a quick slap as he turned her. "I'm going to bury my face between your legs and eat you until you come. Twice."

"Sounds like a challenge," she said, repeating his words back to him. But she didn't protest as she got onto the edge of the bed so he could lick her from behind. She groaned as he slid two fingers inside her, licking her clit at the same time. The roughness of his beard along the inner silk of her thighs sent her over the edge far sooner than she'd planned on. And before she could even call his name, he had speared her with a third finger, twisting just right to press along that inner bundle of nerves that made her come quicker than she thought possible.

"Storm," she panted, so close to the edge she was ready to come again.

In answer, he bit her clit, and she screamed, coming harder than she ever had before in her life.

She was still coming as he slid his fingers out of her and turned her over onto her back.

"Ready for my cock?"

She blinked up at him, her body warm and fuzzy, her breasts heavy, and her nipples hard points. "You're ready already?"

He winked at her. "I seem to never have a problem being hard when it comes to you." He slid a condom over his length and pulled her legs up so they pressed together and lay on one of his shoulders. "I'm going to fuck you like this, but I need you to pinch your nipples. Play with those sweet tits of yours, Ev. Show me how much of a bad girl you are."

"As long as you're my bad boy."

He grinned, showing teeth. "Fuck yeah, Ev. Always."

She licked her lips and cupped her breasts. Her nipples were so sensitive that just the slight brush of her pinkies made her pussy clench. At that same moment, Storm pushed inside, and they both groaned.

"Baby, in this position, you're so fucking tight that I'm going to come way too fast."

"Then think of England and get to fucking," Everly said on a laugh, blushing once again at her words. She'd only read such things in romance novels and had never thought to speak them aloud. But with Storm, she wanted to be dirty. The dirtier, the better.

"That I can do, Your Grace." Then, he *moved*.

She cupped her breasts, playing with her nipples as he fucked her hard into the mattress, and when she came again, he groaned, pulling her legs apart even as he continued to move so he could lay above her, making love to her even as they fucked. Dirty words and all, this was the most romantic moment of her life—or at least one of them. Every time she was with

Storm, she seemed to think it was the most passionate.

"I want you," he rasped. "You're everything to me, Ev. Everything."

He was still moving as he kissed her, and she slid her hands down his sweat-slick back. She wrapped her legs around his waist, meeting him thrust for thrust, even though she was beyond exhausted.

And when she came again, he came with her, filling the condom and heating her up from the inside. His beard had scraped her in the best way possible, and she knew she'd be sore in the morning. Yet it didn't matter. It wouldn't.

After, she lay in his arms without a care in the world.

That would come tomorrow, she knew, but for now, she'd live in the moment.

It was the only thing she could do.

CHAPTER SIXTEEN

Everly needed a nap but knew that wouldn't be happening any time soon. While a bed sounded nice, she'd promised her friends that she'd actually partake in their girls' night. Her boys were with Marie and Harry since they'd volunteered to take care of all of the various children since the men were having a boys' night, as well. How that couple could handle so many children at once, she didn't know, but they'd raised eight kids on their own so she figured they had to have some form of super powers.

She'd dropped the kids off at Austin and Sierra's since the elder Montgomerys were watching the children there that night and now she sat in her car in the parking lot in the back of Montgomery Ink and Taboo. With parking so hard to come by in downtown Denver, the fact that the business owned a freaking parking lot—even a small one—was amazing. She only had one and a half parking spots behind her building and even then her SUV didn't always fit on days with tons of snow or rain.

Everly still couldn't believe that her life had changed so much in such a short time. She'd gone from having only Tabby in her life with Storm running on the periphery, to having a group of friends and an entire family who wasn't her own offering to watch her boys so she could have a few moments to breathe.

The knock on her window forced a scream out of her, and she turned to see Maya standing by her car, her eyes wide.

"You scared the crap out of me." Maya must have yelled it since Everly could hear the other woman through the window.

Everly blew out a breath and opened her door, forcing Maya to take a step back. "You're the one who scared the crap out of *me*." She laughed and shook her head. "I thought you were an ax murderer." *Or Rachel.* Everly held back a frown. Why on earth would it have been Rachel? She didn't know why, but having that other woman and whatever she was planning unresolved made her feel just a bit off. Thank God for the girls' night tonight to keep her mind off the millions of things causing her to stress.

Maya grinned. "Aw, I wouldn't have tapped on the glass with my ax if I was going to murder you. I'd have already been in the back seat to cut your head off from behind, all unsuspecting like."

Everly froze. "You're a very interesting person, Maya."

The other woman laughed. "I try. Now, come on, we're all heading to the new bar down the street. We'll have a drink or two depending on who is driving, eat bar food that will go straight to our hips, then go home to our men all hyped up on sugar and grease and let them go crazy with us."

Well, that was surely far more descriptive than what Everly thought Maya would get into, but now that she thought about it...maybe she could meet up with Storm after she hung out with the girls and have a little *them* time before she went and picked up the boys.

"I can see from the sparkle in your eyes that you're thinking about what I said; however, as you're probably also thinking about my brother, I'm not going to ask for details." Maya gave her a mock shudder, then pulled her arm to get them walking in the right direction. "Let's go. I think we're the last ones to arrive. It took me longer than usual to say goodbye."

"Because you have two men at home waiting on you?" Everly didn't know how Maya handled all that testosterone. She could barely handle Storm, and it wasn't as if they were as serious as marriage and a full-time commitment.

Maya laughed. "Well, usually that would be the case, but this time, I meant my *other* little man, Noah. He's a handful, but really, I only have myself to blame. I was and *am* a holy terror according to multiple sources, so it would only be natural that my baby boy would be, as well. And since I'm a total sap when it comes to him, it took me a while to leave him with my parents."

"I don't blame you. I love my boys so freaking much that sometimes I never want to let them out of my sight."

"It's got to be even harder with Nathan's asthma and James's surgery."

"So true, but somehow, we make it work. Though girls' nights are kind of a new thing for me."

"Well even if you weren't dating Storm, you're Tabby's friend, and Tabby is one of us. We Montgomerys sort of assimilate people. It's what we do." Maya laughed as she said it, and Everly wondered just what she was getting into with the Montgomerys.

They crossed the street and headed to the newly renovated bar that used to be a failed coffee shop. Denver had its share of coffee shops on every corner, but unless they were a big corporation or had something quirky to get people in, they didn't tend to last long. There were just too many. Of course, that could also be said of the bars in Denver.

The music blared as they walked inside, and Everly winced. Maya gave her a look and snorted. "Yeah, this place might be too young for us," the other woman yelled over the din.

"Everly! Maya! Over here!" Tabby yelled from a corner where their friends had already claimed a group of tables.

They made their way over and hugged everyone, laughing as they shouted over the music, though it wasn't as loud in this corner as it had been when they'd first walked in. Meghan and Miranda sat on the other side of the table, looking gorgeous in their green and blue dresses respectively. Maya wore a black jumpsuit thing that looked exquisite and couture and yet punk with all her ink and piercings. Tabby had on a sparkly top and black leather leggings that Everly knew were like wearing pajamas according to the other woman. Autumn wore a black and red dress that made her red curls pop, all seduction and heat with minimal effort. And Sierra had on a purple dress that flowed around her thighs and made her look like she was ready to dance.

Everly had gone with a black dress and shrug since she didn't really own anything else. There hadn't been much need for cocktail dresses or sparkly things for the past three years when she'd been breast-feeding and trying to raise twins while working more than full-time.

"So...what do we think?" Sierra asked, a single brow raised.

Everly pressed her lips together to hold back the laughter as the rest of them tried to look as if they were enjoying themselves.

"I see..." Sierra blew out a breath. "I'm so not with what the kids are doing these days. I thought I was going to be the cool mom with Leif, and now it looks as if I'm not as cool as I thought."

"Is it really called cool these days?" Everly asked and blushed as the others looked at her. "I mean, I know wicked is out, but is there another word for being groovy or whatever?"

Maya held up one of the glasses the others had set out for them and their pitcher of water and margaritas. "To being groovy, cool, wicked, slammin', and whatever else the kids use these days."

Everly laughed and held up a water glass, trying to keep from spilling as they toasted as a group. She didn't drink that much these days, and since she was driving, she wanted to err on the side of caution.

"Okay, let's dance!" Miranda stood up and wiggled her hips. "Quick before the men show up and it's no longer a girls' night."

Everly frowned. "The guys are showing up?" Storm hadn't mentioned that when she'd seen him that morning or when the two of them had texted on and off throughout the day as they went through their many meetings. Maybe the others had planned on coming, but Storm hadn't. She tried not to feel so confused about that.

"They always do," Meghan said with a roll of her eyes. "Doesn't matter that this is a girls' night. Their boys' night always ends up joining ours, even if they don't mention it."

That made her feel slightly better, but she still wasn't sure how she felt about the fact that she'd gotten so disappointed about Storm not joining them. Yes, they were getting serious, but she'd been serious with Jackson, as well.

"Stop frowning," Tabby said as she wrapped an arm around her waist. "Let's dance."

Everly winced. "I don't dance. I mean, I *can't* dance."

"That's why we dance in groups," Miranda explained. "That way, no one can tell."

"Give the predators too many things to look at, and they can't choose what to see," Autumn added and flipped her hair over her shoulder. "Or something along those lines. I don't remember exactly what that nature show said, but come on. Let's dance!"

The group of them took a corner of the dance floor, swinging their hips and arms to the beat and looking downright amazing and hilarious all at the same time. There were far younger people in attendance, but hell, Everly was in her early thirties, it wasn't as if she were the crypt keeper or anything.

Occasionally, a man would try to breach the circle, but Maya or Autumn would either let the guy off nicely if *he* was nice, or threaten his balls if he got a little handsy. It paid to dance in groups.

When one set of arms slid around her waist, Everly turned around, ready to kick the guy in the nuts for touching her without permission, then stopped when he saw it was Storm.

He had on a dark blue shirt over crisp jeans, and yet all she could see was the look in his eyes. He was so damned sexy, and at least for now, he was *hers*. "Hey."

She licked her lips, aware that the other men had joined their women and were saying their hellos in more interesting ways. "Hey," she said softly. "I didn't know you'd be here."

"Wasn't planning on it, but I should have."

"And now I'm going to go get a drink," Wes said dryly. "Somehow, I'm like the thirteenth wheel or something."

Everly winced and looked at the only single Montgomery left if they accounted for the fact that Storm was with her. "You can hang with us if you want."

Storm shook his head. "Not sharing." He kissed her neck, and she held back a shiver.

Wes pinched the bridge of his nose. "We don't share. Though for some reason right after college, a few women thought it would be fun to be with both of us at once..."

Everly's eyes widened. "Huh?"

"We didn't," Wes added, and Storm chuckled. "Not even close. Don't worry. No twin ménages here."

"Good to know." Everly said on a laugh and shook her head as Wes walked away, mumbling under his breath.

Storm kissed the side of her neck again, and she leaned into him. "As much as I love watching your ass move when you dance, how about we head to my place for a bit until you have to pick up the boys?" He bit her earlobe, and she rocked into him.

"Get out of here you two," Maya teased from between Border and Jake. Her husbands weren't wrapped around her like they might have been in other circles, but Everly didn't blame them. There had been a few hate crimes recently against poly couples in the area, so they were being cautious even though everyone wanted to hurt someone on the trio's behalf.

"Don't have to ask me twice." Storm gripped her hand and pulled her away as the two of them waved goodbye to the others. As soon as they had exited the building, Storm pulled her into his arms and kissed her hard. "We can go back in if you want to dance. I just saw you dancing and got so hard I could barely think straight. If you were having fun, we'll do this instead. Promise."

She went up on her tiptoes and kissed his chin. "Let's go to your place. I danced. I laughed. Now I want you."

"Good." He kissed her again and led her down the street. "I take it you parked in the Montgomery lot?"

"Yes, since my spot isn't available at the moment." She pushed thoughts of her store from her mind since she didn't want to think about that right then. All she wanted to do was think of Storm and what they were about to do. All her other worries would be waiting for her in the morning. "Where did you park?" she asked, not wanting to talk about it.

"Wes drove and parked in the same lot. We'd planned on him driving me home but I think this is even better."

She stopped him before they crossed the street and kissed him again. He ran his hands through her hair, and she sighed, aware they were standing on a street corner at night in downtown Denver and not really caring for these few bare moments. "It sounds perfect."

Storm slammed her back into the door, kissing her neck and jaw as she raked her hands down his back through his shirt. They'd only just walked into his home and couldn't keep their hands to themselves.

He slid his hand up her dress and cupped her breast through her strapless bra. She shivered at his touch and arched into him.

"More," she rasped. "Harder."

She tugged on his shirt, and he did the same to her dress. Soon, they were both naked, clothes around their feet, and her shoes kicked to the other side of the room where she would have no chance of finding them in a hurry. He slid his hand between her folds, and she wrapped her fingers around his cock. They both groaned, sweat slicking their bodies as they touched and teased each other.

When he slid two fingers inside her, she came, her body arching as she called his name, her eyelids growing heavy-lidded. Her breasts became heavy, and she grew even slicker around his hand. When he pulled his fingers away, she whimpered, but only long enough for him to sit in the armchair near them and hold out a condom.

"Put it on me."

Her hands shook as she tore open the wrapper and slid the condom down his length. "Ready?"

"Always, Ev. Always ready for you. Now, ride my cock."

With his hands on hers, she straddled him on the chair, slowly sliding herself over his cock. When she was fully seated, she burned, her skin hot to the touch, and her nipples so hard she ached.

"Ride me, Ev. You can do it, baby."

She leaned down and kissed his lips, lowering her hands to his shoulders as she rocked her hips. They both groaned, and he gripped her waist, helping her keep the perfect friction as they lifted higher and higher. Everly leaned back, feeling every inch of him inside of her, filling her up so much she thought she'd break from the ecstasy. Storm took that moment to lean forward and take her nipples into his mouth, one by one.

She squeezed her inner muscles, and Storm let out a curse. "Do that again."

When she lowered her head and met his gaze, squeezing her inner muscles again, they both moaned.

"Harder," she whispered. "Almost there."

"Done," he growled and slammed up into her so hard she called out, pleasure filling her so hard and fast, she came right then. Storm followed her, pumping in and out of her until they both fell together onto the chair, their bodies sweat-slick and limp.

As he ran his hands down her back, he murmured to her, telling her how much he wanted her, how much he craved her...

And she held him close, never wanting this moment to end but knowing it might. Because nothing good in her life ever stayed that way, nothing except for her boys.

Nothing.

CHAPTER SEVENTEEN

S o maybe having him and Everly attend their first family dinner as a couple with twenty plus Montgomerys present hadn't been the smartest idea. But he couldn't back out now, so he rolled with it.

Hopefully.

"I hope they like the potato salad," Everly said from the passenger seat. They'd taken the truck, complete with new car seats for the boys and a special harness for Randy in the back. Storm had taken that as a sign that they were moving forward with their relationship, but with Everly, he didn't know. She was about ready to combust with all the tension riding her, and he couldn't do a damn thing about it.

There was truly only so much a woman could take, and for a man like Storm, it killed him that he couldn't help her.

"They'll like the potato salad," Storm said with a smile. "And you didn't have to bring anything at all. I told you that."

"I'm not going to my first Montgomery Family Barbeque empty-handed. When I called your mother, she said I could bring a side dish if I truly wanted to, and I mentioned my potato salad."

"I like your potato salad," he said, his attention on the road even as he glanced up into the rearview mirror to check on the boys. They were talking to one another in that secret language only twins knew. He and Wes had done the same; though with so many Montgomerys in the family, it hadn't lasted as long as he figured Nathan and James's would.

"When did you have it?" she asked, her tone on the slight edge of panic.

"You used to make it when you had people over on weekends back in the day." When she'd been with Jackson, and Storm had just been the family friend. He didn't mention that since she already knew what he was thinking. Times had changed, but his love for her potato salad had not.

"Oh," she said, her voice deflating. "It's just that people are picky with things like that. They'll either go mustard or vinegar or really mayonnaise filled. Some like it with dill or just paprika. I should have brought an easier dish that would accommodate more people."

Storm held back his laughter since she wouldn't appreciate it and reached out to grip her hand. They tangled their fingers together, and he gave her hand a slight squeeze. "They'll like what you bring. There will be enough of us there that there's bound to be a bunch of people who like your brand of salad. They'll have to fight me for it, though. Just saying."

She sighed and looked over at him as he parked on the side of the road. While the Montgomerys had an ample lot, there were still too many of them for everyone to park near the house. They'd have to walk a block, but that wasn't too bad.

"I'm acting like a nut," she muttered under her breath. "I've never really done this before, you know?"

She looked back at the boys, who were staring at them with rapt attention. That meant he and Everly couldn't exactly go into detail about their relationship and whatever firsts came with it in front of the kids. He figured the boys would know eventually, but he agreed with Everly that they should focus on how they worked together before introducing the twins to a new idea.

He nodded. "I know." He turned off the engine and looked in the back seat. "Okay, gentlemen, are you ready for a Montgomery event?"

"Yes!" Nathan shouted, and James clapped while Randy barked. Everly laughed as Storm rubbed his ear jokingly. Two three-year-old boys, as well as a young puppy, in a small cab of a truck didn't make for a quiet time.

"Then let's do it," Storm said with a laugh before winking at Everly.

It wasn't as easy as he'd thought it would be since he was clearly new to this, but somehow they got Randy on his leash, the boys standing between the two adults with the puppy ahead of them all, and all their bags and even the potato salad to the front door in one trip. Why the twins needed their own bags of toys and other things he didn't know, but he also didn't question Everly. She knew what she was doing.

"You're here!" his mom, Marie Montgomery, said as she opened the door. "Harry, come and help me get all their things. Oh, Everly darling, I'm so glad you brought the potato salad, it looks wonderful. And look at you boys, I swear you've grown two feet since I last saw you. And Randy, darling, I see you, too. You're such a good boy."

His mother said all of that in one long breath and yet hugged them all and ushered them in at the same time. How she could make them all feel welcome *and* individual astounded him daily, though he knew part of it came from raising eight hellion children.

The kids were ushered off to the play area where his sister Maya and her two husbands, Jake and Border, were watching over the herd of children. He hadn't actually added up how many nieces and nephews he had now since the number kept increasing, but the eldest was almost a teenager now, and the youngest still couldn't walk, so they ran the gambit.

Everly tucked herself to Storm's side, and he slid his hand over her hip. "You ready?" he asked. This wasn't her first time meeting most of his family, and she was friends with many of them, but this *was* the first time she was there as his girlfriend.

"No, but let's do this."

Austin and Sierra made their way up first. Sierra immediately went up to Everly to hug her, and Austin gave Storm a head tilt before hugging Everly, as well.

"I'm so sorry about your store," Sierra said softly. "You still haven't heard anything?"

Storm squeezed Everly's hand, and she gave him a soft look. "No," she answered. "Only that they're still looking."

"When do you get the go ahead to start rebuilding?" Austin asked. "If that's what you want to do, that is."

Everly blew out a breath. "Soon, I hope. I just don't know. And, yes, I plan to rebuild. I mean, I hope to. It's all up in the air right now, but darn it, I love that store. And it's *mine*, you know?"

Austin nodded. "I get it. If anything happened to the tattoo shop, Maya and I would be a wreck but would still want to rebuild."

"Same with my shop," Sierra added. She owned the boutique across the street from Montgomery Ink called Eden. In fact, Storm remembered that's how Sierra had met Austin in the first place.

"If you need anything, you let us know," Austin said, his voice that deep growl of authority.

"I will," Everly said. "Thank you so much for even caring."

"Of course, we care," Sierra said.

"Yeah, you're one of us now, even if you weren't dating this dork over here." Austin grinned as he said it, but Storm still punched his brother in the shoulder.

"Men," Sierra said with a smile and rolled her eyes.

They talked for a few more minutes before they parted ways and met up with Luc and Meghan. Miranda and Decker joined them, and soon, Everly was laughing hard, and Storm just held her close, knowing they needed times like these to balance out everything else going on in their lives.

"When you're ready, you call us and we'll help with the rebuild," Decker said. "I know you could go with Jake's brothers, but come on, go with the Montgomerys. You like us better."

"I heard that!" Jake called, and Maya wrapped her arms around his middle to pull him away.

Every laughed, and Storm pinched the bridge of his nose. "It's not a competition, you know," he said.

"Of course, not," Luc said with a wink before kissing his wife's temple. Though the two had been married for a bit now, Meghan blushed and leaned into her husband. "There's no competition."

"Not exactly what I meant," Storm said but still smiled. The two companies had different areas of expertise, and neither of them was lacking for jobs. The fact that they were connected through marriage now just made it more enjoyable to rib each other.

"But, really, we're here to help," Meghan said. "I know you don't have any landscaping needs since you're located downtown, but who knows, you might have a potted plant or something."

Every smiled. "I kill plants, so I might actually need your help."

"I kill them, too," Miranda said with an evil grin toward her sister. "Thankfully, Meghan can bring them back to life."

"If you kept them out of the reach of pets and children, maybe they'd live longer," Meghan argued.

The two of them joked with one another, and Storm waved as he pulled Everly away. He wanted her to meet everyone but not feel so overwhelmed. He also wasn't the most talkative of the bunch, so he tended to stick to one area of the house or backyard and have people come to him, or he'd just float from group to group, listen to what they had to say and move on. He loved them, but hell, his family was so big it got overwhelming at times.

Griffin and Autumn were sitting next to Tabby and Alex around one of the tables his parents had set up, and he gave them a wave. Everly waved, too and the group smiled at them, waving hello. Wes joined them, and they laughed and talked about random things that had happened that week. Since they all saw each other often, it was surprising how much they still had to talk about. He and Everly spoke to them for a bit before hunger got the better of him and he dragged Everly back to the boys.

"It will take another four hours to talk to everyone about their days, so let's get the boys fed and then food in our bellies."

She rolled her eyes at him and poked at his stomach. "You don't have any fat on you, how is that possible?"

He winked. "Good genes and the fact that Alex makes me work out more now."

"I should thank him," she said huskily, and he swallowed hard. He could *not* have a hard dick right then in front of his all-knowing family. He'd never live it down.

He kissed her on the top of the head since they were in the middle of his parents' living room and went to go make sure the boys had their lunch. Of course, he shouldn't have worried since his mom had the kids already set up with their own food. They didn't always split up the kids and adults like they were today, but since the grills were out in full force, it made sense safety-wise.

He and Everly made sure the twins were okay then piled food on their own plates—complete with Everly's potato salad—before taking one of the empty tables near the side of the backyard. They weren't alone for long, however, because three of his cousins decided to join him. As they were of the few Everly hadn't met yet, he didn't mind.

"Everly, this is Adrienne, Thea, and Roxie. They're the Colorado Springs cousins. Shep is their big brother. He's the one who lives in New Orleans now but still helps out at Montgomery Ink when he's in town visiting. Ladies, this is Everly, my girlfriend." He hadn't said that word aloud before, and the two of them stiffened but rolled with it.

Everly smiled at them all and said hello. "Do you go by that band name or do you just like the location?"

Adrienne rolled her eyes. She was the eldest of the three girls, but Shep was also far older than the rest of them, so the girls had been raised a little differently than wild Shep—not that Adrienne had let that stop her from being wild herself. Though in all reality,

Storm wasn't sure Adrienne was as out there as she claimed to be.

"The Denver Montgomerys like to call the rest of us by our city since they outnumber us," she said with a wink.

"But we tend to think of *us* as the Montgomerys," Thea, the next in line said with a smile.

"And we call them the Denver ones rather than the Main Eight like Wes wanted them to be called," Roxie added.

"And there are even more of you?" Everly asked, sounding a little overwhelmed. He didn't blame her since there *were* a lot of them and the Montgomerys tended to be big and loud with even just a few of them at a time. The men were all big, bearded, and inked, while the women were just as big in personality and body art. They tended to stand out.

"A few more," Adrienne answered. "There's like twenty-one of us or so in our generation, I think. I lost count after ten or so, though."

"Wow."

Storm snorted at Everly's breathy word but ran his hand down her back to comfort her. She wasn't used to so many people, and he got that. She'd been an only child just like Jackson had been. And hell, neither of their parents had been overly warm and loving, so being around the Montgomerys had to be a real change for her.

He was just happy that his family hadn't started quizzing her. It would come, maybe not today, but the next time she came with him. He thought it odd that it didn't feel strange to have her by his side. It was as if she'd always been there. She just fit. This was his Ev, and it felt *right*.

He just hoped it felt right to her, too.

They finished their lunches but sat where they were with his cousins as Nathan and James ran to them. They were giggling and chasing Randy, who barked and skidded to a stop at Storm's feet. Storm bent down to rub a hand over the pup's head before holding back a grunt as James landed on his lap. Nathan climbed into Everly's, and the two of them spoke at once about their afternoon. Randy went back to playing with the other family dogs, and Storm just put his arm around the back of Everly's chair and listened to her sons ramble in that kid way they did.

He didn't miss the knowing looks on not only his cousin's faces but also every other person who happened to stop by. He didn't mind the attention as much as he thought he would. After all, he'd ribbed the rest of his family as each of them had found the person they wanted to be with.

He frowned.

Was that was this was? Was she the one he wanted in his life now and always? Did that mean kids and marriage and everything that came with that? He'd always thought he'd end up one of those uncles that were around but didn't have a family of their own. It had taken him a long time to realize he might deserve a life beyond the guilt. By the time that had happened, though, he'd reached his mid-thirties and hadn't found a woman he wanted to be with.

Until Everly.

He let out a breath. Maybe, just maybe, she could be his future.

He just didn't know what to think about that.

The boys had been hyper when they got into the truck later that evening since the barbeque had rolled into dinner and everyone had gone back for more food, but as soon as they hit the highway, everyone in the backseat was out like a light. Even Randy was on his back, feet in the air and mouth open as he snored.

"That damn dog looks like a dork when he sleeps like that," Storm muttered under his breath.

"But adorable," Everly said as she turned in her seat to snap a photo of the trio.

Storm snorted. "That is true." He rubbed the back of his neck, thankful he'd had a cup of coffee before he hit the road. He wasn't tired, necessarily, as nothing on earth would make him think it was okay to drive while tired after what had happened on that rainy night years ago, but he'd needed the pick-me-up.

"I had a lot of fun today," Everly said on a yawn. "More than I thought I would."

Storm glanced at her. "What, you thought we'd be boring?"

She gave him a dramatic eye roll. "As if the Montgomerys could ever be boring. I just meant that I thought I'd be too stressed out to enjoy myself. I'm glad I was wrong."

He reached over and tugged on her hand, bringing it to his mouth so he could lay a gentle kiss on her palm. "I'm glad, too."

She gave him a happy sigh, and they made their way back to her place in peaceful silence.

The boys woke up somewhat as they got them out of their car seats. Randy was ready for a bathroom break, and the boys seemed to be on the same page, so Storm went out back with the dog as Everly got the boys ready for bed. Before heading back to the other side of the house to help out with bedtime, he made sure that Randy had water since the puppy had eaten far too much at his parents'. He and Everly hadn't talked about if he'd sleep over that night, but both of them had clearly assumed it. Even Randy had a set of things over at the house for when Storm stayed the night.

It was feeling more and more like a family, and though Storm was still wary, he was starting to come to rely on it.

"Are you going to kiss Uncle Storm again?" James asked as Everly tugged a shirt over his head. Nathan was already in his PJs and half-asleep in his bed. Since her back was to him, and James had a shirt over his eyes, only Storm saw the way Ev's face went pale at the question.

"What do you mean?" she asked, her voice seemingly calm. Storm didn't say anything, but he knew she realized he was in the doorway. They hadn't discussed how they would handle the boys knowing, and he knew it was her place to decide what to say. He would go with it because while he was falling for the family, she was still the boys' mother.

"You and Uncle Storm kiss. A lot." Nathan gave a big yawn as he said it, and Storm thought the boy had fallen asleep before he continued. "It's okay. We like him."

"You should keep kissing Uncle Storm," James said with a sleepy smile before kissing his mom on the cheek. "That way, Uncle Storm can be our daddy, and we can be a family. We get to have a puppy then, and no one can hurt us because Uncle Storm would beat them up."

"He's strong and awesome and knows about X-men. We love him, and you should, too."

Storm's heart grew ten sizes even as his belly clutched at what the boys thought. Hell, those kids were damn observant. He hadn't broached the subject of marriage with Everly and he damn sure hadn't thought about it much himself, but the boys were apparently on board.

And he needed a damn drink.

"I'm glad you like Storm," Everly said carefully as if she were thinking over every word. He didn't blame her, and that's why he kept silent. This wasn't his place, but he'd support her if she needed it. "I like him, too."

He a hell of a lot more than liked her.

"Okay," James said simply before Everly tucked him into bed. Nathan was already snoring, passed out with one hand over his face. How the kid could fall asleep so easily was beyond him.

Everly kissed her son's head before walking back out of the room and turning off the lights so their Thor night light shined brightly.

"Oh my God," she whispered as she hurried to her room. Storm came with her but turned around as Randy trotted into the boys' room. The dog was potty trained and well behaved, but he didn't know if he should be sleeping with the boys.

"Ev, before we freak out over that, can Randy sleep with the boys? He's already making himself at home next to James from the sound of those giggles."

Everly put her hands over her face and let out a small scream that wasn't all that loud. "That's fine. Everything's fine. Oh my God."

He closed the door behind him and tugged her hands down so he could hug her. "You handled that great, babe." He ran his hands down her back, and she clung to him.

"I didn't think they knew." She buried her face against his chest and let out a groan. "And they were...happy about it."

"Apparently, we suck at hiding." He kissed the top of her head.

"We aren't all that subtle."

He smiled and pulled her back slightly so he could look into her eyes. "No, we aren't."

"I...while I'm relieved they're so okay with everything right now, I just want to forget about the rest of the world for a while. Can we do that?"

He cupped the back of her head and kissed her softly, his dick pressing against his zipper. "We can do that." He wanted her more than he could put into words—this woman, his friend that wasn't just his friend anymore.

"Good," she breathed. She slid her hands down his chest, and he kissed her again, needing her taste.

Slowly, they moved their hands over each other, learning each other, the way they moved as one. He slowly stripped off her top, then her pants. That left her in just her lingerie, perfect in every single way. He loved the way her breasts filled the cups of her bra, and how her hips flared out so they were perfect for his hands to grip.

"You're so beautiful," he whispered.

Ev rolled her eyes. "I have stretch marks, and I'm still not the weight I was before I had the babies. I look better with clothes on. Believe me."

He leaned down and bit her lip. When she gasped, he gave her a grin. "As I've seen you both ways, I'm going to tell you how much you're wrong." He kissed her. "Actually, I'm going to *show* you."

He took off her bra, taking each nipple into his mouth one after the other, then went to his knees and slid her panties down her legs. He gave her a kiss on each thigh, his dick so hard he thought he might burst right there in his jeans like a damned teenager.

"I want you, Ev," he said softly, pressing another kiss on her thigh. She ran a hand through his hair, and he licked where he'd kissed. "I know we still need to use condoms because of birth control, but I want to taste you, Ev."

She tugged on his shoulders when he would have kissed her heat, and he stood up so he could kiss her mouth instead. When he pulled back, she gave him a wicked smile. "I'd rather taste you at the same time."

He grinned back, his cock officially so hard he'd probably last one touch. "I think that can be arranged." She helped him strip out of his shirt and undo his pants. They were both panting as he pulled down his pants and boxer briefs. His cock sprang free, slapping his belly and making them both groan.

"That looks like it hurts."

He winked. "Well, there are a few ways you can help me."

"Let me guess, with my mouth? And if I were to say I had a headache, you'd tell me you have the perfect medicine for me."

He reached out and hugged her, bringing her to his chest so he could nuzzle his face into the crook of her neck. "Let's find out, shall we?"

They kissed and touched until they were lying opposite each other on the bed. He had his face between her legs in the next instant, her thigh resting over his shoulder as he licked and sucked her. She tasted sweet and exotic, and he knew he'd crave her until the end of his days. And when she took him into her mouth, he groaned. She cupped his balls and squeezed the base of his dick as she sucked him down.

"Dear God," he growled before licking up and down her labia. He sucked on her clit, loving the way it swelled under his attention. She was so damn close, and he could feel it. As soon as he speared her with his fingers, she came, and he licked it all, wanting more.

And because he knew he was far too close to coming, he pulled back.

"I wasn't done," she said, her eyes dark and glassy.

"If I come down your throat, I won't recover in time to fuck you hard into the mattress." He turned and slid between her legs as he reached for the condom he'd placed next to the pillows on the bed and sheathing himself.

"I guess if we were having sex when we were both in our twenties it would have been different." She winked as she said it, and he pinched her thigh.

"I'm not that much of an old man," he growled before taking her hips in his hands and thrusting into her with one move.

She gasped, and he let out a groan of his own. "Okay, not an old man."

"Good to hear." Then he leaned down and captured her mouth with his as he thrust in and out of her, their bodies shaking and sweating. Hell, she was additive; he knew he'd never stop wanting her...stop needing her.

And that drug would have to be something he thought of later. For now, he only needed the woman in his arms and the feeling that overwhelmed him at that moment.

He rolled his hips, knowing he hit her at just the right spot when her mouth parted and she arched her back, her breasts pressing into his chest. He thrust in and out, going faster and harder until they both yelled and came at the same time, their bodies shaking, spent, and exhausted.

He collapsed next to her, his dick still semi-hard inside her, and brought her close so he could kiss her.

"That was..." She breathed. "That was..."

"I can't think of a word either," he said with a laugh. "Let's just go with 'that was...'"

"Yeah." She snuggled into him, and he held her close. With her so close and in his arms, he could almost believe that everything would work out and nothing could come at them that they couldn't handle.

Almost, he thought. But for now, he'd hold her in his arms and know that they'd deal with what they needed to eventually. Because he had her next to him, around him, and as a part of him. That was all he needed.

CHAPTER EIGHTEEN

"I know a Celtic knot is generic for some, but hell, I've been collecting them since I was a kid."

Storm looked down at Clay and snorted. "It's only generic for anyone who doesn't realize how difficult the design is."

"Amen," Austin said absently, his attention solely on Clay's new ink.

This was the first time Storm had brought Clay down to Denver to at least meet some of his family. Since Austin knew about Clay and the accident, it made sense to Storm that he be the first person the kid met. Storm knew it was time to tell the others what had happened, even if it broke open something inside him he'd long since closed and buried. But if Everly could face her fears and loss head-on every day, so could he.

So, Storm was here with Clay, watching the kid get his first tattoo. Maya was off that day, and yes, Storm had known that when he'd made the appointment. His sister saw far too much, and Wes needed to be the first person he told when he found the way to do it. *No more hiding*, he told himself. It wasn't fair to anyone.

The one thing he and Clay hadn't discussed, however, was the kid's sister. They'd pointedly left Rachel out of the conversation. Once Everly figured out her plan, he'd be there to help and do what he could, but until then, it wasn't his place. Standing back wasn't easy on him, but he'd learned the hard way what happened when he tried to take over.

"Looking good," Storm said before turning his attention back to his tablet. He'd been up late the night before with the twins when Nathan had begun coughing. Everly had gotten him back to sleep after using his inhaler, but James had been worried, so Storm had rocked him until he too fell back asleep. That meant Storm had been exhausted for his half-day at work, and now needed to finish up a few things during Clay's appointment. Clay hadn't minded, though Wes hadn't been happy. His twin wasn't happy with him most of the time these days. Storm hoped things would change once he told Wes everything he'd been hiding, things might be better, but he wasn't sure. Something had changed between them, and he didn't know how to fix it.

"You okay over there?" Clay asked as Austin cleaned up the tattoo.

Storm nodded. "Yeah, just thinking."

"Been doing a lot of that lately," Austin commented. "Need to talk?"

"I'm good," Storm said honestly. Things were a little off-kilter, but he'd figure it out.

"You'd tell me if you needed to," Austin said, and it wasn't a question. His big brother took care of the lot of them and even tried to take care of all the cousins, too. He was the eldest of the twenty-one cousins, and he acted like it. "Okay, Clay, let's get you up so you can see your new ink."

Clay had been straddling the chair since he'd wanted the knot on his shoulder. He rolled up easily. Storm still couldn't quite believe that Clay hadn't even gotten a bruise during the accident that had claimed his father's life and given Storm back problems for so much of his life, but he was damn grateful for it.

Jax, Brandon, and Derek—the three other tattoo artists on duty at the time—came over to see the new tattoo, as well. Storm didn't know the three of them as well as he knew the other artists who weren't his family, but he liked them. Jax was so new that Storm didn't even know the man's last name, but if Maya and Austin had him working here, they obviously trusted him, and that was all that mattered.

"Dude." Clay's eyes went wide as he turned in the mirror. "That's fucking perfect."

Storm rolled his eyes and took a quick photo of the kid's reaction. He'd taken a few during the process so Clay would have them for later once Storm forwarded them with his phone. He may not be the kid's father, but he'd be there for the moments he could.

"You do good work," he said to Austin as the other artists moved in on Clay to get a closer look.

Austin grinned and rubbed that big beard of his. "Yeah, I do. Speaking of, you coming in to get more ink at some point, or are you good with what you have?"

Storm had a few pieces but not as many as some of his family. And unlike the rest of the Montgomerys, he only had Austin do his ink. Maya would have gotten too close to his scars and asked too many questions. But that might change, he thought.

"I have an idea, but I might get Maya to do it."

Austin's brows rose. "You stepping out on me?"

He rolled his eyes. "Maybe it's time I don't hide everything for so long."

His big brother nodded before punching him in the shoulder. "Good. It's about time. You heading over to Everly's after this? Or back to work?"

Storm shook his head. "I have a few things to do at home, and she's coming over later. Tabby and Alex are playing house with the kids tonight." Storm had a feeling it was because the couple wanted him and Everly to have privacy, and if it helped Alex and Tabby as a couple as well, then he'd take it.

"Things are getting serious between you two." Again, it wasn't a question, but Storm answered anyway.

"Yeah, I think so." He blew out a breath. "Not that I know what I'm going to do about it."

Austin smiled wide. "You'll figure it out. We always do. Just don't do anything stupid."

Storm laughed since, yeah, they all tended to do stupid things when it mattered, but he'd figure it out. Everly was worth that and more.

After Clay had settled up and they parted ways, promising lunch soon, Storm went back to his house to finish up a few things for work. He had a home office set up and worked at home some days when his brain couldn't function with the noise that came with the open floor plan at Montgomery Inc. If Tabby needed him for something, she'd call in a hurry, and it wasn't a big deal. Plus, this way, he could let Randy out of the crate since he hadn't been able to take him to Montgomery Ink even though he'd started bringing him to the office.

But as soon as he pulled into the driveway, he knew things weren't going to go as smoothly as he'd have liked. He sighed, turned off his engine, and gave

Wes's truck parked beside his one last look before making his way into his house.

Wes sat on Storm's couch with Randy on his lap and a frown on his face. When Wes looked up, Storm knew he'd waited far too long by being a coward.

"Hey," Storm said, his voice rough.

Wes was silent a moment before he set Randy down on the floor and stood up. "I've gone through what I needed to say twenty times and even wrote some of it down, but it doesn't seem right. I don't know what I need to say because I don't know what's wrong. All I know is that something *is* wrong and you don't trust me enough to tell me. We're fucking *twins*, Storm. We're not just brothers. We're more than that. And yet you've been hiding something and acting weird and pushing me away. I thought maybe it had something to do with Everly, but that's not it because it happened way before that. And fuck, it happened way before Jillian, too, though I tried to put the blame on her."

Wes raked his hands through his hair, making himself look even more disheveled, even though the man usually looked more put-together than anyone. Storm didn't speak, knowing Wes needed to get everything out first. That's how they worked...or at least how they *used* to work.

"I don't know why things are off, but fuck it, Storm, you're not working like you used to, you don't come to jobsites as much to help out, you're in your head more often than not, and you're keeping secrets." He blew out a breath. "If you don't want to work with the family company anymore, then fine, but tell me. I won't tell you that I get it and that everything will be okay, I'd be fucking lying, but I can't stand back and watch you do this to yourself, do this to *us* because you're not letting me know what's going on in your head."

Storm's brows rose. "The fuck? I'm not leaving the company. Mom and Dad left it to us when they retired. It's *ours*. All of ours. Just because I don't spend as much time doing *your* job, doesn't mean I don't want to be part of what our family built."

"Then why don't you do what you used to? Why aren't you *here*?"

"Because my back can't handle it!" Storm shouted back.

Wes frowned. "What? What's wrong with your back? You never mentioned that you hurt your back. Was it on the jobsite? At home?"

Storm ran a hand over his face and tried to calm down. Nothing could get his blood pumping for a fight like his twin. They were so much alike, even though they had stark differences, as well.

"You should sit down, Wes. I have something to tell you." Dread filled his belly, but he pushed through it. He *had* to get everything off his chest, and damn it, he should have done it years ago and not when everything was about to blow up in their faces.

Wes frowned at him and sat. Randy came up to Storm and nuzzled his legs, and he rubbed the puppy's head, needing the comfort.

"I got in a car accident twenty years ago," Storm blurted, then told the whole story of the accident and Clay—without mentioning Rachel as that wasn't his story to tell—while Wes sat there and listened with wide eyes and a look of hurt on his face.

"Jesus Christ, Storm. You know it wasn't your fault, right? It was an accident. But you blamed yourself this entire damn time, didn't you?"

Storm hung his head and gripped it with his hands. "A man died, Wes. Clay's dad *died,* and my car was the one to hit him." Bile coated his tongue, and he tried to focus, but he couldn't get the sounds of metal clashing against metal out of his head. He counted to ten, and Randy pressed against his legs.

With the weight of that small body along his calf, he was able to breathe again. This was why he had Randy, and why he'd trained those other dogs.

"His car hit *you*." Wes's voice brought him out of his thoughts. "It was a tragic accident, and I'm so sorry that you went through it, but it wasn't your fault." He paused. "I...how could I not have figured something like this had happened? How did I not know? Damn it, I wish you had told me. You told Dad, Austin, and *Jackson*, but not me."

Storm looked up, an old weight off his shoulders now replaced by a new one. *Guilt.* Even more guilt. Damn it, he could do this and be an adult and own up to his mistakes. He might not have been the cause of the accident, but he'd hidden it from Wes for so long. *That* was on him.

"Jackson was an asshole," he ground out. "I can't tell you everything about that. Not yet. It's not my secret to tell, but I will regret having him part of my life at that point for a long fucking time. As for not telling you? I was so fucking scared, man. I was a damn coward. I'm sorry I didn't tell you and that I hid it for so long. I shouldn't have, but it kept snowballing, and somehow, twenty years passed, and I had this big thing...yet I didn't know how to tell you."

"Would you have if I hadn't come here like this?" Wes asked. "I don't agree with why you kept your secret, but I get it. It *was* a big thing, and it's not about me. I'm just glad you had Austin to talk to if you needed to."

Storm sighed. "I was going to." He paused, his hands tensing. "I told Everly. Recently. And I guess that just opened the vault and I found it harder and harder to keep it to myself."

"I'm glad you have her," Wes said after a moment before letting out a groan. "I can't believe how much of an asshole I've been about you working on-site when you've been in pain. You were hurting, and I didn't see."

"I hid it well. It's not your fault."

Wes sighed. "It wasn't yours either." He looked up and met Storm's eyes. "This isn't over, and I want to talk about it more, but I need to let it all sink in. I don't want any more secrets between us. I hate that we used to be best friends and that we aren't anymore."

They each stood up and gave each other a hard hug, Storm's chest and shoulders finally holding a bit less tension. Twenty years. Twenty freaking years of holding everything in, and now his twin knew.

It hadn't hurt as much as he thought it would...and yet he knew it could have been so much worse. They had a long way to go, but he'd taken the first step. Being a Montgomery wasn't easy, but when things got tough, they were there for each other. He'd forgotten that, and he prayed he didn't forget again.

By the time Wes left, and Storm had Randy fed, the doorbell rang and he went to let Everly in. He was still shaking a bit, but he hoped the worst was over.

She took one look at his face and stepped into his arms. "I thought I was going to be the pale one tonight. What's wrong?"

He kissed her, needing her taste to breathe, to *be*. "I told Wes," he whispered, the weight on his chest once again feeling lighter.

She pulled back, her eyes wide. "About the accident?"

He tucked her hair behind her ear, needing to touch her. "Yeah. It went...well, better than I thought, but it's not over. I should have told him before this."

She played with the pocket on the front of his shirt, a frown on her face. "You weren't ready. I hated that you were hurting yourself by keeping it all in, but now you can talk about it more if you're able."

He kissed her again, feeling far younger and freer than he had in years. "You helped. How are *you* doing?"

She shrugged, and he pulled her over to the couch where Randy proceeded to jump on their laps to cuddle with them. The sight brought a smile to her face that made it hard for him to pull Randy off the couch, but he had to since Randy was still in training. The little guy might be small now, but he wouldn't always be.

"Talk to me."

"I just feel a little off. The final arson report should be back soon, and they're saying I can do a walkthrough, but I'm scared."

He gripped her hand. "Do you want me to go with you?"

She nodded as he spoke. "I'd hoped. I mean, before you..." She took a deep breath. "Before you and I started this thing, I would have done it on my own, but I want you with me. Is that okay?"

He leaned forward and cupped her face. "It's more than okay." Then he kissed her, first soft and slow, then a little hotter, a little deeper. "I want you," he growled out. "I know we have so many things to talk about, but I need you."

"Make love to me?" she asked, her voice breathy.

In answer, he tipped her head back and kissed her again.

Storm pulled her closer, and she straddled his lap. His dick pressed against his zipper and her heat, and he groaned when she rocked into him. "You're so fucking sexy, Ev."

She tossed her hair over her shoulder and reached around to take off her top. "You make me feel this way. I've always been a sex-in-bed-on-my-back sort of woman, but apparently, I'm in an exploring mood."

"And I'm one lucky bastard." He kissed her again, and slowly, they began to strip off the rest of their clothes. He slid his hands over her and then inside her. She was soft, wet, and oh so hot. If he weren't careful, he'd bend her over the couch and pound into her until they were both sated and exhausted, but that wasn't what either of them needed right then.

They both ended up lying on their sides, her back to his front, as he lifted her thigh and slid his condom-covered cock into her heat. She tilted her head back and kissed her hard, at the same time playing with her nipples and sliding in and out of her.

"Holy God, you go so deep at this angle."

He kissed her shoulder and lowered her thigh, pressing down with the palm of his hand. "Let's try this, too."

"Oh?" She moaned. "Oh..." She drew out the last word as he slid into her hard and fast from behind with her legs pressed tightly together. He was so close to coming that all it would take would be a slight squeeze of her inner muscles and he'd blow. And because he didn't want to come without her going first, he let go of her thigh and slid his hand around the front to slide his fingers over her clit.

"Oh God," she moaned as she came. "Storm."

He thrust hard two more times before he came with her, his body shaking and his back burning. He'd ache later, but it would be worth it. His woman was worth everything.

Afterward, they lay in a tangle of limbs, their breathing coming in pants. He was trying to put his thoughts in order when she blurted, "I love you."

He froze then turned her in his arms so he could look down at her.

"Oh my God. I can't believe I just said that out loud."

His heart beat faster, and he tried to take in every nuance, every taste, every sound. He'd never loved a woman, not as he should, but everything was different with Everly. Always had been. And he figured, always would.

"I love you, too," he said softly.

Her eyes filled, and she blinked the tears back. "What are we going to do about it? I was wrong the last time, and I don't want to be again."

He ran his thumb over her cheek, knowing there were important words he had to say, and yet he came up blank. "I don't know what's to come, but we've both spent so long looking back, maybe it's time to look at the now and what might be. I'm not going anywhere, Ev." He kissed her again. "But we don't have to make every plan right now." He kissed her once more. "I love you."

She smiled softly. "I love you, too."

He grinned and rolled on top of her. "Let me show you how much."

She laughed, arching into him. "I thought you were an old man who needed time to recover."

"Hush your mouth." He lowered his head to kiss her again, but her phone rang. With a sigh, he reached for it since his arms were longer. He handed it over to her and helped her cover up with a throw blanket so she wouldn't have to talk on the phone while naked.

When she stiffened after she answered the call, he put his arm around her. Randy pressed himself against her legs and nuzzled as if to comfort.

"Can you repeat that?" she gasped. "Are you sure? No, thank you. Yes, I realize. Thank you." She hung up, her hands shaking as she turned to him.

"What is it?"

She blew out a breath, her eyes wide. "It's Rachel."

"What? She called? What did she want?" Everly still hadn't made her mind up about the other woman, and Storm hadn't blamed her with everything going on. Her kids and store came first. Now and always.

"It wasn't her on the phone. It was the arson investigator. Apparently, it took so long to get back to me because they found DNA but needed to process it." She looked at Storm, her face pale. "It was Rachel. She was the one who set the fire. I don't know how they know, but they do. She was in the system because of an assault charge when she was younger or something. God, Storm. Rachel burned down my bookstore. I don't know why, but it all has to do with Jackson, doesn't it? How could she do that?" Tears slid down her cheeks, and he pulled her into his arms.

"They'll find her," he promised, his brain slowly processing everything. "We'll make sure everyone is safe.

Everly pulled back. "The kids! I need to call Tabby and Alex. What if Rachel comes by the house again?"

He nodded, trying to remain calm. Let's get dressed and call to warn them. Then we'll head over to your place and bring Randy with us. We won't let anyone else get hurt, babe."

Everly pulled on her clothes even as she shook her head. "It all comes back to Jackson's lying. All of it. I...I can't believe this."

He couldn't either, but it was their reality. Somehow, they'd figure it all out. Everything was snapping into place like a puzzle he couldn't quite see, but in the end, it didn't matter. As long as he kept Everly and the boys safe, they'd figure it out.

They had to.

CHAPTER NINETEEN

Everly tried to take a deep breath, but the air wouldn't come. The authorities had let her walk into Beneath the Cover that morning, and with the boys hanging with some of the Montgomerys who now knew the entire Rachel situation—and wasn't *that* a fun conversation—she and Storm could do a walkthrough.

She'd been expecting the worst.

She hadn't been expecting *this*.

It was so much worse than she'd thought.

"Everything's gone," she whispered into the darkness. "Nothing's left."

Storm wrapped his arms around her from behind, but she didn't lean into him. She couldn't. But the idea that he was there if she were to fall let her stand up straighter. Everything had a black tinge to it with streaks and burn marks covering what was left of the walls. By some mercy, the fire hadn't spread to any of the connecting buildings. Though the alarms hadn't gone off to warn her or the fire department, people had called the emergency lines right away, and the fire had been contained easily.

Only not fast enough to save any of her things.

She had insurance, and now with Rachel's name being attached rather than an unknown, her insurance could start helping. There hadn't been another unknown phone call that set her on edge, but she still didn't know if all of that was connected. She also didn't know if the note was from Rachel, or why it would have been sent to Jackson, but Everly had a feeling it *was* all connected. It had to be.

She'd be able to rebuild from the ground up, but she'd lost so much. Even with the Montgomerys' help, rebuilding couldn't bring back the way the old stone had looked against the pale cream of the walls. It couldn't bring back the hours and hours of work she'd put into building the shelves and picking out her inventory. It wouldn't bring back the tiny decorations she'd put in for the fairies that the children loved to imagine existed within the walls of her store. It wouldn't bring back the memories she'd had with her children within these walls.

Everything was gone.

Even her staff had been forced to find other work while she waited to reopen. She couldn't pay them with no income herself, and they'd understood. But now, she felt just that much more alone in what remained of her home away from home.

Storm kissed the top of her head, and she was reminded that no, she wasn't truly alone, even if the ash-soaked walls wanted her to feel it.

"Jesus Christ," Austin muttered under his breath.

"I'm so sorry, Everly," Sierra, Austin's wife added. She owned the boutique named Eden a few doors down and could have lost her place, too if the fire had spread.

Every one of the Montgomerys except Marie and Harry who had chosen to stay at their place with all the grandbabies—including her twins—was with her in her shop so she wouldn't feel alone. Even Jillian had come to hold her hand, and damn it, she'd needed it. The two of them had grown close over the past few weeks—something that completely surprised her. But they both loved Storm—if in different ways—and that connected them.

Wes and Decker moved through the place in front of her, looking at the damage with their technical eyes. The others moved around, as well, taking photos and notes for her on what the insurance company needed. The adjuster had already been out, but no one was taking any chances. Tabby had brought coffee for everyone and kept hugging Everly as they both tried to hold back tears. It was all just too much.

But with the fact that Rachel had been the one to do this, everything had come full circle. They were still searching for her, as they couldn't find her at home. Clay was inconsolable and had called to apologize over and over again. She never blamed Clay for how their lives had been connected through Storm and would never blame him for his aunt. But with Rachel's cruel streak coming to light, Everly now knew what she had to do about Jackson's other children.

There was no way her twins could have anything to do with Rachel, but with Clay and his grandparents, she'd find a way for the five siblings to get to know one another. That would happen eventually, but first...first, she needed to make sure her store was salvageable.

Storm kissed her temple, and she sighed. "Love you."

"Love you, too," she whispered. She couldn't believe that she loved Storm Montgomery, or that his entire family had rallied around her when she'd needed them. Somehow, she'd gone from her own tiny island to the continent that was the Montgomerys.

Shocking didn't even begin to cover it.

But she wasn't alone. She had her sons and the man she loved...and perhaps a future she could depend on. Even a few months ago, she never would have thought that would be the case, but now, here she was, in Storm's arms. She was even *happy,* despite where she stood. Because in the end, she could rebuild.

She *would.*

"I'm going to rebuild," she said softly. Only it must not have been as soft as she thought because everyone stopped what they were doing, mixtures of pride and understanding showing in their eyes.

"We'll make it exactly what you want. We can't replace what you have, but we can make it work."

She turned into Storm's arms and kissed his chin. "Yes, *we* can." She wasn't sure when they'd become a *we,* but she wouldn't change it for anything. *We can do this,* she told herself. As long as she had Storm and the Montgomerys, she could do anything.

****

Storm was one lucky man. He didn't know how it had happened, but somehow, he was living a life he'd never even dreamed of. Nothing like what he had with Everly and the twins had been on his radar, and yet he *knew* it was the life he'd always needed.

He was in love with a woman with so much courage and strength, his own paled in comparison, and all of that just made him want to be a better man. He didn't know exactly what would happen next, as neither of them was ready for marriage, but they were finding their way through this new aspect of their relationship and enjoying it.

At least, he was.

And from the happy smile on her face right then, he figured she was, as well.

"Okay, so the diner for dinner then?" Storm asked as he and Everly buckled the boys into their car seats.

"I'm craving country-fried chicken and gravy," she answered with a laugh. "I know it'll go right to my hips, but I had dreams about that black pepper cream gravy."

Storm's mouth watered, and he snorted. "That sounds amazing. I guess we'll just have to get a workout in tonight if we're going to have all that fried food."

Her eyes darkened, and he winked. Damn, he loved this woman.

James grinned up at him from his seat, and Storm buckled him in. "You ready for dinner, buddy?"

"French fries!" James squealed, his voice sounding clearer by the week. His speech therapy was working, and his body had taken to the cochlear implant amazingly well.

"Yay! Fries!" Nathan clapped his hands as he said it, his voice loud and bright. His lungs were doing well that week, and that was another thing in the plus column.

"Can Randy come?" James asked. The boys loved his dog and considered the puppy theirs, as well.

"Not in the restaurant, but he'll be with you when you sleep tonight."

"Good," Nathan said solemnly. "He shouldn't be lonely."

"No one should, buddy."

As Storm got into the front seat and took Everly's hand as she got into the truck with them, he smiled. Their lives had been in the negative column over and over again recently, but now things were looking up. He and his family were talking about the accident and getting everything out in the open. Both of the twins were getting healthier and loved the fact that Storm was around more and more. Everly's store might be in shambles at the moment, but that wouldn't always be the case. The Montgomerys would help rebuild and had all rallied around her the moment she'd needed help—probably even before she realized it.

The only thing hovering over them was Rachel. He held back a scowl at that thought. The police hadn't found her yet since she'd apparently gone to ground, but Storm knew they would. There wasn't another acceptable outcome.

"You're frowning," Everly whispered. "What's wrong?"

Storm kept his attention on the road but pulled their clasped hands to his lips to leave a soft kiss on her even softer skin. "Just thinking, but I'm pushing those thoughts from my head and am going to focus on gravy."

Everly gave him a worried look that he caught out of the corner of his eye but smiled anyway. "And mashed potatoes. And possibly apple pie."

Storm groaned. "All the food, Ev. All the food."

"All the food!" James repeated.

"Food! Food! Food!" Nathan chanted.

Everly laughed and turned on the sound system. "How about a song?" She leaned closer to Storm and lowered her voice. "They're hyper at the moment, so we might as well let them sing a song rather than scream about food."

"Sounds like a plan."

She turned on the song they'd played about two hundred times since he and Ev had started dating, and the boys began to sing along about dancing and feelings. James and Nathan were also addicted to the brightly colored and shiny movie that the song came from, so Storm had the words down by heart.

The kids were enthusiastic if not adept at their singing, so Storm shrugged and joined them. Everly laughed and did the same, and soon, the four of them were singing and laughing and on their way to dinner as...well, as a family. He wasn't their father and never would be, but he loved those boys and loved the woman next to him. That was all he needed.

Storm squeezed Everly's hand, feeling the happiest he'd been for a long time, and if he hadn't had his eyes on the road, he would have missed the bright shine of headlights coming at the car head-on.

Only he didn't have time to turn out of the way or hit his brakes. Everly screamed, and the boys cried out. Metal smashed, and rubber burned. Glass shattered around them, and for a moment, he thought he was back where this had all started. But that wasn't the case. He was here...with his family...with Ev and the boys...and the world had shattered around them.

A sharp pain radiated down his arms and legs, then nothing.

There was nothing.

Only numbness.

And darkness.

And nothing.

CHAPTER TWENTY

Everly blinked her eyes open, her head a little fuzzy and something sticky coating her hands, but she could breathe, and she could *feel*. And once she focused, she could see.

Everything.

Something had hit their car. Something had made them crash.

Her boys.

"Mommy!" James was crying, and Nathan was doing the same. She turned, ignoring the ache in her head to see that her boys were still in their car seats and from what she could tell, didn't have a cut or bruise on them. That could all change though in an instant.

"Everything's fine, babies. Someone will come and help us soon. Are you hurt? Tell Mommy where it hurts."

"I'm scared," Nathan said with a cry.

"I want hugs," James cried with him.

She tried to soothe them, but she couldn't reach her boys. They had to be okay. They had to be.

She pressed her hand to her head and winced, knowing she had to have a cut there. People were screaming around her, but it was like they were in a vacuum. She needed to make sure her family was safe.

Storm.

She turned to him in the front seat, and he sat still. His eyes were closed, and his breath came in labored pants. Tears streamed down her face, and she tried to reach for him but couldn't as her seatbelt stopped her. She couldn't get her hands to work right to undo the buckle, and she winced with each movement.

"Storm," she gasped.

He opened his eyes slowly, his gaze dark with pain. "Hey, baby, are you okay? The kids?"

"I'm fine," she lied. She wasn't fine, and wouldn't be until she had her family in her arms. "Can you move? Can you help me get the boys out?"

"Storm?" Nathan cried. "I want Storm."

"Mommy!" James cried.

Her body shook as sobs took over, and she tried to be strong, but she was so tired. No, she reminded herself, her exhaustion didn't matter. The *only* thing that mattered was her kids and Storm. Once they were safe and healed, *then* she could break down. Not now. Not anytime soon."

"I'm right here, boys," Storm said calmly, though she knew he had to be anything but calm. He looked directly at Everly and lowered his voice. "I can't reach the boys." He took a deep, shaky breath. "I can't feel my legs right now, baby, but we'll get out. Everything will be fine. I love you, Everly. I love you so fucking much."

Tears fell in earnest, and she choked back a sob. He couldn't feel his legs? Oh, God, his back. "I love you, too."

With the way the truck had been crushed on Storm's side, she was just far enough away from him that she couldn't reach anyone. She'd never felt so helpless.

"We'll get out of this," she promised, her hands shaking, and bile filling her throat as her head throbbed. "We will."

"I know, baby. I know."

The sirens came closer, and she looked back at her boys, doing her best to keep awake. People were coming to help. They wouldn't be alone.

She wouldn't lose everything.

Again.

She had a partial concussion but not a full one, and the boys were perfectly fine. So fine, in fact, they were cuddling on Marie's and Harry's laps after having cuddled on Nancy's and Peter's. Her in-laws had shown up at the hospital after Marie had called them—somehow finding their number—and had not only wanted to ensure their grandsons were okay, but Everly and Storm, as well. Nancy had gone so far as to hug her softly and cry on her shoulder.

Apparently, almost losing the last of Nancy's family after everything had changed had altered her thinking. Everly wasn't sure what to think about that because she had more important things to worry about just then, though she would keep that in the back of her mind.

"He's going to be fine," Jillian whispered from Everly's side. The other woman had shown up with the rest of the Montgomerys—minus the few that had stayed home to take care of the children—and she hadn't left Everly's side since. They held hands tightly and would every once in a while hug even if they didn't speak.

"I know." She put force behind her words, willing them to be true. "He's just been in surgery for so long."

"And he'll make it out when the doctors are done," Wes said, his voice hollow. "Because he doesn't get a choice. He's going to be grumpy and growly when he gets out, but he's going to be *fine*."

"Surgeries take time," Austin said from Sierra's side. "But I'm fucking tired of our family having to constantly figure that out in a waiting room that looks just like this." He winced and looked over at Jackson's parents as well as the boys.

Peter waved him off, and the twins were asleep. If Everly had had any left over energy in her body, she'd have probably smiled. But she couldn't find a way to smile at all, not when she didn't know if Storm was going to be okay or not.

Because of the size of the Montgomery family, they had the entire waiting room to themselves. There were a few others on the surgical floor, so she knew others were taken care of, but she was still trying to get over the fact that she wasn't alone in this. This entire family had not only dropped everything for Storm but for her, as well.

How her life had become this, she didn't know, but she'd focus on it later and even say her thanks for that blessing. For now, she could only worry and try not to think about the throbbing in her head. Her doctors had only let her out of bed because the entire Montgomery clan had said they'd make sure she didn't overdo it, but if she looked like she was in pain, she knew all of them would push her back into the hospital bed where she wouldn't be around to hear what happened with Storm. She couldn't let that happen.

The doors opened, and everyone stood, only to see two detectives walk in, not the doctor. "Mrs. Law?" the older one asked. "May we have a moment?"

Everly looked around at the people in the room and knew everyone was exactly where they should be. "They can stay. If that's all right. How can I help you?"

The detectives looked around again before giving her a nod. "We've ID'd the other driver. Unfortunately, they didn't make it."

Everly's breath caught. "They died? What happened?"

"From what we can tell, she hit you head-on without hitting the brakes on purpose. And, as it turns out, she's connected to another ongoing investigation you're involved in. It seems the same woman who sent your deceased husband that note to your shop that you gave us, was also the one who hit you tonight. The same woman who set fire to your bookstore. The arson investigator will be in touch shortly, but based on fingerprint analysis, we know that she sent Mr. Jackson Law the letter. We assume it was to get you to open it and scare you, as Mr. Law didn't own the shop with you, though we haven't pieced together what she meant by the message. We also found a burner phone in her vehicle that only called one number over the past few weeks. Yours. And now that we know it was her DNA found in the shop at the time of the fire, we know that it's all connected."

She blinked, her head throbbing. "Rachel? Rachel did this?" And now, she was dead. The first thing Everly thought of was Rachel's children, the second...the second thought filled her with rage, which only made her head hurt more. Why had she done this? For money? How could she gain anything by taking away Everly's livelihood or trying to kill her and her family? None of it added up. There was no logic to any of it. What... What was wrong with that woman? No, what *had* been wrong with that woman? She had to be crazy. It was the only reasonable explanation.

"Rachel did this," she said again.

"Yes, ma'am. We have a few questions for you."

"Can they wait?" Wes asked. His voice sounded a bit stronger this time, and for that, she was grateful. "She's hurt, and we're still waiting on news about Storm. Plus, her kids might be sleeping, but they're still in the room. Rachel isn't going anywhere," he growled, not kindly.

The detectives nodded and explained to Everly that they'd be seeing her soon before leaving the waiting room. Everyone let out a collective breath, and Everly just wanted to curl into herself and cry. Instead, she shoved down the emotions, stood up slowly, waved off Jillian's glare, and went to where her babies slept.

"Thank you for holding them," she whispered to the elder Montgomerys as well as Jackson's parents. "Just...thank you."

Marie patted the seat next to her, and Everly sank down with a sigh. "You need to rest, honey. And don't tell me you can't because I know that. Once we know Storm is fine and out of surgery, then you will rest and heal." There was a firmness in the other woman's tone that told Everly that Storm's mom was just as scared as she was, but not showing it because of her children. The woman was so tough, and Everly wanted to be her when she grew up.

She just needed to make sure Storm was okay first.

As soon as that thought slid through her mind, the doors opened again, and this time, Storm's doctor came through. The room went quiet, and she stood up on shaky legs.

"The Montgomery family?"

"That would be all of us," Griffin said dryly, though she heard the worry in his tone.

"Okay, then," the doctor said as he ran a hand through his hair.

"How is he?" Everly asked, surprised at how strong her voice sounded.

"He's going to be fine. He has a few cuts and lacerations as well as a concussion, but he'll be okay. Before this accident, his L1 and L2 vertebra were fused, and now there is a hairline fracture on his L1. His spinal cord is intact, and he'll have to be off his feet for a decent time period, but with physical therapy and time, he *will* walk again and be just fine."

Everly didn't even know she was crying until Wes pulled her into his arms and she soaked his shirt. The others asked questions, and she vaguely heard the answers. She was aware her boys were up and talking, asking why their mommy was crying, but she couldn't stop almost hyperventilating to tell them she'd be okay.

And she *would* be okay.

Because Storm would be fine.

He was alive. Hurt, but alive.

With that relief crushing her chest, she knew they could face everything else. She had her Montgomery and her family. Her boys and Storm.

Life would move on because *finally,* she'd found her future...with her architect.

EPILOGUE

"We're teaching Randy to roll over," James said solemnly, and Storm grinned from his place on his new memory foam chair. "How's he doing?" Storm asked and laughed when he saw Nathan rolling over in front of a confused-looking Randy as if showing the dog how to do a new trick.

"Not good, but we'll learn him," Nathan said with a smile.

"You'll teach him," Everly corrected before sinking into the large cushion next to Storm.

"That's what I said," Nathan said before rolling over again. Randy sank down on his belly and rested his head on his paws.

"He's not doing it," James sighed.

"He'll learn eventually," Storm said. "We'll get Wes over here to help since I can't crawl on the ground with you right now."

"Just don't overdo it. Any of you." Everly sounded calm when she said it, but he heard the tension in her tone. Storm slowly lifted his arm, and Everly cautiously leaned against him. They were always so careful since the accident, and he didn't fault either of them for it, but he was beyond ready to be able to hold her in his arms or have him on top of her...or under her...or behind her.

Everly bit his earlobe, and he groaned. "Stop thinking about that right now, mister."

He looked down at his sweats and pulled a blanket on top of his lap. "Oops. Well, at least that still works."

"Don't even joke like that," Everly whispered. "Okay, boys, show us what you've done with Randy so far."

The boys started rolling over and Randy plopped on his back. Storm called that a win. "Good job." He moved slowly to kiss the top of Everly's head and was damned happy that he didn't feel any pain. It was odd, but the surgery he'd gone through had actually helped his earlier back pain. He would never be one hundred percent, but he'd be able to move around better than he used to in a couple of months if not weeks.

Storm tried not to think about how everything had changed so quickly over the past few weeks, months. He'd talked to Clay earlier while the boys had been in the tub with Everly watching over them and still couldn't get that conversation out of his head. The kid had been distraught over everything that had happened.

It wasn't just the fact that his aunt was dead, because damn it, Storm felt for the kid, but now there were three children out there that were now orphans, and Clay would have to be there, trying to help with everything he possibly could. According to Clay, the kids would be taken care of by his grandparents, with Clay helping when he could. Storm wasn't sure what the right answer was, he just knew that things would get harder before they got easier.

Everly knew James and Nathan needed to spend time with their brothers and sister, though they were too young to understand that now. No one knew how things would work out or how much damage might occur along the way, but Storm and Everly would be part of Clay's life for a long time to come.

Things had definitely changed and hadn't gotten any easier, but now he wasn't alone.

"I should do more unpacking," Everly said after a few more minutes.

Storm shook his head. "Wait until my sisters get here to help. That way, I can have you in my arms a bit longer." He still couldn't believe Everly had moved in that week. Between his recovery time and the fact that Jackson's memory had been in each room of Everly's old home, they had decided that she and the boys would move in to see how it all worked out. *So far so good*, he thought, and knew that as soon as he was able to get down on one knee, he'd propose.

Things had moved fast for them, yet in reality, it had taken years for them to see who they were to each other. He'd fallen in love with his friend's wife and hadn't realized it. Everly was everything to him, her and the boys. He'd gone from being a confirmed bachelor with pain in his heart that he never thought he'd overcome, and had ended up with a woman he loved, and two children whose lives he was honored to be a part of.

"So..."

He looked down at Everly and smiled. "What?"

"I know we're not engaged, but your mother has practically adopted me...can I get the Montgomery Ink brand?" She fluttered her eyelashes at him, and he fell that much more in love with her.

"You want our MI tattoo?" he asked, surprised. "I didn't think you'd want ink."

"It's kind of your family's thing, and your ink is kind of hot. Just saying." She kissed his jaw, and he moved so he could take her mouth.

"I think you with our ink would be fucking sexy. So, yes, get the ink, and when we're ready, you'll get a ring, too."

She kissed him again, and the boys laughed and clapped as Randy barked, the noise increasing with each passing moment, and Storm wouldn't have it any other way. His life had changed so much he could barely keep up, but he was one damned lucky man.

"You're so romantic."

"Yeah? Well, later, when the boys are in bed, I'll show you exactly how romantic I can be." He bit her lip before licking the sting away. "You'll have to be on top, of course."

She rolled her eyes. "I'll go slow, baby. Don't worry."

"Sounds like a plan to me." He kissed her again, and knew that no matter what happened from this point on, he had everything he wanted.

He just hadn't known he'd fall the way the other Montgomerys in his life had in order to get it.

THE END

Up Next:
Wes and Jillian. Finally.

A Note from Carrie Ann

Thank you so much for reading **INKED EXPRESSIONS**. I do hope if you liked this story, that you would please leave a review. Not only does a review spread the word to other readers, they let us authors know if you'd like to see more stories like this from us. I love hearing from readers and talking to them when I can. If you want to make sure you know what's coming next from me, you can sign up for my newsletter at www.CarrieAnnRyan.com; follow me on twitter at @CarrieAnnRyan, or like my Facebook page. I also have a Facebook Fan Club where we have trivia, chats, and other goodies. You guys are the reason I get to do what I do and I thank you.

Make sure you're signed up for my MAILING LIST so you can know when the next releases are available as well as find giveaways and FREE READS.

The Montgomery Ink series is an ongoing series and there's more to come! Wes and Jillian are up next in INKED MEMORIES. While Wes might be the last Denver Montgomery to find his HEA, they aren't the last of the Montgomerys. Once Wes and Jillian have their book, Shep's sisters from Colorado Springs are getting their own romances! The Montgomery Ink: Colorado Springs series might have a new series name, but you'll still get glimpse of the Denver Montgomerys.

Up first? FALLEN INK will begin the new series and I cannot wait to not only continue the Montgomery Ink series but introduce more Montgomerys soon!

And don't forget that you can check out the Gallagher Brothers and Whiskey and Lies series set in the same world as the Montgomerys as well!

Happy Reading!

Montgomery Ink:
Book 0.5: Ink Inspired
Book 0.6: Ink Reunited
Book 1: Delicate Ink
The Montgomery Ink Box Set (Contains Books 0.5, 0.6, 1)
Book 1.5: Forever Ink
Book 2: Tempting Boundaries
Book 3: Harder than Words
Book 4: Written in Ink
Book 4.5: Hidden Ink
Book 5: Ink Enduring
Book 6: Ink Exposed
Book 6.5: Adoring Ink
Book 6.6: Love, Honor, & Ink
Book 7: Inked Expressions
Book 8: Inked Memories (Coming Oct 2017)

Montgomery Ink: Colorado Springs
Book 1: Fallen Ink (Coming Apr 2018)

Want to keep up to date with the next Carrie Ann Ryan Release? Receive Text Alerts easily!
Text CARRIE to 24587

About Carrie Ann and her Books

Carrie Ann Ryan is the New York Times and USA Today bestselling author of contemporary and paranormal romance. Her works include the Montgomery Ink, Redwood Pack, Talon Pack, and Gallagher Brothers series, which have sold over 2.0 million books worldwide. She started writing while in graduate school for her advanced degree in chemistry and hasn't stopped since. Carrie Ann has written over fifty novels and novellas with more in the works. When she's not writing about bearded tattooed men or alpha wolves that need to find their mates, she's reading as much as she can and exploring the world of baking and gourmet cooking.

www.CarrieAnnRyan.com

Montgomery Ink:
Book 0.5: Ink Inspired
Book 0.6: Ink Reunited
Book 1: Delicate Ink
The Montgomery Ink Box Set (Contains Books 0.5, 0.6, 1)
Book 1.5: Forever Ink
Book 2: Tempting Boundaries
Book 3: Harder than Words
Book 4: Written in Ink
Book 4.5: Hidden Ink
Book 5: Ink Enduring
Book 6: Ink Exposed
Book 6.5: Adoring Ink
Book 6.6: Love, Honor, & Ink
Book 7: Inked Expressions

Book 8: Inked Memories (Coming Oct 2017)

Montgomery Ink: Colorado Springs
Book 1: Fallen Ink (Coming Apr 2018)

The Gallagher Brothers Series:
A Montgomery Ink Spin Off Series
Book 1: Love Restored
Book 2: Passion Restored
Book 3: Hope Restored (Coming July 2017)

The Whiskey and Lies Series:
A Montgomery Ink Spin Off Series
Book 1: Whiskey Secrets (Coming Jan 2018)

The Talon Pack:
Book 1: Tattered Loyalties
Book 2: An Alpha's Choice
Book 3: Mated in Mist
Book 4: Wolf Betrayed
Book 5: Fractured Silence
Book 6: Destiny Disgraced (Coming Sept 2017)
Book 7: Eternal Mourning (Coming Feb 2018)

Redwood Pack Series:
Book 1: An Alpha's Path
Book 2: A Taste for a Mate
Book 3: Trinity Bound
Redwood Pack Box Set (Contains Books 1-3)
Book 3.5: A Night Away
Book 4: Enforcer's Redemption
Book 4.5: Blurred Expectations
Book 4.7: Forgiveness
Book 5: Shattered Emotions
Book 6: Hidden Destiny
Book 6.5: A Beta's Haven

Book 7: Fighting Fate
Book 7.5: Loving the Omega
Book 7.7: The Hunted Heart
Book 8: Wicked Wolf
The Complete Redwood Pack Box Set (Contains Books 1-7.7)

The Branded Pack Series:
(Written with Alexandra Ivy)
Book 1: Stolen and Forgiven
Book 2: Abandoned and Unseen
Book 3: Buried and Shadowed

Dante's Circle Series:
Book 1: Dust of My Wings
Book 2: Her Warriors' Three Wishes
Book 3: An Unlucky Moon
The Dante's Circle Box Set (Contains Books 1-3)
Book 3.5: His Choice
Book 4: Tangled Innocence
Book 5: Fierce Enchantment
Book 6: An Immortal's Song
Book 7: Prowled Darkness
The Complete Dante's Circle Series (Contains Books 1-7)

Holiday, Montana Series:
Book 1: Charmed Spirits
Book 2: Santa's Executive
Book 3: Finding Abigail
The Holiday, Montana Box Set (Contains Books 1-3)
Book 4: Her Lucky Love
Book 5: Dreams of Ivory
The Complete Holiday, Montana Box Set (Contains Books 1-5)

Stand Alone Romances:
Finally Found You
Flame and Ink
Dropout (Coming June 2017)

Excerpt: Delicate Ink

From New York Times Bestselling Author Carrie Ann Ryan's Montgomery Ink Series

"If you don't turn that fucking music down, I'm going to ram this tattoo gun up a place no one on this earth should ever see."

Austin Montgomery lifted the needle from his client's arm so he could hold back a rough chuckle. He let his foot slide off the pedal so he could keep his composure. Dear Lord, his sister Maya clearly needed more coffee in her life.

Or for someone to turn down the fucking music in the shop.

"You're not even working, Maya. Let me have my tunes," Sloane, another artist, mumbled under his breath. Yeah, he didn't yell it. Didn't need to. No one wanted to yell at Austin's sister. The man might be as big as a house and made of pure muscle, but no one messed with Maya.

Not if they wanted to live.

"I'm sketching, you dumbass," Maya sniped, even though the smile in her eyes belied her wrath. His sister loved Sloane like a brother. Not that she didn't have enough brothers and sisters to begin with, but the Montgomerys always had their arms open for strays and spares.

Austin rolled his eyes at the pair's antics and stood up from his stool, his body aching from being bent over for too long. He refrained from saying that aloud as Maya and Sloane would have a joke for that. He usually preferred to have the other person in bed—

or in the kitchen, office, doorway, etc—bent over, but that wasn't where he would allow his mind to go. As it was, he was too damn old to be sitting in that position for too long, but he wanted to get this sleeve done for his customer.

"Hold on a sec, Rick," he said to the man in the chair. "Want juice or anything? I'm going to stretch my legs and make sure Maya doesn't kill Sloane." He winked as he said it, just in case his client didn't get the joke.

People could be so touchy when siblings threatened each other with bodily harm even while they smiled as they said it.

"Juice sounds good," Rick slurred, a sappy smile on his face. "Don't let Maya kill you."

Rick blinked his eyes open, the adrenaline running through his system giving him the high that a few patrons got once they were in the chair for a couple hours. To Austin, there was nothing better than having Maya ink his skin—or doing it himself—and letting the needle do its work. He wasn't a pain junkie, far from it if he was honest with himself, but he liked the adrenaline that led the way into fucking fantastic art. While some people thought bodies were sacred and tattoos only marred them, he knew it differently. Art on canvas, any canvas, could have the potential to be art worth bleeding for. As such, he was particular as to who laid a needle on his skin. He only let Maya ink him when he couldn't do it himself. Maya was the same way. Whatever she couldn't do herself, he did.

They were brother and sister, friends, and co-owners of Montgomery Ink.

He and Maya had opened the shop a decade ago when she'd turned twenty. He probably could have opened it a few years earlier since he was eight years older than Maya, but he'd wanted to wait until she was ready. They were joint owners. It had never been his shop while she worked with him. They both had equal say, although with the way Maya spoke, sometimes her voice seemed louder. His deeper one carried just as much weight, even if he didn't yell as much.

Barely.

Sure, he wasn't as loud as Maya, but he got his point across when needed. His voice held control and authority.

He picked up a juice box for Rick from their mini-fridge and turned down the music on his way back. Sloane scowled at him, but the corner of his mouth twitched as if he held back a laugh.

"Thank God one of you has a brain in his head," Maya mumbled in the now quieter room. She rolled her eyes as both he and Sloane flipped her off then went back to her sketch. Yeah, she could have gotten up to turn the music down herself, but then she couldn't have vented her excess energy at the two of them. That was just how his sister worked, and there would be no changing that.

He went back to his station situated in the back so he had the corner space, handed Rick his juice, then rubbed his back. Damn, he was getting old. Thirty-eight wasn't that far up there on the scales, but ever since he'd gotten back from New Orleans, he hadn't been able to shake the weight of something off of his chest.

He needed to be honest. He'd started feeling this way since before New Orleans. He'd gone down to the city to visit his cousin Shep and try to get out of his funk. He'd broken up with Shannon right before then; however, in reality, it wasn't as much a breakup as a lack of connection and communication. They hadn't cared about each other enough to move on to the next level, and as sad as that was, he was fine with it. If he couldn't get up the energy to pursue a woman beyond a couple of weeks or months of heat, then he knew he was the problem. He just didn't know the solution. Shannon hadn't been the first woman who had ended the relationship in that fashion. There'd been Brenda, Sandrine, and another one named Maggie.

He'd cared for all of them at the time. He wasn't a complete asshole, but he'd known deep down that they weren't going to be with him forever, and they thought the same of him. He also knew that it was time to actually find a woman to settle down with. If he wanted a future, a family, he was running out of time.

Going to New Orleans hadn't worked out in the least considering, at the time, Shep was falling in love with a pretty blonde named Shea. Not that Austin begrudged the man that. Shep had been his best friend growing up, closer to him than his four brothers and three sisters. It'd helped that he and Shep were the same age while the next of his siblings, the twins Storm and Wes, were four years younger.

His parents had taken their time to have eight kids, meaning he was a full fifteen years older than the baby, Miranda, but he hadn't cared. The eight of them, most of his cousins, and a few strays were as close as ever. He'd helped raise the youngest ones as an older brother but had never felt like he had to. His parents, Marie and Harry, loved each of their kids equally and had put their whole beings into their roles as parents. Every single concert, game, ceremony, or even parent-teacher meeting was attended by at least one of them. On the good days, the ones where Dad could get off work and Mom had the day off from

Montgomery Inc., they both would attend. They loved their kids.

He loved being a Montgomery.

The sound of Sloane's needle buzzing as he sang whatever tune played in his head made Austin grin.

And he fucking *loved* his shop.

Every bare brick and block of polished wood, every splash of black and hot pink—colors he and Maya had fought on and he'd eventually given in to—made him feel at home. He'd taken the family crest and symbol, the large MI surrounded by a broken floral circle, and used it as their logo. His brothers, Storm and Wes, owned Montgomery Inc., a family construction company that their father had once owned and where their mother had worked at his side before they'd retired. They, too, used the same logo since it meant family to them.

In fact, the MI was tattooed on every single immediate family member—including his parents. His own was on his right forearm tangled in the rest of his sleeve but given a place of meaning. It meant Montgomery Iris—*open your eyes, see the beauty, remember who you are.* It was only natural to use it for their two respective companies.

Not that the Ink vs Inc. wasn't confusing as hell, but fuck, they were Montgomerys. They could do whatever they wanted. As long as they were together, they'd get through it.

Montgomery Ink was just as much his home as his house on the ravine. While Shep had gone on to work at Midnight Ink and created another family there, Austin had always wanted to own his shop. Maya growing up to want to do the same thing had only helped.

Montgomery Ink was now a thriving business in downtown Denver right off 16th Street Mall. They were near parking, food, and coffee. There really wasn't more he needed. The drive in most mornings could suck once he got on I-25, but it was worth it to live out in Arvada. The 'burbs around Denver made it easy to live in one area of the city and work in another. Commutes, though hellish at rush hour, weren't as bad as some. This way he got the city living when it came to work and play, and the option to hide behind the trees pressed up against the foothills of the Rocky Mountains once he got home.

It was the best of both worlds.

At least for him.

Austin got back on his stool and concentrated on Rick's sleeve for another hour before calling it quits. He needed a break for his lower back, and Rick needed a break from the pain. Not that Rick was feeling much since the man currently looked like he'd just gotten laid—pain freaks, Austin loved them—but he didn't want to push either of them too far. Also, Plus Rick's arm had started to swell slightly from all the shading and multiple colors. They'd do another session, the last, hopefully, in a month or so when both of them could work it in their schedules and then finish up.

Austin scowled at the computer at the front of shop, his fingers too big for the damn keys on the prissy computer Maya had demanded they buy.

"Fuck!"

He'd just deleted Rick's whole account because he couldn't find the right button.

"Maya, get your ass over here and fix this. I don't know what the hell I did."

Maya lifted one pierced brow as she worked on a lower back tattoo for some teenage girl who didn't look old enough to get ink in the first place.

"I'm busy, Austin. You're not an idiot, though evidence at the moment points to the contrary. Fix it yourself. I can't help it if you have ape hands."

Austin flipped her off then took a sip of his Coke, wishing he had something stronger considering he hated paperwork. "I was fine with the old keyboard and the PC, Maya. You're the one who wanted to go with the Mac because it looked pretty."

"Fuck you, Austin. I wanted a Mac because I like the software."

Austin snorted while trying to figure out how to find Rick's file. He was pretty sure it was a lost cause at this point. "You hate the software as much as I do. You hit the damn red X and close out files more than I do. Everything's in the wrong place, and the keyboard is way too fucking dainty."

"I'm going to go with Austin on this one," Sloane added in, his beefy hands in the air.

"See? I'm not alone."

Maya let out a breath. "We can get another keyboard for you and Gigantor's hands, but we need to keep the Mac."

"And why is that?" he demanded.

"Because we just spent a whole lot of money on it, and once it goes, we can get another PC. Fuck the idea that everything can be all in one. I can't figure it out either." She held up a hand. "And don't even think about breaking it. I'll know, Austin. I *always* know."

Austin held back a grin. He wouldn't be surprised if the computer met with an earlier than expected unfortunate fate now that Maya had relented.

Right then, however, that idea didn't help. He needed to find Rick's file.

"Callie!" Austin yelled over the buzz of needles and soft music Maya had allowed them to play.

"What?" His apprentice came out of the break room, a sketchbook in one hand and a smirk on her face. She'd dyed her hair again so it had black and red highlights. It looked good on her, but honestly, he never knew what color she'd have next. "Break something on the computer again with those big man hands?"

"Shut up, minion," he teased. Callie was an up-and-coming artist, and if she kept on the track she was on, he and Maya knew she'd be getting her own chair at Montgomery Ink soon. Not that he'd tell Callie that, though. He liked keeping her on her toes. She reminded him of his little sister Miranda so much that he couldn't help but treat her as such.

She pushed him out of the way and groaned. "Did you have to press *every* button as you rampaged through the operating system?"

Austin could have sworn he felt his cheeks heat, but since he had a thick enough beard, he knew no one would have been able to tell.

Hopefully.

He hated feeling as if he didn't know what he was doing. It wasn't as if he didn't know how to use a computer. He wasn't an idiot. He just didn't know *this* computer. And it bugged the shit out of him.

After a couple of keystrokes and a click of the mouse, Callie stepped back with a smug smile on her face. "Okay, boss, you're all ready to go, and Rick's file is back where it should be. What else do you need from me?"

He bopped her on the head, messing up her red and black hair he knew she spent an hour on every morning with a flat iron. He couldn't help it.

"Go clean a toilet or something."

Callie rolled her eyes. "I'm going to go sketch. And you're welcome."

"Thanks for fixing the damn thing. And really, go clean the bathroom."

"Not gonna do it," she sang as she skipped to the break room.

"You really have no control over your apprentice," Sloane commented from his station.

Because he didn't want that type of control with her. Well, hell, his mind kept going to that dark place every few minutes it seemed.

"Shut up, asshole."

"I see your vocabulary hasn't changed much," Shannon purred from the doorway.

He closed his eyes and prayed for patience. Okay, maybe he'd lied to himself when he said it was mutual and easy to break up with her. The damn woman kept showing up. He didn't think she wanted him, but she didn't want him to forget her either.

He did not understand women.

Especially this one.

"What do you want, Shannon?" he bit out, needing that drink now more than ever.

She sauntered over to him and scraped her long, red nail down his chest. He'd liked that once. Now, not even a little. They were decent together when they'd dated, but he'd had to hide most of himself from her. She'd never tasted the edge of his flogger or felt his hand on her ass when she'd been bent over his lap. That hadn't been what she wanted, and Austin was into the kind of kink that meant he wanted what he wanted when he wanted. It didn't mean he wanted it every time.

Not that Shannon would ever understand that.

"Oh, baby, you know what I want."

He barely resisted the urge to roll his eyes. As he took a step back, he saw the gleam in her eyes and decided to head it off at the pass. He was in no mood to play her games, or whatever she wanted to do that night. He wanted to go home, drink a beer, and forget this oddly annoying day.

"If you don't want ink, then I don't know what you're doing here, Shannon. We're done." He tried to say it quietly, but his voice was deep, and it carried.

"How could you be so cruel?" She pouted.

"Oh, for the love of God," Maya sneered. "Go home, little girl. You and Austin are through, and I'm pretty sure it was mutual. Oh, and you're not getting any ink here. You're not getting Austin's hands on you this way, and there's no way in hell I'm putting my art on you. Not if you keep coming back to bug the man you didn't really date in the first place."

"Bi—" Shannon cut herself off as Austin glared. Nobody called his sister a bitch. Nobody.

"Goodbye, Shannon." Jesus, he was too old for this shit.

"Fine. I see how it is. Whatever. You were only an okay lay anyway." She shook her ass as she left, bumping into a woman in a linen skirt and blouse.

The woman, whose long honey-brown hair hung in waves down to her breasts, raised a brow. "I see your business has an...interesting clientele."

Austin clenched his jaw. Seriously the wrong thing to say after Shannon.

"If you've got a problem, you can head on right back to where you came from, Legs," he bit out, his voice harsher than he'd intended.

She stiffened then raised her chin, a clear sense of disdain radiating off of her.

Oh yes, he knew who this was, legs and all. Ms. Elder. He hadn't caught a first name. Hadn't wanted to. She had to be in her late twenties, maybe, and owned the soon-to-be-opened boutique across the street. He'd seen her strut around in her too-tall heels and short skirts but hadn't been formally introduced.

Not that he wanted an introduction.

She was too damn stuffy and ritzy for his taste. Not only her store but the woman herself. The look of disdain on her face made him want to show her the door and never let her back in.

He knew what he looked like. Longish dark brown hair, thick beard, muscles covered in ink with a hint of more ink coming out of his shirt. He looked like a felon to some people who didn't know the difference, though he'd never seen the inside of a jail cell in his life. But he knew people like Ms. Elder. They judged people like him. And that one eyebrow pissed him the fuck off.

He didn't want this woman's boutique across the street from him. He'd liked it when it was an old record store. People didn't glare at his store that way. Now he had to walk past the mannequins with the rich clothes and tiny lacy scraps of things if he wanted a fucking coffee from the shop next door.

Damn it, this woman pissed him off, and he had no idea why.

"Nice to meet you too. Callie!" he shouted, his eyes still on Ms. Elder as if he couldn't pull his gaze from her. Her green eyes never left his either, and the uncomfortable feeling in his gut wouldn't go away.

Callie ran up beside him and held out her hand. "Hi, I'm Callie. How can I help you?"

Ms. Elder blinked once. Twice. "I think I made a mistake," she whispered.

Fuck. Now he felt like a heel. He didn't know what it was with this woman, but he couldn't help but act like an ass. She hadn't even done anything but lift an eyebrow at him, and he'd already set out to hate her.

Callie shook her head then reached for Ms. Elder's elbow. "I'm sure you haven't. Ignore the growly, bearded man over there. He needs more caffeine. And his ex was just in here; that alone would make anyone want to jump off the Royal Gorge. So, tell me, how can I help you? Oh! And what's your name?"

Ms. Elder followed Callie to the sitting area with leather couches and portfolios spread over the coffee table and then sat down.

"I'm Sierra, and I want a tattoo." She looked over her shoulder and glared at Austin. "Or, at least, I thought I did."

Austin held back a wince when she turned her attention from him and cursed himself. Well, fuck. He needed to learn not to put his foot in his mouth, but damn it, how was he supposed to know she wanted a tattoo? For all he knew, she wanted to come in there and look down on the place. That was his own prejudice coming into play. He needed to make it up to her. After all, they were neighbors now. However, from the cross look on her face and the feeling in the room, he knew that he wasn't going to be able to make it up to her today. He'd let Callie help her out to start with, and then he'd make sure he was the one who laid ink on her skin.

After all, it was the least he could do. Besides, his hands all of a sudden—or not so suddenly if he really thought about it—wanted to touch that delicate skin of hers and find out her secrets.

Austin cursed. He wouldn't let his thoughts go down that path. She'd break under his care, under his needs. Sure, Sierra Elder might be hot, but she wasn't the woman for him.

If he knew anything, he knew *that* for sure.

Tattered Loyalties

From New York Times Bestselling Author Carrie Ann Ryan's Talon Pack Series

When the great war between the Redwoods and the Centrals occurred three decades ago, the Talon Pack risked their lives for the side of good. After tragedy struck, Gideon Brentwood became the Alpha of the Talons. But the Pack's stability is threatened, and he's forced to take mate—only the one fate puts in his path is the woman he shouldn't want.

Though the daughter of the Redwood Pack's Beta, Brie Jamenson has known peace for most of her life. When she finds the man who could be her mate, she's shocked to discover Gideon is the Alpha wolf of the Talon Pack. As a submissive, her strength lies in her heart, not her claws. But if her new Pack disagrees or disapproves, the consequences could be fatal.

As the worlds Brie and Gideon have always known begin to shift, they must face their challenges together in order to help their Pack and seal their bond. But when the Pack is threatened from the inside, Gideon doesn't know who he can trust and Brie's life could be forfeit in the crossfire. It will take the strength of an Alpha and the courage of his mate to realize where true loyalties lie.

Stolen and Forgiven

From New York Times Bestselling Author Carrie Ann Ryan's Branded Packs Series Series

Stolen

The first rule of being Alpha of the Canine Pack is to protect their secrets from the humans at all cost. One look at the dying human at his doorstep and Holden Carter knows he will have to break it. The broken woman with no hope at survival is his mate. When he forces the change on her to save her life, he not only sets forth motions that could risk both their lives, but the lives of every shifter in the world.

Ariel Sands grew up in a post-Verona infection world and under the care of the very humans she thought had cured the disease. When they betray her in the worst ways imaginable, she finds herself not only mated to the Alpha of a the very species she's been taught to fear, but the focal point of a traitor and path to destruction for everyone's way of life. It will take more than trust and a mating bond for Ariel and Holden to not only survive their enemies, but the burn of their own temptations.

Forgiven

Soren Slater is a Beta wolf who understands that duty to his Pack comes before his own needs. At a young age he takes a position as a liaison between his Pack and the other species of shifters. He never expected his enticing flirtations with Cora Wilder, a Tiger Princess, would encourage her cat to consider him a potential mate. He's forced to walk away, choosing a partner among the wolves to try and strengthen his Pack.

Cora has no intention of forgiving or forgetting Soren's rejection. Not even when the Packs are forced to live together and she discovers Soren's former mate has died. But then, she's kidnapped by the SAU and she has no choice but to work with Soren to escape. Together they must put the past behind them if they're to survive the human's evil plot.

Dust of My Wings

From New York Times Bestselling Author Carrie Ann Ryan's Dante's Circle Series

Humans aren't as alone as they choose to believe. Every human possesses a trait of supernatural that lays dormant within their genetic make-up. Centuries of diluting and breeding have allowed humans to think they are alone and untouched by magic. But what happens when something changes?

Neat freak lab tech, Lily Banner lives her life as any ordinary human. She's dedicated to her work and loves to hang out with her friends at Dante's Circle, their local bar. When she discovers a strange blue dust at work she meets a handsome stranger holding secrets – and maybe her heart. But after a close call with a thunderstorm, she may not be as ordinary as she thinks.

Shade Griffin is a warrior angel sent to Earth to protect the supernaturals' secrets. One problem, he can't stop leaving dust in odd places around town. Now he has to find every ounce of his dust and keep the presence of the supernatural a secret. But after a close encounter with a sexy lab tech and a lightning quick connection, his millennia old loyalties may shift and he could lose more than just his wings in the chaos.

Warning: Contains a sexy angel with a choice to make and a green-eyed lab tech who dreams of a dark-winged stranger. Oh yeah, and a shocking spark that's sure to leave them begging for more.

Printed in Great Britain
by Amazon

JOHN WA

A Life from Beginning to End

Copyright © 2019 by Hourly History.

Table of Contents

Introduction

Shakespeare once asked, "What's in a name?" And when you think about the name of John Wayne, it is a very famous name indeed. The funny thing is, John Wayne was not born with this moniker at all—it was actually one that had been fixed onto his person later in life. He came into this world not as John Wayne, but as Marion Robert Morrison. Later, his name changed to Marion Mitchell Morrison because his parents decided to name their next son Robert. To eliminate confusion, however, we will from henceforward primarily refer to this famous movie legend as the larger world knows him, by the name of John Wayne.

Wayne graced the screen as a cowboy, an all-around rugged hero of the plains. With his "pull yourself up by your bootstraps" determination and raw sense of individualism, in many ways he came to symbolize everything that Americans held dear. His characters, tough as nails, were always idealistic adventurers seeking to right the wrongs of the world. In this book, we will cut through all the hype and get to the real man behind the legend of John Wayne.

Chapter One

The Boy Named Marion Morrison

"Tomorrow hopes we have learned something from yesterday."

—John Wayne

John Wayne was born as Marion Robert Morrison on May 26, 1907, in the town of Winterset, Iowa, to Clyde Morrison and Mary "Molly" Morrison. His mother and father were merely 20 and 19 years old when they got married. The couple did not wait for the official blessings of their parents or the church; instead, they were wed by the Justice of the Peace on September 29, 1905. At first, Molly was thrilled with her new husband and thought that she had made a good catch. Clyde was handsome, educated, and had prospects lined up to get a job as a pharmacist in Waterloo, Iowa. He seemed like a good pick, someone that would take care of her and set her mind at ease.

Unfortunately, Molly would be mistaken, because although Clyde could be a hard worker (when he did work), he was also just as hard of a drinker. It was this lethal combination that would threaten to send the family into ruin. As a result, as soon as Wayne was old enough to work he did so in order to help provide for his family and their ever-increasing bills. At the tender age of ten, he was leaving early in the morning to deliver papers, just to bring home extra cash to put food on the table. Things began to look up, however, when Wayne's father received gainful employment in 1916 as a pharmacist in Glendale, California.

The home that Wayne's family lived in was a small but comfortable house situated right in the middle of downtown. It was maybe a little rough around the edges, but it was home. Rather than a playground or a baseball diamond, the two main places that John Wayne spent time at was a sawmill and the local lumberyard. Wayne also had some rather interesting neighbors. He apparently lived right next door to a gun runner for the famous Mexican revolutionary Pancho Villa. According to Wayne's later recollection, the neighboring family's fortunes would fluctuate depending on how well the gun trade was going. When the gun trade was doing well, they had a lot of money, and when business was scarce they would be "eating beans."

After the move, little John Wayne was signed up to attend the fourth grade at nearby Sixth Street Elementary School. Besides work and school, the family also began to attend the local Methodist church. Wayne, eager to escape the dysfunction of his parents, when he wasn't working found time to join the Boy Scouts and logged hours at the local YMCA. By 1919, at the age of 12, Wayne was in the prestigious Troop Four level of the scouts, and although he never attained the rank of Eagle Scout, he would stay an active member all the way up to his High School graduation.

Wayne became a student at Union High School. Here he managed to make some pretty good grades as well as excel in school athletics—especially football, a sport which he would use to produce the physique for which he was later famous. He was also quite active in the drama department of his school, an activity that turned out to be the training wheels of his future career.

One eccentricity that Wayne became known for early on was the fact that he would always walk to school accompanied by his huge Airedale Terrier named Duke. The locals got a kick out of this and began calling Wayne "Little Duke" as a result. The name stuck, and he would carry it for the rest of his life. Even after he had developed the stage name of John Wayne, he always told those who knew him best, "Just call me Duke."

Chapter Two

College Football and Family Troubles

"Talk low, talk slow, and don't say too much."

—John Wayne

In many ways for John Wayne, childhood came to an end when his parents divorced and went their separate ways. In this breakup, not only did Wayne's parents go their separate ways, but he and his brother Robert would part company as well, with Bobby opting to stay with his mother while Wayne would continue living with his dad in Glendale. Wayne knew that his family had reached a point of no return, and sadly, family life and childhood would never be the same again.

In the midst of the turmoil, Wayne tried his best to stay busy. His days usually consisted of getting up in the early morning to deliver papers, then spending the day in school, and helping out at his father's pharmacy after that. During his teenage years he also often helped out at a local horseshoe manufacturer. Believe it or not, it was this gig making horseshoes that ended up being Wayne's first connection to Hollywood since the horses that his employer shod shoes for were used in productions based out of Hollywood studios.

Immediately after John Wayne graduated from High School in 1925, he put in an application for the United States Naval Academy hoping to try his luck in naval command, but after filling out the paperwork, his application was ultimately rejected. As fate would have it, Wayne ended up going to the University of Southern California instead. Due to his football prowess he was offered a full-ride scholarship, covering all of his tuition and even meals in the student cafeteria, which meant a lot back in the 1920s when academic funding was typically much more scarce and hard to come by.

It is said that in considering a major, Wayne figured that studying law would be the most prudent course to take, since real estate was so big in California, and there was always need of someone to interpret the legal dealings of property. In college, Wayne also pursued his avid interest of football, playing on the University of Southern California football team. By this time, Wayne is said to have reached his full 6-foot 4 height and weighed around 170 pounds.

According to many of his female acquaintances at the time, Wayne was also said to have been "drop dead gorgeous." With dark brown, curly hair, blue eyes, and delicate cheekbones, he was said to really stand out from a crowd. In fact, according to a former classmate, "his looks alone could stop traffic." But apparently as good looking as the young John Wayne was, he was a bit awkward around the opposite sex. It is said that he was quite shy, and it took quite a while for him to warm up to someone. He is said to have been very well liked, but his dates at that point were actually few and far between. Wayne's main outlet in college was always football—at least until a fateful injury would stop his athletic career.

Chapter Three

On the Set with Ford

"The man was my heart. There was a communion between us that not many men have. I have never been closer to any person in my life."

—John Wayne on John Ford

The next major milestone in Wayne's life was in the spring of 1926 when Wayne's coach Howard Jones managed to get him and a couple of other guys on the team a summer job on a set for Fox Studios. Jones was a friend of Tom Mix, who just so happened to be a director. As Jones explained to his players, "I got Tom Mix a good box for the football games. He said if there was ever anything, he could do for me, he would do it." And he was right, as a favor for Jones, Mix did indeed hire some of his players—including Wayne—to work as extra stagehands for the summer. According to Wayne, they got the job after going to the studio and presenting a letter of recommendation from Jones. They were then introduced to Mix who happily informed them, "a star owes it to his public to keep in fine physical condition. I want you to be my trainers."

Shortly after this statement, the players were put on the official payroll for the production of the latest western that Mix and his crew were shooting. As Wayne recalls, they were introduced to Mix on Friday and then reported to work the following Monday. Yet according to Wayne, the short weekend in between was still enough time for the busy movie mogul to forget all about him. Wayne would later recall that once they were on the lot, they encountered Mix driving up in his car. Wayne greeted Mix with, "Good morning, Mr. Mix," but all he received was a blank look in return. Nevertheless, the group was indeed on the payroll whether the guy who hired them remembered them or not. For the rest of the summer, Wayne would make $35 a week lugging heavy props and other furnishings across the stage, from set to set. This was a great boon for Wayne who was able to pay off the debt that he had been accumulating.

After this production, Wayne's next big break came to pass in September of 1926, in the form of a film called *Mother Machree*. In this film, Wayne had the distinction of herding a wild flock of geese. As bizarre as it sounds, this was the odd job that he held down—herding geese that were used in certain scenes back into their pens when they were not needed. Wayne didn't take such a mediocre role very seriously, and he would often joke with other members of the crew about his lowly position on the set. Wayne was doing as much one day when he suddenly heard someone shout, "Hey goose herder!" It was the director, a blowhard kind of boss by the name of John Ford.

Ford, who himself used to be a ball player back in college, had apparently heard that Wayne was hired on under the recommendation of USC's football coach. This had sparked his interest, prompting him to inquire, "You're one of Howard Jones' bright boys?" At which Wayne responded, "Yes." Ford, an aggressive and naturally combative kind of character, then shot back with the challenge, "And you call yourself a football player?" Wayne is said to have blithely responded with something like, "I guess so," as Ford continued, "You're a guard, eh? Let's see you get down in position." Upon hearing this, as if on cue, Wayne then dropped down into a classic three-point stance.

Ford then mercilessly kicked Wayne's hand out from under him, causing Wayne to fall down flat on his stomach. As Wayne struggled to get up, Ford then mocked him, "And you call yourself a guard. I'll bet you couldn't even take me out." At which Wayne defiantly mumbled, "I'd like to try." Without another word, Ford accepted this challenge and after marching off several feet spun around and charged at John Wayne. But instead of simply tackling Ford, Wayne chose to place a foot out and trip the director, causing him to dive headlong to the ground. Ford sat there stunned for a moment. A dangerous silence filled the set, as everyone stared and watched to see what the director would do. Suddenly, Ford burst into raucous laughter. Hearing their boss laugh, the crew then loosened up and began to laugh as well. The friendship Wayne forged with Ford that day would last a lifetime.

Chapter Four

Becoming John Wayne

"I'm not the sort to back away from a fight. I don't believe in shrinking from anything. It's not my speed; I'm a guy who meets adversities head on."

—John Wayne

In one of those classic turning points in life, Wayne would be delivered a severe setback during his days at USC in the form of a shoulder injury. The accounts of exactly what happened vary. But according to those who say they were there, the incident occurred at a California beach where Wayne attempted to body surf. Wayne was apparently trying to impress some girls with his moves when he hit some rough waters and ended up getting thrown by the waves back onto the beach where his shoulder was violently dislocated and his collarbone broken.

Rendering him unable to play football any longer, Wayne's injury would not only sideline him from the game, but it would also sideline him from the university since it took away his only means to pay for his tuition—his scholarship. There was no way around it; if he couldn't get his scholarship renewed, Wayne would have to find another way to pay. This meant taking on odd jobs on studio sets and—if he could manage it—signing on for small walk-on roles in films.

Times were hard for Wayne, and he was getting threadbare. But although his financial situation was turning rather grim, his personal life would soon perk up in a big way when a blind date arranged by a friend would turn into nothing short of a date with destiny. John Wayne was still a little shy in college, and his friends thought that a blind date might help get him socially motivated. The date was with a local girl named Carmen Saenz, in which the pair arrived along with a few other couples at the Rendezvous Ballroom located in the vicinity of California's Newport Beach.

The date went fairly well, and afterward Carmen invited Wayne over to her house. Carmen still lived with her parents at the time, so this was by all means an innocent extension of their date. It was here at Carmen's family home, however, that Wayne found himself caught in what could only be called love at first sight. The object of his love wasn't Carmen—it was her sister Josephine. As soon as Wayne laid eyes on her, he knew he wanted to be with her, and apparently with Carmen's blessing, they began to go out together on a regular basis.

But as much as Wayne and Josephine enjoyed each other's company, her parents were none too thrilled. First of all, they didn't care for the age gap the couple presented, since Wayne was a 19-year-old university student and Josephine was a 16-year-old high schooler. Even if they could get past the age difference, they couldn't quite get past Wayne's background. The Saenz family was fairly well to do, and they knew that Wayne came from a disadvantaged family which was unable to pay his own way in college.

Today, such concerns would be absurd. But back in the 1920s, in affluent circles, being able to put your kids through college was a sign of wealth and prestige. The few poorer students that managed to get their tuition paid with a scholarship, such as the one John Wayne had, were derisively referred to as "scholarship boys." Josephine's father, José Saenz, wasn't about to have his daughter get into a serious relationship with a scholarship boy. Truth be told, even Wayne's grip on his scholarship was tenuous at best. Without his scholarship, he was on his own, and unable to pay he was ultimately forced to drop out.

Wayne was now really not sure what to do with himself, but as fate would have it, his old football coach provided him some unforeseen direction. Back to the drawing board once again, Wayne would then spend the summer of 1927 working as a prop handler. He decided to take a year off school so that he could save money for the rest of his tuition and hopefully return to USC in the fall of 1928. The first job that Wayne was able to get with Fox was another Ford production entitled *Four Sons*.

His main role was as the guy who dumped leaves onto a fan just off screen so that they would float down onto the set, in full mimicry of fall weather. Although innocuous in nature, this scene was very important for the production team and had to be done several times in order to get it just right. This put John Wayne in the tedious position of continuously dumping leaves, sweeping them up, and then dumping them again. Wayne was growing weary of the retakes, and somewhere along the way lost his order of operations and found himself sweeping up leaves when he should have been dumping them, completely messing up the shot. The crew was frustrated, but when Wayne realized what he had done, he was even more aggravated and threw his broom down, marching right off the set in what amounted to an exasperated tantrum.

Even though Wayne had just walked off the job, Ford was apparently once again entertained by what he perceived to be John Wayne's sense of comic relief in action. Wayne was then brought back to Ford where Wayne actually bent over as Ford proceeded to give him a "kick in the ass." Wayne had clearly endeared himself with John Ford, but it wouldn't be long before he would get on the temperamental director's bad side as well.

The next Ford production that Wayne was a part of was called *Hangman's House*—a 1928 film that was an epic depiction of legal troubles, discord, and angst. The role that Wayne was placed in was small but somewhat memorable. He was a fiery young Irish youth who worked up a fury and stomped down a section of a picket fence. This troubled character was then eventually brought before a hanging judge who mouthed the words, "You shall hang by the neck until you are dead, dead, dead." The actors merely mouthed their lines since this was a silent film with subtitles. But upon being exposed to such an odd line, Wayne couldn't help but laugh, and instead of following the script he let out a comical, "Amen!" This bit of adlibbing did not sit well with the director, Ford, at all, and he immediately began shouting for Wayne's removal, screaming, "Get that son of a bitch out of the prisoner's box! Get him off the stage! Get him off the damned lot! I don't ever want to see him again!" But this time, the bark was much worse than the bite, and after a couple of days, John Wayne was brought right back onto the set.

Wishing to check out some of the other studios, Wayne next sought a job with Warner Brothers, getting a stint in a production of *Noah's Ark*, where he got paid $15 an hour as an extra. He was then able to get a significant upgrade, being cast in 1929's *Salute*, increasing his pay to $75 a week. In this film, Wayne played a Navy officer by the name of Bill who subjected his crew members to constant hazing. Wayne then got his next big break by chance when the director Raoul Walsh observed Wayne lugging furniture in one of his prop jobs and thought that the ruggedly handsome young man would be the perfect pick for his new leading role.

Walsh wanted to make a big-time western based upon a popular *Saturday Evening Post* serial called "The Shaggy Legion." This was the beginnings of an epic production that Walsh would ultimately call *The Big Trail*. Walsh was looking for a young cowboy pioneer to ride the plains, and he thought that he saw that in John Wayne. He approached Wayne and struck up a conversation, "What else can you do besides handle props?" At which Wayne responded, "I can play football." Raoul then agreed, "I believe you."

Shortly after this exchange, Wayne was taken for his screen test. At first, it didn't go so well with Wayne later recalling that the effort was just a bit too Shakespearean for him. But they tried again shortly thereafter, and Wayne was finally able to find his groove. The screen test consisted of someone asking him various basic questions pertaining to the script, such as, "How long was the trip? Will we see buffalo?" Instead of answering them, however, Wayne shot back his own improvised questions in a defiant style that would become characteristic of his film persona. He cagily asked, "Why do you want to go west? Can you handle a rifle?"

Apparently, Raoul Walsh was very pleased with Wayne's delivery, and feeling he found his star yelled, "Cut!" Wayne was hired. It was shortly after this that the head of the studio, Winfield Sheehan, came up with the idea of giving John Wayne, who up until this point had been known as Marion Morrison, a new name. It is said that Sheehan and Walsh had come up with the idea of naming Morrison after a general from the Revolutionary War called "Mad" Anthony Wayne. But after some discussion, it was decided that Anthony was just a bit too Italian, so the first name of John was settled upon instead. Wayne himself was not even present for the discussion.

At any rate, this is how John Wayne came to be. The Little Duke from Glendale had come a long way and was—in every sense of the word—making a name for himself.

Chapter Five

The Big Trail and the Big Disappointment

"When you come to see a picture of mine, I want you to know that I'm not going to do anything that will make you uncomfortable. I want you to know that you won't be disappointed with me."

—John Wayne

The Big Trail, living up to its name, was a big production, and as such the studio purchased and built multiple props and used several miles of land in the creation of the film. The production team also partnered with a cattle rustler by the name of Jack Padjan, using him as a talent scout for Native Americans at a nearby reservation in Wyoming. Here Padjan gathered several members of the Arapaho tribe who were interested in making their debut as extras in the movie.

It was while John Wayne was lost in the shuffle of production for this feature film that his parents' long-time separation was finally, officially settled as a formal divorce on February 20, 1930. Wayne's father Clyde would later go on to marry a 29-year-old divorcee, who was not too much older than John Wayne himself. Such facts didn't bother Wayne much; in the end, he just wanted his dear old father to be happy.

During the spring, Wayne began to work on the production in earnest, starting with publicity shots of him standing with guns drawn. The official shooting of the film then began on April 20, 1930, and wouldn't finish until August 20. During this window of time, Wayne was dedicated and determined, waking up every single day around five in the morning and working well into the night. Under this heavy workload, Wayne was struck with a severe bout of diarrhea—not exactly the stuff of star power—but apparently it was so bad that Wayne had to call off work for a couple of days just to recover. He didn't want to stay gone long, however, because he knew that he could be very easily replaced.

Struggling to get back on set, Wayne had lost about 18 pounds at this point. He was exhausted, but through sheer force of will, he got himself back behind the camera. The first scene he shot was certainly not very considerate of his condition, as he was made to film a scene in which he and a few other cowboys guzzled down hard liquor. The combination of whiskey and the previous sickness took their toll, and immediately after shooting, Wayne would recall that he quite literally, "puked and crapped" blood for several days thereafter.

There was a lot of other intrigue going on the set of *The Big Trail* as well. For one, there has long been a rumor that Wayne was having a fling with leading lady Marguerite Churchill. In addition to this drama, there was also frequent fights on and off the set among extras and stagehands. Robert Parrish, who was a young extra at the time, would recall that the grandson of Geronimo, Charlie Stevens, would get into it with a rugged stagehand by the name of Cheyenne Flynn. Geronimo's grandson had apparently been accused of cheating at cards, and Flynn wasn't going to take such things lying down. It is said that Flynn leaped upon Stevens, and in a moment of pure primal aggression that predated Mike Tyson's famous ear biting by several decades, he screamed, "I'm going to bite your ear off!" The next thing anyone knew Stevens let out a horrible scream. Flynn let him go, and Stevens took off running in the other direction.

The witness to this altercation, Parrish, would then claim that the very next day he stumbled upon what appeared to be a "piece of Steven's ear covered with ants." The story sounds rather far-fetched, but there can be no doubt that the world of Hollywood was much rougher in the early twentieth century than it is today. And there were indeed regular fights among participants. Just as they were wrapping up filming of *The Big Trail*, Wayne would be pulled into one of these tussles himself.

Wayne had been sitting in his train car, making a trip back to the Hollywood set, playing a game of cards, when he was alerted to a horrible altercation ensuing a few train cars down from him. A stagehand had come back to inform him that some stuntmen were mercilessly pummeling Frederick Burton, a fellow actor from the film. In being given this bit of information, Wayne, viewed as a cool-headed peacemaker, had apparently been automatically volunteered to break up the fight. As it turns out, the man was being attacked at the behest of none other than the direction of film, Raoul Walsh. Walsh believed that the man had been fooling around with his wife, so he sicked his stuntmen onto the actor to "teach him a lesson." Wayne was the one who learned a lesson, however: he learned that he didn't care much for Raoul Walsh, and on that day lost any admiration or esteem that he may have had for him.

Nevertheless, despite all of the drama, *The Big Trail* finished production and made its debut at Grauman's Chinese Theatre in October of 1930. The movie was not exactly a big hit, but it was a major production, clocking in at just over $2 million. For his work on the film, John Wayne made about $105 a week, which was decent money back in those days. But since the film did so dismally, in the end it proved a big letdown for John Wayne. As a result of the lackluster reception, Wayne would not get offered another leading role until about a decade later. He had set his fortunes with *The Big Trail*, and it had turned into one of the biggest disappointments of his life.

Chapter Six

Stuck in the B-List

"I suppose my best attribute—if you want to call it that—is sincerity. I can sell sincerity because that's the way I am."

—John Wayne

After *The Big Trail* turned into the big disappointment, Wayne was now once again struggling to find work, and for his next role, he only managed to get a small part in the production of *Girls Demand Excitement* which he began work on in November of 1930. Shortly after production of this piece came to a conclusion, Wayne received a six-month contract with Columbia for a movie called *Men Are Like That*, which was actually an adaptation of the play *Arizona*. Although the name may sound like a typical cowboy film, it isn't. In this feature, Wayne is cast in the role of a football player who falls in love with several women before abandoning them. A typical film drama that only received moderate success but in retrospect is believed to have captured much of Wayne's early style.

Wayne's next move was to sign on with Mascot in late 1931, where he agreed to do several serial features. One of which was a piece called *The Shadow of the Eagle* which was shot during December of 1931. Wayne worked hard during the production process of all these projects and was once again engaged in a breakneck schedule of arriving on set early in the morning and not leaving until late at night.

Following *The Shadow of the Eagle*, Wayne then got to work on another Mascot serial, this time a version of *The Three Musketeers* which was filmed between April of 1932 and April of 1933. It was later that summer, on June 24, 1933, in the midst of this heavy workload, that John Wayne married his long-time girlfriend Josephine. A priest married the pair in traditional Catholic fashion at the Church of the Immaculate Conception. Soon after this union, the couple would have a steady line of children, starting with the birth of their son Michael in 1934, their daughter Antonia in 1936, their son Patrick in 1939, and another daughter they named Melinda in 1940.

In between the creation of all of these descendants, John Wayne continued his habitual mediocre roles in mediocre films. Even though Wayne was getting paid well for his work, the longer he was stuck in this rut of lackluster productions, his star was growing dimmer and dimmer by the day. Wayne knew that he was at serious risk of being permanently typecast as a B movie hack. He was tremendously depressed about this condition, but there wasn't much he could do about it, staying the course was the only means he had to make a living.

In the middle of all of this professional frustration, Wayne would also have a tragic turn of events in his personal life with the news of the death of his father. His passing was sudden. Clyde had just dropped his step daughter off at school when he mentioned that he wasn't feeling well. After saying bye to his step daughter, he then apparently laid down in bed and died of a massive heart attack. Wayne was beside himself with grief—he had always greatly loved and respected his father despite his flaws.

But nevertheless, as he had done his whole life, Wayne quickly learned to compartmentalize his emotions. The extent to which he had done so would be demonstrated several years after his father's passing. While attending a burial for one of his fellow associates in the film industry, he suddenly looked around the graveyard and offhandedly remarked, "My dad is buried up here someplace. I've never been back since the funeral."

His frustration with his professional situation meanwhile was becoming palpable, and shortly after the passing of his father in 1937, he vented his frustration on his old friend and director Ford, asking him, "When is it my turn?" Wayne recalls that Ford calmly responded, "Just wait. I'll let you know when I get the right script." It was shortly thereafter that Ford would introduce Wayne to the right script—a simple little piece called *Stagecoach* which would forever change John Wayne's life.

Chapter Seven

Riding the Stagecoach to Success

"Nobody should come to the movies unless he believes in heroes."

—John Wayne

Stagecoach was produced by Walter Wanger in the fall of 1938, and Wayne began working on set for the film on October 31. It was Halloween, but when it came to his career prospects, Wayne wasn't hoping for any tricks this time around, and fortunately for him he was in for a real treat. *Stagecoach* wrapped up filming in December of 1938 and was released in February of 1939.

The film had actually been adapted from a play written by Eugene O'Neill. The original story shadows the lives of a group of steamship sailors. John Wayne's character is a freewheeling young man who falls in love with an actress. In the film, Wayne strayed away from the do-gooder type roles that he had previously played and instead stared as a slightly villainous tough guy. It seemed that the new approach did wonders for Wayne, because upon completion, *Variety Magazine* had the following review ready and waiting for him: "John Wayne, as the outlaw, displays talent hitherto only partially used—a forthright, restrained delivery and an appealing personality which here gets a new impetus." Wayne had finally hit the sweet spot of his acting modality—he had now reached mainstream star status, and there was no turning back.

After *Stagecoach*, John Wayne was cast for a role in the film *Seven Sinners* in 1940. In this film, he starred opposite of Marlene Dietrich, and the two soon developed an intimate relationship both on and off the set. Wayne later relayed the story of their first encounter as being a rapid descent into unbridled passion, and it was Marlene Dietrich that had played the major role in bringing them to such a juncture. Marlene, who invited Wayne to her dressing room, allegedly made the first move. As the story goes, Wayne was awkwardly standing around, hovering over Marlene's shoulder as she put on makeup. He tried some small talk but was so nervous that all he could come up with was an awkward, "What time is it?" To which Marlene cut right through Wayne's anxiety by pulling up her dress and showing him a leg with a watch strategically placed in a garter, bluntly informing him, "It's very early darling. We have plenty of time."

In the movie, Dietrich played a woman intent on seducing Wayne's character, and in real life she appears to have done very much the same. Theirs was a brief romance, however, and they would break it off shortly after it had begun. Unlike many other leading men, Wayne truly did love his wife despite his indiscretions and was usually wracked with guilt whenever he did partake in forbidden Hollywood fruit.

But when his wife eventually found out about some of the goings-on behind the scenes of some of Wayne's films, she was heartbroken all the same. She, of course, did not want her husband to be around such women anymore. Wayne couldn't avoid these starlets, and despite any protestations on his wife's part, he and Marlene Dietrich would remain friends and star in a few more movies together afterward. Most notably they both played a role in the movies *Pittsburgh* and *The Spoilers*, both films produced in 1942.

When she had finally had enough of Wayne's extramarital misadventures, Josephine sought intervention in the form of a priest named Father McCoy who she brought to the Wayne home for marriage counseling. Wayne didn't appreciate the interference, but for the sake of his wife assented to the intervention. The end result had Wayne promising to stop being personally involved with Dietrich, as long as Josie stopped talking about the whole ordeal. He hoped that she would forget about the whole thing and move on, but he was mistaken. Eventually the rift would become so insurmountable that Josephine felt that she had no choice but to file for divorce. John Wayne had apparently ridden the stagecoach to success but had left his marriage vows somewhere back at the station.

Chapter Eight

War and Love Affairs

"All I'm for is the liberty of the individual."

—John Wayne

After the Dietrich affair, the Wayne marriage was already on the rocks, but it hit absolute rock bottom when Wayne began seeing his new paramour, a lively Mexican woman named Esperanza Baur. Wayne was introduced to Bauer through Dietrich's business manager, a man who went by the name of Bo Roos. In August of 1941, Wayne had accompanied Roos along with a troop of other actors, including fellow star Ray Milland, to Mexico on the premise of finding investors for a new movie studio.

But Wayne found more than he had bargained for when while hanging out at their hotel Milland brought him to the acquaintance of Esperanza Baur, a woman he referred to as "Chata." Almost immediately, Wayne was completely enamored with Chata, and soon she was all that he talked about. He told Roos on one occasion that "the great thing about Latin women was that they liked the simple things—marriage, family, children, a home." Chata was not exactly a simple woman, however, she had been seeing Milland, and she was known to be linked to several other people as well. On top of that, her mother was said to be an actual madam, who ran a brothel in Mexico. Still, Wayne was bitten by the love bug and could not be convinced otherwise. He continued to see Chata regularly even after returning to the United States.

The last straw for Josephine came when she began to receive nightly calls from Wayne's latest mistress asking about his whereabouts. Josie may have been able to look past some of Wayne's indiscretions when they occurred far afield, but now his latest lover was actively infiltrating her private life. This was more than she could take. As a result, shortly thereafter Wayne came home to find all of his clothing piled up on the front lawn, a clear indication that Josephine was done dealing with his extra liaisons. The couple would then file for a separation on June 20, 1942, which would ultimately lead to divorce a few years later in 1945. Shortly after the divorce was finalized, Chata and Wayne were married on January 17, 1946.

While the initial stages of his divorce were underway, the year 1942 also saw John Wayne make his debut on the radio, in which he stared in several serial radio dramas. As the country became more and more involved in World War II, the main bread and butter for all Hollywood stars soon became aimed at the war effort. Wayne was actually able to escape the draft because he had four children to support. His film studio also advocated for him to be excused from the draft "in support of national interest." Additionally, Wayne was in his early 30s at the time and considered past the usual age for the draft.

But even though John Wayne was exempt from the draft, he was not exempt from doing SSO tours for the troops. In all, Wayne would tour countless bases and hospital units in the Pacific theater over the course of three months from 1943 to 1944. He also toyed with the idea of volunteering like some other Hollywood leading men had done, but in the end, he kept finding excuses not to. This fact would come to haunt him for the rest of his life. Many would later claim that Wayne's often great—some would say even exaggerated—show of patriotism stemmed from his guilt over the fact that he failed to serve his nation during the war.

As John Wayne continued to reprise his roles both in film and in real life, he would recast himself as a producer by the end of the decade, directing such films as *Angel and the Badman* in 1947. Playing the lead role in the production, Wayne took on the persona of a conflicted gun slinger who was torn between his wild life and the beautiful Quaker girl that he had become infatuated with. Playing the role of this girl was acclaimed actress Gail Russell. She seemed excellent for the part, and her and Wayne's screen chemistry was almost immediate. This smooth interaction, however, soon made Chata fear that Wayne was cheating on her with his new onscreen love interest. Chata, who had brazenly engaged in an affair with Wayne under the nose of his first wife, was now fearing that she was getting a taste of her own medicine from someone else. Her fear and resentment reached a boiling point on the night of the wrap party for *Angel and the Badman*. When Wayne arrived home late, drunk, he was greeted by Chata who pointed a gun at him and nearly shot him.

Shortly after filming for *Angel and the Badman* drew to a close, reviews of the film began to pour in. Contrary to many of his previous works, this piece was actually well received by most of the critics who viewed his performance in the film as employing a much more complex and dynamic approach. His personal fanbase, however, was not quite so thrilled. This film tended to focus more on the protagonist's romantic entanglements rather than gun battles. This served to alienate much of his audience. Many of the die-hard action enthusiasts were a bit disappointed from this deviation from what had been the standard, shoot-'em-up John Wayne formula.

But John Wayne learned long ago in the movie business that you can't always please everyone. He knew that now that he had found his direction, the best thing for him to do was to keep moving forward. So that was exactly what he did.

Chapter Nine

Sands of Iwo Jima

"Get off your butt and join the marines!"

—John Wayne

The next major milestone in Wayne's life came with the release of the film *Red River* in 1948. The piece had actually been rather quickly put together on the heels of *Angel and the Badman* and had already been all but wrapped up by the Christmas season of 1946. Here Wayne played a conflicted cattleman named Tom Dunson. It was a darker sort of character, and to Wayne's pleasant surprise, he seemed to play it well. He was a natural in displaying the character's breakdowns and especially his strained relationship with his son, a role that was performed by Montgomery Clift. Wayne was at first skeptical that Clift, who was in his 20s at the time and straight off of Broadway, would be a good fit to play his antagonist in the film. But Clift, an extremely studious actor, soon proved his weight in gold when it came to complementing Wayne's style and persona.

The only problem Clift seemed to have was with drinking, but this was common ground he shared with Wayne, who was already a habitual alcoholic both on and off the set. Nevertheless, some $2 million in production costs later, the movie proved to be a major blockbuster hit. *Red River* is still considered one of John Wayne's best films to this day. But as was often the case in John Wayne's life, this professional positive coincided with a personal negative.

Right after finishing up *Red River*, Wayne had taken his new wife Chata on what they viewed as a belated honeymoon. The couple went off to Honolulu along with Wayne's friend and frequent screenwriter, James Edward Grant, and his wife. Chata didn't approve of the company and claimed that Grant was a bad influence on Wayne who encouraged him to be promiscuous with other women on the set. This viewpoint of Chata's only festered and became worse as she proceeded to drink her way through the occasion. Soon she was becoming unhinged, shouting obscenities at Wayne and embarrassing him in public. It is said that Wayne came back from the trip completely distraught but still reluctant to admit that his marriage to Chata was ill-advised. Chata seemed to have a hold on Wayne and was able to manipulate him into doing whatever she wanted.

The only escape Wayne could find from his ever-increasing marital troubles was by burying his head in his work. Some of his concerned friends might even say he was burying his head in the sand by doing so and merely delaying the inevitable. But speaking of sand, at least this volatile period with Chata was artistically productive for Wayne since it was during this period of turmoil that he starred in the iconic war film *Sands of Iwo Jima*. This film was originally inspired by the famous wartime photo of

U.S. troops struggling to raise the American flag over the war-torn Pacific island of Iwo Jima. Just 750 miles from mainland Japan, this island was to be a stepping stone for an American invasion of the Japanese Empire that had bombed the naval base of Pearl Harbor a few years prior.

Ultimately, the Japanese were brought into submission not by a mainland invasion launched from Iwo Jima, but through the dropping of two atomic bombs. The immense struggle and loss of life (around 7,000 U.S. Marines and 18,000 Japanese troops were killed) that occurred in taking this island was one of the most dramatic episodes of World War II. The folks at Hollywood rightly guessed that the events of Iwo Jima had all of the makings of a blockbuster film if only they could write a captivating script and cast the roles with competent actors. To their credit, the producers of this piece did indeed do their homework, partnering directly with the Marine Corps for onscreen advisors, as well as the use of a whole unit of actual troops to serve as extras on the set. As for John Wayne, with his ever-growing image as the all-American patriot, he seemed perfect for the role he was given.

Cast as the character of Sergeant John Stryker, Wayne played the part of a no-nonsense career soldier who was often disliked by his troops for his harsh demeanor. As he leads his men to battle, however, they come to a new understanding of their commander and grow to respect his dedicated leadership. *Sands of Iwo Jima* was shot over the summer of 1949, from July to August, and released to the public before the year was out. It was an instant success and did well enough to gain Wayne a nomination for Best Actor at the Oscars. Wayne wouldn't take home the coveted prize, however, until 20 years later for his role in the smash hit *True Grit*. But with *Sands of Iwo Jima*, he was well on his way all the same.

Chapter Ten

Wayne's Final Marriage

"We had a pretty good time together, when she wasn't trying to kill me!"

—John Wayne on Esperanza "Chata" Baur

Despite their previous marital troubles, Wayne and his second wife Chata endured most of 1949 together without incident. But throughout much of 1950, the relationship became strained once again. Before the year was out Chata was demanding that she be allowed to make a trip to Mexico City to visit her mother over the Christmas holiday. Even though it would take her away from her husband during the Christmas season, Chata claimed the visit was needed to cure her of her "nervous condition."

This holiday trip turned into an extended stay, with Wayne's wife not returning to him until the summer of 1951. If this time away from Wayne helped her nerves remains unclear, but Wayne's nerves certainly were not at his best; during this time, he was beset by a personal crisis of a whole other order as his hair began to thin and fall out. Wayne, who always prided himself in his appearance, was at first hesitant to do so, but ultimately decided to start wearing a toupee.

Wayne was in transition in his life, perhaps even hitting what many would refer to as a midlife crisis, when he left Chata behind in their Encino home in 1952 to go to Peru under the pretense of planning a new movie in the Peruvian environs. It was on a local film site in Peru that Wayne would meet the woman that would become his third wife, a young Peruvian woman named Pilar Pallete. Pilar was actually in a similar condition as Wayne—she was married but separated with her long-estranged husband and on the verge of divorce. She later recalled that at the time of the fateful meeting with John Wayne she had not even seen her husband for many months. Her estranged husband was deeply involved with another woman at the time.

After meeting this new love interest, Wayne wasn't wasting any time in moving forward, and shortly after returning to the states, on September 12, 1952, he filed for divorce. Chata appeared more than ready for this official split and quickly contacted all the gossip columns in order to run John Wayne's name in the mud as much as she possibly could. As the divorce proceedings came to a close in October of 1953, Chata would portray John Wayne as a habitual drunk and an abusive husband. Wayne denied any such accusations, and in the end, he was able to get a settlement that was fairly favorable to his estate. Chata meanwhile managed to receive a lump sum of $150,000 and a limited six-year alimony payment of $50,000 per year.

Chata always felt that she received the short end of the stick after the divorce, and sadly her life afterward would not be a very happy one. Following the divorce, she holed herself up in a hotel in Mexico City where she proceeded to drink herself to death. As if her own life was the result of a tragic Hollywood plot twist, Chata was found dead in her hotel room surrounded by empty bottles of booze as her only companions. She was not even 40 years old.

If Wayne mourned the death of his second wife, he was not quite so forthcoming with his emotions. On November 1, 1954, Wayne officially married for the third time, to his new wife, Pilar Pallete. Wed in the luxurious surroundings of Kona, Hawaii, John Wayne was most certainly hoping that the third time would be the charm.

Chapter Eleven

Late Life and Lung Cancer

"Courage is being scared to death—and saddling up anyway."

—John Wayne

Right around the time of his marriage to Pilar, John Wayne had been commissioned to play the role of Genghis Khan in the film *The Conqueror*. Produced by the reclusive Howard Hughes, the film was meant to be an epic blockbuster but turned out more to be an epic bust. First of all was the glaring fact of just how miscast Wayne was in the role of the Mongolian warlord. In his fake Fu Manchu mustache, bad makeup, and cheesy time period clothing, he stood out like a sore thumb. Secondly, the dialogue was considered completely lacking to anyone who heard it, with Wayne grunting in his fake accent phrases that were barely even coherent. In one scene, he proclaimed to his co-star Susan Hayward, "Know this, woman: I take you for wife."

By today's standards, such a bizarre film wouldn't have got off the drawing boards. Even back in the 1950s, it didn't take much to realize that the production was a complete flop. It was so bad, in fact, that *The Conqueror* would come to haunt Wayne for the rest of his life. Some would argue that filming on-site in the Escalante Desert of Utah, in the fake mustaches, wigs, and makeup of a Mongolian warlord, not only damaged Wayne's credibility but also may have damaged his health. As it turns out, the set wasn't far from where the infamous nuclear bomb tests in Nevada were being carried out. Several years later, it would come to the cast and crew's attention that the desert sand where they shot the film was most likely full of radioactive dust. Wayne himself would have to wonder if the lung cancer he would later develop was contributed to by inhaling this radioactive dirt. Then again, it was no secret that Wayne smoked several packs of cigarettes a day, which in itself was enough to cause lung cancer without any aid from radioactive fallout.

By 1955, Wayne was seeking to recoup from the losses that he experienced from *The Conqueror* in what seemed to be yet another promising western, *The Searchers*. This movie had Wayne back in familiar territory as a gunslinging cowboy. *The Searchers* lived up to every bit of Wayne's cowboy image, and it was the first film that had him utter the phrase that would be his trademark, calling other characters "pilgrim." The film also had an all-star cast consisting of a young Natalie Wood, Jeffrey Hunter, Vera Miles, and Ward Bond.

The plot is built around the character of Debbie played by Natalie Wood and her uncle Ethan Edwards played by John Wayne. Debbie has been kidnaped by a roving band of Comanches, and her uncle is part of a party of searchers attempting to find her. In the end, they do indeed rescue the woman, but she has already been forcefully wed to a Comanche warrior, provoking all kinds of painful drama among the main group of characters. The film is more than just an action adventure—it showcases a dynamic and complex narrative. Along with these big emotions and plot devices, it was also quite an expensive enterprise with a budget that clocked in at almost $4 million. But even at this high cost, it would eventually provide a great return for all of those that invested in it.

Production of *The Searchers* came to a close on August 16, 1955. Shortly after Wayne wrapped up his work on the set, he and his wife Pilar welcomed their first child into the world. Born on March 31, 1956, the happy mother and father named the new baby Aissa. This child—the first of three that he and Pilar would have—came when Wayne was just a few weeks shy of turning 49 years old.

Wayne would continue attempting to balance his film and family life until he hit an unexpected roadblock in 1964 when he was given his lung cancer diagnosis. The cancer at this point was already at such a late stage that he had to have four ribs and his entire left lung removed. After his experience, Wayne, contrary to what his handlers had advised, was inspired to go on a public awareness campaign about his illness, in which he stressed the importance of early cancer screenings. Interestingly enough, it is from these efforts of public awareness that has John Wayne being cited as the originator of using the phrase the "Big C" as a nickname for cancer.

Five years after his original diagnosis, Wayne would be declared cancer-free in 1969. It was that same year, after displaying so much tenacity and courage in his personal life, that he embarked upon one of the greatest films of his professional career, a piece entitled *True Grit*. Another epic western taking place in the latter half of the nineteenth century, *True Grit* casts Wayne in the role of Rooster Cogburn, an intrepid U.S. Marshal. In the film, Rooster Cogburn, a man described as having "true grit," is dispatched to capture a dangerous fugitive and murderer named Tom Chaney. The film debuted at Radio City Music Hall on July 3, 1969, and was a stunning success. It had John Wayne back at what he did best—playing the rugged onscreen hero.

For his efforts, Wayne would ultimately win both the Golden Globe and the academy award for Best Actor. The film was so popular that a sequel would be made in 1975 titled after the main character, *Rooster Cogburn*. Thanks to this success, Wayne would remain a household name for many years to come.

Conclusion

Despite his success in the box office, the 1970s would be a decade of slow decline for John Wayne. He and his wife Pilar had begun to drift apart, a fact that was ultimately realized in their official separation in 1973. Left to his own devices, Wayne continued to bury himself in his work. He lived his last few years in quiet isolation, with his personal secretary—and sometimes lover—Pat as his main source of company.

Wayne would finally succumb to the dreaded "Big C" as he referred to it, on June 11, 1979, after it made its return as an aggressive form of stomach cancer. After stubbornly resisting the Catholic religion of his past three wives, it is said that on his death bed Wayne was finally won over to the Roman Catholic faith. After his funeral service, John Wayne was put to rest at Pacific View Memorial Park Cemetery in California. He lived an exceptional life. Like so many of the characters he played, John Wayne simply rode off into the sunset while the rest of the world looked on.

Printed in Great Britain
by Amazon

81939555R00031